Annja knew there was no way she could turn her back on her friend

Jenny had to be protected—if not from the external threats, like the mysterious gunmen, then from herself. Annja had seen obsession kill people and knew that Jenny could easily fall prey to the same fate. *I won't let her die*, she thought.

Joey came back into the camp, dragging branches behind him. "She still out?" he asked.

"Yeah."

Suddenly Annja heard a low howl of some sort. It sounded like a cross between a coyote and a banshee. She looked at Joey. "What the heck is that?"

Joey busied himself thatching a roof together. "I don't know. Now, if you'll help me make this shelter, we can get to bed and hopefully forget we ever heard that. Because it's not something I've ever heard before."

"Never?" Annja asked.

"Never," Joey said. "But whatever it is, it sounds like it's coming this way."

Titles in this series:

ROGUE Angel

Alex Archer

FOOTPRINTS

A GOLD EAGLE BOOK FROM

W❂RLDWIDE®

TORONTO • NEW YORK • LONDON
AMSTERDAM • PARIS • SYDNEY • HAMBURG
STOCKHOLM • ATHENS • TOKYO • MILAN
MADRID • WARSAW • BUDAPEST • AUCKLAND

Recycling programs
for this product may
not exist in your area.

First edition September 2009

ISBN-13: 978-0-373-62138-5

FOOTPRINTS

Special thanks and acknowledgment to
Jon Merz for his contribution to this work.

Printed in U.S.A.

The
LEGEND

...THE ENGLISH COMMANDER TOOK
JOAN'S SWORD AND RAISED IT HIGH.

The broadsword, plain and unadorned,
gleamed in the firelight. He put the tip against
the ground and his foot at the center of the blade.
The broadsword shattered, fragments falling
into the mud. The crowd surged forward,
peasant and soldier, and snatched the shards
from the trampled mud. The commander tossed
the hilt deep into the crowd.
Smoke almost obscured Joan, but she continued
praying till the end, until finally the flames climbed
her body and she sagged against the restraints.

Joan of Arc died that fateful day in France,
but her legend and sword are reborn....

1

Annja Creed ducked around another thick pine tree and paused. A cool breeze blew through her hair, which she'd recently had cut, thinking she should take a chance and go for a new look. After her stylist had taken a good six inches off, she realized she'd made a mistake.

"You're always on the go," Rachel said, looking almost guilty. "It's so much easier to take care of it like this, and besides, a lot of guys like short hair."

"Yeah, but I'm not sure I do," Annja said.

Rachel smiled at her and shrugged. "You can always grow it back."

Two days after the haircut, Annja hid out in her Brooklyn loft, desperately wondering how long she could get away with her self-imposed hibernation. She didn't have any urgent commitments and she wasn't due to film another segment of her popular cable television series, *Chasing History's Monsters*, for a few weeks. She realized that having a lot of downtime made her restless and led to rash decisions like ill-advised makeovers. Then the e-mail had arrived that changed her plans and suddenly she was flying out to the Pacific Northwest.

Now she stood in the forest on a trail that the guy who ran the combined gas station and grocery store had assured her would lead all the way to a small encampment hidden deep in the woods.

"Stay on the trail," he'd said sternly. "Don't get off it—whatever happens."

"What is that supposed to mean?" Annja asked.

He'd smiled at her. "That forest is like a maze of pine trees and vines that'll trip you up and suck you under where no one can find you. You stay on the path, you'll be all right. Venture off, and you'll be lucky to be found by next spring."

She could see what he meant. Since parking her rented Jeep at the entrance to the trailhead, she'd had a hard enough time just trying to find the trail itself. It was incredibly overgrown, almost as if the woods themselves were desperate to reclaim it from civilization.

The crack of a branch somewhere behind her caused her to freeze. Was someone coming up the trail behind her?

Annja hadn't gotten the impression that this was a busy recreational hiking area. And the appearance of the trail itself didn't exactly make a convincing argument about its popularity. So who else might be wandering in the woods?

The e-mail Annja had received was from an old friend named Jenny Chu. She and Jenny had taken many undergraduate courses together and their friendship had blossomed over in-depth discussions about American folklore and legends. Jenny's passion was for things like the Lake Champlain monster and the legends of the Sasquatch.

The Sasquatch legend was why Annja was traipsing through the Oregon woods. Jenny's e-mail suggested that she'd found new evidence of the creature's existence. It was evidence she wanted Annja to see, as well, in case she wanted to do a segment about it on *Chasing History's Monsters*. Annja didn't believe for a second there would be any proof of a giant hairy creature roaming the woods, but her producer, Doug Morrell, was a sucker for those types of stories. Besides, Annja figured, I can buy some time before anyone I know sees my hair.

Annja smirked, thinking about the last time she'd seen Jenny, and their debate. Jenny had gone on and on about how it was anthropologically possible for a giant ape-man to exist in the farthest reaches of the forest of the North American continent.

Annja hadn't been swayed. "You're talking about a missing link, here, Jen. And it's just not possible. Not with the technology we have nowadays. You'd think we could float a satellite over certain areas and just get readings if there was anything there."

Jenny, her hair in two braids with her glasses slung low on her nose, had fired back. "You trust technology way too much. It's not the magic bullet you think it is."

"I don't think it's a magic bullet, per se," Annja said. "Just that we have to acknowledge it could solve mysteries that we've created for ourselves."

"I'll prove you wrong, Annja. One day. You'll see."

Was this the day Jenny had forecast? Annja smiled and started walking again. She'd have to wait and see. Jenny's campsite was supposed to be set up about two miles farther down the trail.

Annja took another five steps and paused again. She didn't hear anything but something didn't feel right.

She turned and looked back the way she'd come. How many times, she wondered, had she suspected that someone had followed her? The feeling was so ingrained that it had become the norm.

Still, she couldn't discount it. Her safety might well be in jeopardy. It often was these days. And that meant she'd have to take precautions.

The words of the gnarled shopkeeper rang in her ears. "Stick to the trail."

Annja frowned. If she stuck to the trail, there was a good chance that whoever or whatever was following her would overtake her.

*What*ever?

She caught the mental slip and frowned. Was she already supposing that some giant creature might be tailing her? She chuckled. It couldn't be helped. Despite the sunny start to the day, bloated clouds had moved in, threatening to drench the forest below. The forest itself had gone quiet, almost as if the animals and insects knew what was coming.

Or did they?

One thing was certain—if Annja didn't make some progress and reach the campsite, she was going to get soaked to the bone and face the threat of hypothermia. Even though the day was relatively warm, it was still early spring and she knew that temperatures could fluctuate rapidly. In the space of a few hours, alone, wet and cold, Annja could easily become disoriented and disappear. Unfortuately, she knew such things happened all the time.

Not the best way to start off the trip, she decided.

Ahead of her, she spotted what looked like a redwood tree, its massive trunk almost too large to even attempt to hug. It's been here for hundreds upon hundreds of years, Annja thought. Too bad Jenny can't ask the tree what lives here. I'll bet it could clear up the whole big-foot mystery right quick.

She walked around the tree, marveling at the sheer size of it, its branches reaching toward the heavens.

Fantastic, she thought. This alone was worth the trip.

She heard the noise as a twig snapped again, about thirty yards back.

Annja whirled. I need cover, she thought.

Another twig cracked. She spotted a clump of bushes and ducked toward it, squeezing her tall frame under the overhang until she could just about peer out from under the foliage.

She sensed movement farther back on the path. Was it the creature Jenny had been hunting for?

Or something else entirely?

She spotted a set of boots and relaxed somewhat. The last she'd heard, the Sasquatch didn't wear trendy hiking boots. The feet were moving along at a casual pace. There wasn't any sense of menace.

Annja poked her head out from under the bush and heard a shout of surprise.

The hiking boots belonged to a boy of about fourteen. His jet-black hair spiked out of his head at odd angles and he toppled back, landing on his butt as he reacted with shock to seeing Annja's head emerge from the bush.

"Who are you?" he asked.

Annja climbed to her feet. "Sorry about that. I thought someone might be following me."

The boy frowned. "You always go around hiding in blueberry bushes?"

Annja shrugged. "I've been known to hide in Dumpsters, too. Trees, sand dunes, snow caves. You name it, I've done it."

She helped him to his feet. "Who are you?"

"Joey," he said easily.

Annja smiled. "Nice to meet you."

He frowned. "That's some haircut you got there. You pay someone to do that or did you hack it off yourself?"

Annja frowned. "She took too much off. I wanted a change, but not this much."

Joey smirked. "Well, I think it looks killer."

Annja laughed. "Thanks. So where are you heading with that backpack stuffed as it is?"

Joey pointed down the trail. "I'm spending my vacation working for an expedition that's camped farther in. I get to hang out, run some errands and see what they're up to."

"That wouldn't be Jenny Chu's expedition, would it?"

Joey nodded. "Yeah. You know her?"

"She's an old friend of mine. She asked me to come out here and see what she was up to."

Joey's eyes went wide. "You're Annja Creed?"

"Guilty."

Joey frowned. "Wow, you don't look anything like you do on television."

"Yeah, well I didn't bother going to hair and makeup before hiking through the woods. I wasn't expecting to run into any fans," she said, winking. "How about you showing me exactly where the camp is? Those clouds look as if they're going to open up any second and I don't want to be out here when it pours."

"No sweat, Annja. Follow me."

Joey hefted his pack and set off. Annja followed along behind him. "You know this area well?" she asked.

Joey shrugged. "This is the land of my ancestors. We've been around here longer than anyone else."

Annja nodded. "You made a lot of noise on the trail back there. Might be time to study the skills of your ancestors."

Joey stopped walking. "What are you talking about?"

"On the trail. I heard you coming a mile away. Lots of twigs snapping, that kind of thing. Not very stealthy, huh?"

"Lady, I move pretty quiet. I don't know what you heard, but it wasn't me. They don't call me Creeping Wolf for nothing."

Annja frowned. "If I didn't hear you, then what—"

Joey held up his hand. "Let's not even go there, okay?

No offense to your friend or anything, but she's kind of obsessed with the whole Sasquatch thing, you know? I can dig having an interest and all, but she's really going full speed into nut job."

Annja smiled. "That sounds like Jenny."

"It's cool," Joey said. "I get that way about things. Girls, mostly. But you have to know when to draw the line at becoming a lunatic."

"Good advice."

The trail started to descend into what looked like a valley. Annja could see the trees starting to part as they entered a clearing. Ahead of her, she saw the bright reds and yellows of tents.

"So there it is," she said.

Joey nodded. "I've been gone all day. I had to go back to town and get some more supplies."

"Did you drive?"

Joey looked at her. "I walked."

"Yeah, but town's six miles away."

"And?"

Annja raised her eyebrows. "Nothing. Never mind."

Joey smiled. "Like I said, I've been cruising these woods my whole life. I know them better than almost anyone else. And as the crow flies, the distance back to town is only three miles."

"You fly, too?"

"Sometimes that's exactly what it feels like."

They broke out of the forest and into the clearing. Joey walked ahead of Annja, leaving her to take in the camp.

It was strangely quiet.

"Joey."

He stopped. "What?"

Annja frowned. "Where is everyone?"

Joey turned and glanced around. They both stood for a

moment, taking in the fact that there seemed to be absolutely no noise anywhere in the camp. Overhead, the clouds jostled together and Annja felt the first few drops of rain starting to flick down at her.

She felt uneasy and turned to see the barrel of a gun aiming at her.

The man standing behind the rifle did not look very friendly.

"How nice. Another guest," he said.

Annja turned to warn Joey, but he had vanished.

Startled, Annja turned back to the man. He was looking her up and down and then he nodded. "Walk that way. Try anything funny and I'll be more than happy to put a couple of holes into you."

Annja turned and started moving. One of these days, she thought, I'm going to have to find a deserted island. Maybe then I can get away from everyone who wants to kill me.

2

Annja felt the rifle barrel jab into her spine for the third time. She risked a glance back at the man standing behind her. "That's not necessary. I'm perfectly capable of walking without you stabbing me with your gun every few seconds," she said angrily.

"Shut up and walk."

Annja glanced around the camp as he escorted her past the tents. Everything seemed to be in good order and there wasn't an air of chaos. Annja wondered if the guy with the rifle had surprised Jenny's camp. She also wondered if he was alone.

She found the answer to that question when they turned the corner and she saw two other men similarly armed. One of them looked at Annja's escort.

"Where'd she come from?"

"She's been on the trail leading here. I followed her for a few miles."

"Noisily, I might add," Annja said.

"Sit her down with the others."

Annja felt the jab of the rifle barrel again and sat down.

Jenny's expedition consisted of a number of college students—an even mix of boys and girls who looked quite frightened.

But where was Jenny?

Annja watched as the three armed men huddled together and spoke for a few seconds. They parted and the one who seemed to be in charge, a guy of maybe forty with thick pork-chop sideburns and a long scar down one side of his face, nodded at her. "You."

"What?" she asked.

"Stand up."

Annja tensed. Were they going to shoot her now? She closed her eyes and pictured the powerful sword she'd inherited from Joan of Arc. The weapon was ready for her to call forth. She knew her timing would have to be perfect.

Annja stood and asked, "What's this all about?"

"Shut up. We've got a message for the professor."

Annja frowned. So this wasn't just some random occurrence. These guys wanted to speak to Jenny. But what had happened to her?

"What's the message?"

The man leveled a finger at Annja. "Tell her to back off. She's not wanted here. These woods belong to us. And we'll do whatever it takes to keep it that way."

Annja wanted to argue, but decided it would be better to just accept things and try to figure out what was going on once the danger had passed. "Okay. I'll give her the message."

"You do that. And tell her we'll be watching. If we don't like what we see, then bad things will start happening."

Annja nodded. "I get it."

The lead man regarded her for one more second and then turned. The three men walked toward the trees that bordered the clearing. In minutes, they had vanished back into the gloom.

Annja frowned. She turned and pulled one of the young men to his feet. "What the hell is going on around here?" she asked him.

"Who are you?" he said, sounding terrified.

"I'm Annja Creed. Where is Jenny?"

"Jenny?"

"Professor Chu," Annja said.

Although he was big and strapping, the student looked frightened. Probably hasn't had the experience of being shot, stabbed and blown up, Annja thought

"Professor Chu went out on a hike this morning. We haven't seen her since."

Annja looked around. "None of you have seen her?"

"No. And those guys showed up about an hour ago. I guess they just got tired of waiting for her."

Annja peered out into the woods. "Maybe."

"Maybe?"

"Perhaps they were only supposed to deliver the message. Maybe it's a scare tactic."

"Those guns looked real enough."

Annja smiled. "They were."

"Hey," a voice called out.

Annja turned and saw Joey standing behind her, sliding his backpack off.

"Where the hell did you disappear to?"

Joey grinned. "Creeping Wolf, remember? I can disappear in the blink of an eye."

"Yeah, well, thanks for sticking around to defend the weak and all that jazz."

Joey smirked. "Yeah, right. You defenseless? That's a joke. And besides, I don't do guns, man. I'm a lover, not a fighter."

"Great. So, my creeping friend, maybe you can tell me what happened to Jenny?"

"How could I do that? I've been gone all day getting supplies," Joey said.

Annja frowned. He had a point. And none of the college kids looked as if they were going to be particularly keen to set out on a search through the woods. Annja could hear them all talking in hushed tones. She knew what was coming.

Annja looked at Joey again. "They'll want to leave," she told him.

Joey frowned. "Because of those guys? That's weak."

"Didn't you just tell me you're a lover, not a fighter?"

"Sure, but I don't lay down for anyone, either. I did that, I wouldn't be much of a credit to my tribe."

"Well, I don't think any of these kids signed on for this kind of thing. The thought of gun-wielding dudes is probably giving them images of *Deliverance*."

"Deliverance?"

"It's a movie," Annja said. "Rent it when you're older."

Joey shook his head. "I can download it for free. But thanks for dating yourself."

"You've got quite the mouth on you, don't you?" Annja said, attempting to sound stern.

Joey held up his hands. "No disrespect intended, ma'am."

Annja smirked. "Wiseass." She turned back to the student she'd spoken to initially. "Get your gear packed up. You guys aren't staying here."

He looked as if Annja had just promised him several bars of gold. Instantly, the college students all sprang into action, taking down tents and getting their packs squared away.

Annja watched them. She felt hesitant about taking command of the situation but, with Jenny nowhere to be seen, someone had to. She couldn't tell a bunch of kids to hang around with gun-toting nuts lurking in the woods. And she was pretty confident that Jenny would tell them to get out of there, as well. There was no way Jenny would want kids under her care to be in danger.

It took them twenty minutes to break down the camp. Annja found Jenny's tent and started to pack it up, too.

Joey spent most of the time complaining about the supplies he'd lugged back from town. "Hey, man, I'm still getting paid for this, right? I mean, charity's nice and all, but I have to look out for numero uno."

Annja fished out her wallet and gave him fifty dollars. "That enough?"

Joey's eyes lit up. "Not bad. Jenny promised me a hundred per day out here, though."

"Don't push your luck. Jenny's on a university grant and has to watch all of her expenses. That fifty's a gift and you know it."

Joey smiled. "Can't blame a dude for trying."

Annja finished breaking down Jenny's tent and wrapped up the stakes in the nylon. "I've got one final assignment for you, Creeping Wolf."

"Yeah?"

"You need to lead these kids back to the trailhead."

Joey frowned. "They stay on the trail, they'll be fine. They don't need me."

Annja pulled him close. "Take a look at their faces. Every one of them is terrified. Being confronted with guns isn't a normal occurrence for these kids. And they're probably considering very seriously the idea that they came close to being killed. If I let them go like this, they'll wander off the trail and die from exposure. You know that's true."

Joey nodded. "Yeah, I guess you're right. They do look pretty shell-shocked."

"As opposed to you."

"I left, man. I don't stick around for trouble. That's bad medicine."

"Well, do me this one favor and then you can get lost, as well."

"What about you?" Joey asked.

Annja looked out into the trees. "I'll leave with you guys as a group. But somewhere along the trail, I'll bleed off. Don't try to find me. I'll search for Jenny and we'll figure out what to do next."

"You're going to find Jenny in these woods alone? You?"

"I'm pretty good at finding my way around, Joey. I've been in a lot worse environments than this," Annja said.

At that moment, the clouds finally opened up and rain pelted down from the sky, soaking everyone in seconds. The students shouted and complained that they had no tents to use for shelter.

Annja sighed and called them all together. "You're leaving."

"Now?" one of them said. "It's raining."

"So the quicker we get out onto the trail and headed back to the trailhead, the better off you'll be. Move quickly and you'll stay warm, too. Joey here is going to lead us all out."

"Can he do it?"

Joey looked as if he was going to punch the person who asked, but Annja held him back. "Yes, he knows these woods better than anyone."

"What if we get lost?"

"You won't," Annja said. "And I'll be bringing up the rear so I'll make sure no one gets left behind. Now, are we ready?"

They all nodded. Annja breathed a sigh of relief. If she could just keep them focused on the task at hand, getting back to the safety of town and away from here, then they'd be all right.

She looked at Joey. "You all set?"

"Of course," he said.

"All right, then. Lead on."

Joey started off down the trail. One by one, the students fell in, forming a ragged line. Rain continued to drench them all. Annja knew she'd have to find shelter pretty quickly if she had any hope of surviving long enough to find Jenny.

She figured the trio of gunmen were probably watching them leave. She hoped they would think that Annja had just wanted to get everyone out in one piece. Hopefully, they would believe that their threats had worked.

Even though they hadn't.

The trees seemed to reach in over them as they walked down the trail. Overhead, the long spindly branches with leaf shoots and pine branches deflected some of the rain, but it was still getting very squishy on the ground. Annja's boots left footprints behind her that quickly filled with water.

The trail was turning into a muddy mess.

"Joey?"

He turned back, hearing Annja call him. "Yeah?"

"Thanks for your help."

He frowned for a moment and then simply nodded. He understood that Annja would simply take off on her own at the right time and not announce her departure. The quieter she was, the better. The last thing those kids needed was something else weighing on their minds.

Annja did find it peculiar that none of them had asked about Jenny's welfare. But then again, when faced with mortal danger, most people do end up only considering their own personal safety.

Jenny was on her own.

Well, not quite. As Joey led the group around a bend in the trail, Annja saw her chance and quietly stepped off the trail. She crouched low and then slipped behind a thick pine tree.

The rain continued to fall and the light in the sky seemed to be dimming by the second. It was already late afternoon and the addition of bad weather meant that she was looking at spending a truly dark night in the woods.

Annja, soaked and not really knowing where she was or how to even begin looking for Jenny, was facing the very real threat of staying warm enough to survive her first night out here.

She smirked. Funny how her bad haircut paled in comparison to the dangers she faced now.

3

If Annja had initially believed that the rain would taper off as the evening progressed, she was wrong. Indeed, as the sky continued to darken, the rain increased until sheets fell from the clouds above her. The forest floor ran with mud and debris while a strong wind howled around her.

If I stay here, I'll die, Annja decided. The good news was that the weather was a great equalizer. The men with the guns would also have to seek refuge from the storm. That meant Annja could risk setting herself up properly without fear of them showing up to shoot her dead.

She hauled Jenny's tent out of her backpack and immediately got it staked into the sodden ground. There was no guarantee that the tent wouldn't fly away at the next gust of wind, but she was grateful she at least had something that would keep her reasonably dry.

Her next task was fire. Annja could already feel herself starting to shiver. And she knew from experience that the onset of hypothermia would render her useless very soon.

Her system would literally start to shut down, as her core drew heat away from her extremities and her brain.

She pulled out her knife and started scraping at the bark of the tree closest to her. The exterior of the bark was wet but the interior would still be reasonably dry. Annja produced a handful of shavings that would easily catch a spark. She put them into a plastic bag and then in her pocket to keep them as dry as possible.

Twenty yards from her makeshift camp, she spotted a downed tree. Closer inspection showed it overhung a fairly large area and provided substantial shelter from the rain. It was almost dry under the canopy of the dense pine. Annja could see the splintered trunk and reasoned it must have come down during a recent thunderstorm.

She hurried back and pulled Jenny's tent from the muddy ground. Back under the canopy, the ground was much drier. It wasn't high enough to set up the tent under the branches, but she could stretch the tent out and use it as a tarp. It was perfect to further protect her from the elements.

Annja also found a large pile of deadfall and the branches were almost all dry. She hacked several into smaller lengths and then scraped out a fire bowl depression in the ground. On the bottom she laid the tinder bundle and set some thin kindling sticks above it.

Here goes nothing, she thought. She scraped her fire starter against her knife blade and saw the sparks fly into the tinder bundle. They caught almost immediately, and even with the cacophony of noise from the rainstorm, Annja could still hear the snap and crackle of the wood as it caught.

Heat radiated up toward her and Annja shivered again, as if trying to throw the water off her skin.

I need to get these clothes dry, she thought.

She added more wood to the flames and set two of the

thicker logs nearby to begin burning. When she was satisfied she had a sustainable fire going, Annja removed her clothes.

Her jacket was still fairly dry, but she'd gotten wet pretty much everywhere else. She stripped off all of her clothes until she huddled around the fire nude, feeling the wood smoke curl up around her, wrapping her in its warmth.

On the branches above her, Annja draped her clothes, letting the heat and smoke dry them out.

The area was littered with pine boughs and Annja knew that sleeping on them could be almost a luxury if they were soft enough. The spring growth hadn't occurred yet so they were obviously dead leftovers from before the winter snows. Still, when she gathered enough of them and lay down, it was quite comfortable.

The wind howled around her sanctuary. I wonder where Jenny is in this mess? Annja frowned. She knew there was a chance that her friend would not survive the night without any of her camping gear. The wind, rain and falling temperature together could kill even an experienced outdoors type.

Still, Annja knew that Jenny was remarkably resilient. And she also had a lot of training. Annja rooted through her pack and found the energy bar she always kept there along with the bottle of water she'd packed. Some feast, she thought, but at least she had something.

The rain continued to hammer the forest. Annja couldn't remember hearing about any major storm systems threatening this area, but that didn't mean much in the mountains where the weather could change from minute to minute.

She finished her meal and then leaned back against the thick tree trunk. Thanks to the way the branches drooped almost to the ground, the heat from the fire warmed the area nicely. Annja felt relaxed and comfortable, despite the fact that she was sitting naked in the midst of a terrible storm. If she wasn't worried about Jenny's whereabouts she'd actually be having a great time.

But it was definitely not a night to be out alone. Still, she had her sword. And she had a fire and shelter. Water wasn't an issue yet. She'd just eaten. So even though she was out in the woods with three armed guys who had warned her not to hang around, Annja didn't feel too bad. As soon as the rain let up she'd start her search for Jenny.

She touched her clothes. The heat and smoke were doing their job nicely. She pulled them down and slid them back on. Her body heat would finish drying them.

She fed another log onto the fire, watching the flames jump around in the slight breeze that had managed to work its way inside the relative safety of the drooping tree. The heat enveloped her. Annja felt her eyelids drooping. She tried to blink away sleep, but she took another deep breath and nodded off.

When she woke, the sun wasn't shining. In fact, it was still pitch-black outside. It was dark inside the shelter, as well. The fire had died out and only red coals remained, smoldering from a lack of fuel.

Annja reached for a branch to toss onto the fire. She felt a small chill run up her back and knew she would need to keep better alert to ensure the fire didn't die out entirely.

Fortunately, the coals were still hot enough, and with a quick huff of air over them, they flared and caught on the branches, resurrecting the fire into a reputable condition. Annja shivered again.

The rain had tapered off. But the wind continued to blast through the trees.

Had she just heard something?

It was tough trusting her ears when the wind seemed to overpower her ability to pick out details.

The fire blazed to full strength. Annja sat with her back

against the tree. The fire had compromised her relative invisibility. If those goons were out there looking for her, they would see its glow through the branches and know someone was in there.

Annja closed her eyes and made sure the sword was ready to wield. It would be tough in the close confines of the overhang, so she would have to get out of it in case a fight broke out.

She paused, waiting for another indicator that something was moving around in the woods. But she doubted that she'd be able to detect a twig breaking underfoot. The wind continued to howl and it was roaring in her ears.

Any telltale sounds would die long before they reached her.

She'd have to go on her instincts alone.

Annja took a deep breath and allowed herself to relax, slowly enabling her focus to expand outward like a circle around her. She hoped it would act almost like a radar and let her know if there was any reason to be afraid.

She had no evidence but she couldn't shake the feeling that something was out there.

But what was it?

Maybe it was Jenny.

Maybe it was one of the gunmen.

Annja frowned. Did she really believe that gang would abandon the comforts of their camp to come out in the storm? It was doubtful. Having seen them up close, Annja knew they were probably sleeping off an alcohol-induced state of euphoria by now. In the morning, they would become a problem.

But right now?

No.

That meant there was something else out there.

Annja frowned. There it was again. *Something*. She shook her head. Being in the dark woods during a rainstorm all by

yourself could certainly make the idea of something like big
foot seem possible.

But Annja would have to see the creature face-to-face
before she bought into that. She knew of a bunch of expedi-
tions that had tried to prove the existence of the mighty
Sasquatch, without anything to show for their efforts.

Meanwhile, the true believers insisted that something like
the Sasquatch had the ability to make itself as visible or invisible as needed. Just because a bunch of humans tramped
through its woods didn't mean they'd find it.

Annja sighed. In all likelihood, there was probably an
animal out there just looking for a bit of something to eat.
Maybe it had gotten a whiff of the fire and had come to see
if there was any food to be had.

Annja smiled. Not this time.

Suddenly, though, she felt a sense of trouble.

Annja slowly got up on her haunches. She reached for her
boots and slid them on, tucking the laces inside so she
wouldn't have to tie them up. She was on full alert.

What was out there?

The wind blew another blast through the overhang, rattling
the branches around her. Annja felt a small shower of water
rain down on her from somewhere high overhead.

She racked her brain for all of the animals that lived in
these woods. She knew that there was fox, bear, coyote, but
what else might call this place home?

A wolf?

Maybe a werewolf.

Annja grinned in spite of herself. There were times when
her internal dialogue made her crack up. This was one of
them. She'd been working with Doug Morrell for too long.
Werewolves were exactly what he'd be thinking about.

But she had to find out what was threatening her safety.

She glanced up. She could climb into the branches for a look-see. She might be able to figure it out.

The wind died then and she heard a large crack somewhere outside of her shelter.

That didn't sound like a small animal.

Annja fed another log onto the fire, letting the flames blaze up. It wasn't doing her night vision any good, but seeing the fire made her feel a lot better about being alone.

Annja had no idea what she might be facing. And although she had her sword, the thought of running out of the shelter, blindly hacking at something, didn't make sense.

She'd have to go up.

Annja reached up and threaded her way into the branches. With every move, more drops of rain fell on her.

I'll need to strip off after this just to get dry again.

More sounds reached her ears. Something was definitely trying to get closer to the shelter.

She had to move fast.

Annja let her feet carry her into the higher branches of the tree. She still had her knife on her belt. And she had her sword. But she'd left her pack down at the base of the tree.

The branches below her yawned and then snapped back.

Annja kept climbing.

Was that a snarl?

Her pulse quickened. Wild packs of dogs sometimes roamed through the woods. And they would gladly tear a lone female apart without hesitation.

She knew she was far better to be off the ground. She reached for the next series of branches and pulled herself into a seated position about twenty feet up before pausing to catch her breath.

Below her, a series of snaps made her look. Something was destroying her camp. She could just make out the black shape moving back and forth. But it wasn't unrestrained carnage. More like calculated destruction.

Whatever it was seemed to be searching for something.

She could easily jump down and attack them, but what would be the point? She was safe, and the idea of facing an unknown adversary didn't sit well with her. She frowned and climbed even higher.

Annja's foot slipped. And the branch supporting her cracked.

She gulped as her stomach spasmed.

The branch gave way.

Annja fell toward the unseen danger.

4

As Annja plummeted through the branches, time seemed to slow down long enough for her to feel every poke, prod and stab from the mighty tree's limbs. She kept her eyes closed and prayed that her body would relax enough to somehow survive the fall. As she waited for the inevitable thump, she kept her eyes firmly locked on the sword. If, as she suspected, something nasty was waiting down there for her, she'd need it as soon as she landed.

If she could move.

But instead of a hard impact and broken bones for her trouble, as Annja's body hit the ground she tucked and turned into a roll. She exhaled hard, rolling several feet before coming to her feet.

Underneath the canopy, something still lurked.

And now she heard a distinct growl.

Last I checked, the legend of big foot didn't include any growling. Howling maybe, but growling? No way.

Annja closed her eyes and summoned the sword. In the darkness, its blade glowed a dull silver.

A gust of wind nearly knocked her off her feet but she bent her knees and kept her balance. What was rustling through her backpack? A bear? Was it late enough for a bear to come out of its hibernation? Annja wondered if the bears around these parts were grizzlies and then decided that pretty much any animal would be dangerous.

She caught a sudden glimpse of yellow and realized that there were two eyes staring out from under the tree canopy at her.

It had to be a wolf.

Annja stepped forward, keeping the blade in front of her. The last thing she wanted to do was kill an animal but if she had to defend herself, she wouldn't hesitate. She knew it was highly unlikely the animal was maliciously trying to kill her. She had inadvertently stumbled onto its territory and the wolf was simply defending its home turf.

Still, a threat was a threat.

The wolf growled louder now, clearly threatened with Annja's advance. But she kept moving. There were things in the backpack she wanted, and letting the wolf tear it apart wasn't going to happen. Annja had already suffered through enough headaches thus far on the trip and she had no intention of giving in so easily for this.

"Get out of here! Scat!"

Annja thought it sounded ridiculous yelling into the night, but if she could scare the wolf off, that would be the best outcome.

The wolf, however, continued to growl, and it grew even louder. Annja took a glance around her and tried to recall if wolves hunted alone. As pack animals, she reasoned there could be others nearby. That would drastically reduce her chances of winning a confrontation.

She heard more rustling under the canopy and frowned.

The wolf was probably tearing everything apart as punishment for Annja trespassing on his land. Great.

She stepped closer to the overhang and slashed the air in front of her with the sword. It cut several branches off with a dull singing sound that made the wolf stop and regard her again.

This time it didn't growl.

Annja paused.

Had the blade convinced it? Could it see that if Annja pressed forward, it would probably die on her sword? Maybe it didn't want any part of violence tonight. Maybe it was simply out hunting for something to eat after the terrible storm.

Annja looked around, but saw nothing else lurking in the night. It seemed likely that the wolf was alone. A lone hunter. Annja smiled. I know the feeling.

"You're not going to kill him, are you?"

Annja nearly fainted from fright, but recovered quickly enough to pivot and aim her sword into the darkness.

"Hey, whoa, be careful with that thing, lady. I don't want to be run through."

Annja squinted and could just make out the form of another person in the shadows nearby. The voice was familiar enough for her to guess who it belonged to.

"Joey?"

"Yep."

Annja exhaled. "Want to tell me what you're doing wandering around out here in the dark?"

"Isn't it obvious? I'm looking for you."

"Why? I can take care of myself, thank you."

Joey stepped out of the shadows, his eyes running along the length of the blade. "I can see that. Where did you ever get that thing? I didn't see you with it earlier today."

"It's a tool I carry around with me."

"Something that looks like that isn't what I'd call a tool, Annja. That thing has one purpose—to kill."

Annja shook her head. "You'd be surprised what else it can do other than just take a life."

"Yeah, you'll have to explain it to me. So you got a wolf rummaging through your gear, huh?"

"You know it's a wolf?"

Joey pointed at the ground. "Tracks. Yep, it's a wolf."

Annja smirked. "One wolf under the canopy and one creeping wolf outside. I'm surrounded, I guess."

"At least you had the good sense to find some shelter. I smelled your fire a ways back, too. I would have come in sooner, but I picked up the wolf stalking you and couldn't interfere."

"Why not?"

Joey shrugged. "He's just doing what a wolf does. No sense interrupting him, you know?"

"Is it dangerous?"

"Sure. If he feels threatened. Most likely he's just checking out your stuff. We don't get a lot of humans out this way and the animals around here tend to be naturally suspicious, anyway. He's probably making sure he understands what your intentions are."

Annja raised her eyebrows and glanced back at the canopy. She couldn't tell what the wolf was doing right then. There wasn't any movement in the darkness under the canopy.

"You should probably put that away," Joey said.

"Why?"

Joey smiled. "He's not going to hurt you. Let him get on with what he's doing and he'll leave. He's got other things to be doing tonight, like finding dinner somewhere. He was tracking rabbits when he veered off to check you out. Probably found you the same way I did—the fire."

"I really needed it or else I would never have had one."

Joey nodded. "No sweat. With all that rain, it was a good thing you did build one. You must have been soaked."

"I was." Annja thought about Jenny. She would be soaked, too. "You didn't happen to find any sign of Jenny while you were out looking for me, did you?"

Joey shook his head. "No, but I thought I'd start with you first."

"You took the kids back to town?"

"Yeah, they're fine. I think they're leaving tomorrow. They couldn't stop talking about the guns and stuff the entire way back. I've never heard so much talking in my life. It got ridiculous and I had to tell them to shut up."

Annja smiled. "Thanks for taking care of them."

"They wouldn't have lasted without me. Guess you were right."

"Well, every once in a while I get something correct."

Joey pointed behind her. "You really should put that away. The wolf doesn't want to hurt you."

Annja turned her back to Joey and let the sword return to the otherwhere. She wasn't sure how to explain the sword's behavior to Joey. When she opened her eyes and looked at him, he didn't seem the slightest bit fazed by the sudden disappearance.

"I guess you don't want me telling anyone about that, huh?"

"I'd prefer that we kept it between us, yes."

"People find out, there'll be way too many questions. I can dig it."

"You sure?"

"Well, another fifty would help seal the deal."

Annja pointed at the tree overhang. "Tell you what. If you help me get my stuff back from the wolf it's a deal."

Joey smiled. "No sweat."

He knelt in the muddy ground and put his hands to his mouth. In a split second, he exhaled and made a strange sound that resembled a type of bark, but nothing like anything Annja had ever heard before.

The effect, however, was instantaneous. From under the tree, there was a rustle of movement. And then Annja saw a large shape dislodge itself from the branches and come through the darkness toward Joey.

Her heart raced but she stayed where she was. Joey must know what he was doing to tempt fate this way. She had to trust him.

The wolf trotted out and sniffed Joey's hand. He spoke to the wolf in a low voice and a different language. With a casual glance at Annja, the dark gray predator stood at Joey's feet and let himself be stroked.

Joey looked up at Annja. "You want to pet him?"

Annja held up her hands. "Are you kidding?"

Joey smiled. "Humans spend too much time thinking that animals are different from them. The truth is, we're all just the same, made by the Creator. We're not different—we all belong to the earth. And the spirit that moves in all things moves in this guy just as much as it moves in you."

Annja watched the wolf loll its head back to better expose his ears to Joey's fingers. From its throat, Annja heard a low rumble come out, but it didn't sound remotely menacing. It almost reminded Annja of a cat purring. But somehow she thought maybe the wolf wouldn't appreciate the comparison.

Joey waved her over. "Trust me, okay? I wouldn't tell you it was safe if it wasn't. This guy is one of the protectors of his forest."

"You know him?"

Joey shrugged. "We've kind of grown up together. I've been coming here for years, ever since I was old enough to run around on my own. Cheehawk here has been around about the same time as me."

"It's got a name?"

Joey frowned. "Well, what's wrong with that? I've got a name—several, actually. And so do you. Why shouldn't this guy?"

"Cheehawk, huh?"

The wolf turned its head again to better see Annja as she started to approach. Joey held up his other hand.

"Take it nice and slow. Don't do anything to upset him and you'll be fine. Just like any other animal, you've got to give him time to scent you and get used to your smell. Once he does, he'll be fine. Just come to him without the intent to harm him."

Annja approached very cautiously. This was, without a doubt, one of the stranger things she'd done. Making friends with a wild predatory animal like a wolf wasn't what she'd expected to happen when she responded to Jenny's e-mail from her New York City loft.

Cheehawk continued to appraise her as Annja drew nearer. When she was within a few feet of the wolf, she sat down and extended her hand until it was under Cheehawk's snout.

She could feel the wolf's hot breath on the back of her hand as he sniffed her. And then she felt the curious sensation of his tongue lapping at it.

Joey chuckled. "I guess you passed."

Annja let her hand wander up behind Cheehawk's ears and ran her fingers through his coarse fur. It was almost like patting a big dog, but not quite. Even though Cheehawk seemed to have accepted her, Annja couldn't shake the idea that this animal could easily tear her throat out if it wanted to.

Joey shook his head. "Don't believe that."

Annja looked at him. "What?"

"Cheehawk would only attack if he felt threatened, just the same as you." He smiled at Annja. "Don't look so surprised.

The expression on your face was enough for me to figure out what you were thinking."

"Oh. Well, this is a bit new for me."

Joey nodded. "For Cheehawk, too. You're only the second human he's let pet him."

"Really?"

"I'm the first," Joey said proudly.

"I'm honored, then," Annja said. She looked into Cheehawk's eyes. "Thank you."

Cheehawk rose without making a sound, looked once at Annja and then at Joey, before turning and stalking off into the night.

"Where's he going?"

Joey got to his feet. "I told you. He's looking for his dinner."

Annja stood, awed by what had just happened. Then she thought about why she was even in the Oregon woods in the first place. "We need to find Jenny. If she wasn't able to make a fire, she might die of exposure out here."

Joey frowned. "All right, but we've got to be careful. Those lunatics with the guns are probably still around. And I don't feel like running into them."

Annja got her gear from under the canopy. Despite the awful sounds, very little of her stuff was damaged at all. She emerged and saw Joey standing on the trail.

"Ready?" the young man asked.

Annja nodded. It was still terribly dark and she had no idea how they were going to find their way. But Joey didn't seem to notice and before she knew what was happening, they were headed down the trail.

5

"How long have your people lived here?"

Joey picked his way along the path without making a sound. Annja marveled at his ability to stay quiet. He was very much every bit his namesake.

"Hundreds of years. We're a splinter group of Apache."

"Apache? I thought that tribe was from the Southwest," Annja said.

"It was. We came up north to escape the persecution of the Spaniards and the white man. It took us a long time to find a suitable home, but this was it. We had a need to remain hidden until such time as we could prosper."

"Has that happened yet?"

Joey shrugged. "There's always the future to look forward to. Life on a reservation doesn't offer very many Native Americans a lot of hope. Crime's rampant. Kids drop out of school. It's a mess."

"You lived on one?"

"Me? Nah. I visited a cousin one summer. It was all I could do to hope for September to hurry up and get there so I could come home and go back to school. Not the kind of place I'd choose to live, you know?"

"So you live here?"

"Sure. My grandfather takes care of me. My parents died in a car accident when I was really young."

Annja ducked under a tree branch. The wind had died down some and she lowered her voice since shouting wasn't necessary anymore. "I'm sorry to hear that."

"Yeah, well, I didn't really know them. It makes me sad to think of them sometimes, but my grandfather is all the family I need. Him and the animals who live here."

"I don't blame you. I never knew my parents, either." She nodded at the trail. "You really know your way all over these parts?"

"Yep. I've been running around here for about five years now. My grandfather insists I come out here to practice my skills so they aren't lost. He was a scout for his tribe when he was young."

"That must have been a long time ago."

Joey nodded. "Yep."

"And he taught you how to do all of this stuff? The tracking? The stalking? All of it?"

Joey paused and studied the ground. "Skills like that are what made my people such a tough enemy. They're also what protected us when we needed them. My grandfather says it's my duty to ensure they never die out. When I have a son, I'll teach them to him, as well. Just the way it goes, I guess. Stuff gets passed on this way like it has for hundreds, maybe thousands, of years."

"Incredible," Annja said. "You're very lucky to have someone like your grandfather in your life."

"Yep, he's pretty cool. He once walked from Alaska to South America. He called it the spirit journey where he learned how to beat his own limitations. Eventually, I'll probably do something similar. Kind of a rite of passage for my tribe."

"How many of you are left?"

Joey ran his hands over the ground. "Your friend passed this way about an hour ago."

"Really?"

Joey glanced at Annja. "She's stumbling, though. You see how her footprints are staggered? There's not a rhythm to them anymore. She's in danger, most likely from the wind and the rain."

"You're certain these tracks were made about an hour ago?"

"I might be off by fifteen minutes or so, given the degradation of the track from the weather, but yes, it's pretty accurate."

"Can you find her?"

Joey frowned. "Be a lot easier if she was in better shape. As it is, she'll be unpredictable. Her footwork will make it tough to follow her along a set course. In her state she might easily stumble and fall and we'd never find her."

"We've got to try," Annja said. "Lead the way."

"Can you keep up? I'll move faster if I know you can hang with me as I go along."

"Don't worry about me. If I can't keep up, I'll call out and ask you to slow down."

Joey eyed her. "Okay, then. Let's go." He turned and started moving quickly. With his body stooped lower, Annja watched him move at a crouching run, checking the ground every few minutes for more signs and then continuing on.

Annja kept pace pretty well for a while, but then her own stamina took a bit of a hit. She felt herself starting to grow weary from the fast pace. Joey kept moving. Annja forced herself to push on, concerned that Jenny could well be dying somewhere close by.

Joey paused. "You okay?"

Annja bent over and breathed deeply. "Fine. Why?"

"I can hear you panting. You sound like a train huffing along back there. Honestly, I thought you were in better shape."

Annja frowned. "I'm in fine shape, thanks. I'm a bit tired, though."

"You want to rest?"

"No. Jenny needs us."

Joey pointed to a nearby tree. "Stay there and get some rest. I'll go on alone and find her. When I do, I'll come back and lead you there. Right now someone needs to make sure she's okay."

"I'm slowing you down, aren't I?"

"Yep."

Annja nodded. "All right, then. Go."

Joey turned and vanished into the night. Annja watched him disappear and then leaned her head back. The trunk of the tree behind her felt solid and somehow comfortable. Within a few moments, her eyelids dipped shut and she fell asleep.

And then she felt herself being shaken.

"Annja!"

She popped her eyes open. Joey's face was close to hers. "Come on and wake up, sleepyhead."

Annja got to her feet. "You found her?"

Joey nodded. "About a mile farther on. She was in a bad way but I got a fire going and huddled her up close to it. Hypothermia, I'd guess. The rain and wind probably took her down, but she should be okay. I made some pine-needle tea for her to drink, to warm her from the inside out. She was coherent when I left."

"What did she say?"

"I guess she went back to camp and found it deserted."

Annja frowned. Of course there was no way she could have let those kids stay in danger with gunmen threatening them. She had to break camp and send the students away. Jenny would understand, Annja felt certain of it.

"So what happened? She just went hiking around, looking for us?"

Joey shook his head. "Nah, she says she found her way back to the trailhead. She assumed something must have happened that made the camp leave. She was trying to get to town when the storm came down. Totally disoriented her. Before she knew it, she was in a bad state."

"Thank God we found her," Annja said. "She might have died otherwise."

"Definitely," Joey said. "Another thirty minutes and she would have been a goner."

He led Annja over the trail and down a steep precipice. Bits of shale and gravel broke free, skittering along the path toward the muddy lower ground. Annja thought she could hear something in the distance.

"Is that a waterfall?"

Joey nodded. "Yep. Better to see it in the daylight, though. At night it's not the same thing. Unless, of course, there's a full moon. Then it's pretty spectacular."

"I'll have to remember that. How much farther along is she?"

Joey stopped and pointed through the trees. "There. You see the fire? She's right there."

Annja couldn't see Jenny but she could make out the glow of the firelight. So could anyone else who might be out tonight. "You think that was such a good move? That fire's like a spotlight."

"It was either that or your friend dies," Joey said. "I thought saving her was a little more important than being stealthy about it."

Annja nodded. "You're right, sorry. It's just I can't help thinking about those guys roaming around in the night, looking for someone to kill."

Joey waved his hand. "Those guys are probably back in their tents, sleeping off a drunk. I saw an empty beer can in one of their jackets."

"What about animals? Would any of them attack Jenny if they knew she couldn't defend herself?"

"Highly unlikely. Cheehawk is about as big a predator as we get around here and he wouldn't bother her."

"Mountain lion?"

"Last report was from twenty years back," Joey said. "Long before my time. And I've explored these woods well enough to think that if there was one around, I would have run into him."

"Okay."

Joey led her farther down the trail and then the ground sloped upward again. "How she made it as far as she did is pretty amazing. I would have guessed that she'd lie down close to the waterfall, but she apparently wanted to get to high ground and try to use it as a navigational aid."

"Jenny's made of tough stuff," Annja said. "She knows how to handle herself."

"Well, weather can break anyone down," Joey said. "Even with training and various other tools, the weather can still beat you. You've got to respect it. She should have just hunkered down and gotten shelter and waited out the storm."

"Good advice," Annja said. "I'll make sure she gets the message."

Joey smirked. "I already read her the riot act. She knows she screwed up. But she's looking forward to seeing you."

"So am I," Annja said. "Is it much farther?"

"Just over the next rise."

Annja smiled. It would be good to see Jenny again, even

if she was in a state. At least she was alive. That was the important thing. All they had to do was get her back to town so she could be checked by a local doctor to make sure she had no lingering problems.

Joey ducked off the trail.

"She went this way?" Annja asked.

Joey nodded. "As I said before, in her condition, her travel wasn't orderly. The stumbling kept her going along downhill, but once she started to climb, she veered from the trail and ended up a few yards off the beaten path, so to speak."

"How'd you find her, then?"

"I cast around looking for her tracks and found them. As I got closer, I could hear her murmuring something and that was it."

"Lucky the wind died down enough so you could hear her."

"I can filter the effects of the wind on my ears," Joey said. "It's an old trick I learned a long time ago from my grandfather. It helps to always be able to hear even when the wind is screaming."

"That grandfather of yours is something else."

"Just old family traditions, Annja. Nothing more."

"So you say."

Joey pointed. "It's just over the next hill there. I moved her out of the wind and got a fire wall built to reflect the heat back on to her. Then I covered her up with a bunch of pine boughs. She should be nice and toasty by now."

Annja crested the hill with Joey still in the lead.

Joey stopped abruptly. "Hey…"

Annja came up behind him. "What's the matter?"

Joey pointed down the hill. "What the hell?"

Annja looked. She could see the fire with its flames still eagerly eating their way through the wood. The fire wall and pine boughs were also nearby.

But Jenny was nowhere to be seen.

6

"Where is she?"

Joey shook his head. "She was here, I swear it! I left her right there. She was sound asleep. Exhausted. There's no way she could have just gotten up and walked away."

"Are you sure?"

Joey eyed her. "Of course, I'm sure. You don't think I had something to do with this, do you?"

Annja had to remind herself that Joey was only fourteen years old. The way he carried himself, he seemed so much older. But did it make any sense for him to somehow hurt Jenny? She frowned. Of course it didn't.

"Sorry. I guess I'm used to too many people in my life not being what they claim to be."

Joey scampered down the slope and began checking the area around the pine boughs. "There are no tracks here."

"What? How is that possible?"

He pointed. "You can see the impression her body weight made on the bed of pine boughs. That's where I left her. But look at the ground. There's nothing much here to read. Even for someone like me."

"Is it possible she just got up and walked away?"

"Not without leaving some type of sign. I'd be able to read it, especially since I've grown pretty familiar with her track type. There's nothing here. It's like she just up and vanished."

Annja looked around. The approach to the knoll was fairly well sheltered. Would the gunmen have been able to spot the fire and mount a kidnapping so quickly? And if they had, shouldn't there be some type of track for Joey to find?

"This doesn't make sense. She's got to be around here," Annja said.

Joey shook his head. "Impossible. She'd need to have a stride like King Kong in order to walk away without me having anything to follow. No way. She's not here—she somehow got snatched by someone skillful enough to erase their tracks like they weren't even there. And that's some major skill. I don't know anyone but my grandfather who could pull it off."

"And yet someone clearly has."

"Yep."

Annja frowned. "My real concern right now is that Jenny might be in some serious trouble. She might be close to death again, being away from the fire."

Joey nodded. "Well, whoever grabbed her, they at least had the good sense to take the tea I made for her. It's gone, too."

Overhead, the storm clouds finally broke apart and drifted away, illuminating the area with moonlight. Annja was amazed at how much better she could see the surrounding area now. It was almost, but not quite, like being out in the daylight.

"Well, that will help," Joey said.

"How long did it take you to get her settled before you came to see me?"

"About twenty minutes to get her squared away, and it was long enough for me to make sure she was in a good state. I would never have left her otherwise."

"I believe you," Annja said. "And how long did it take for you to get back to me after you left Jenny?"

Joey shrugged. "Under ten minutes. It's not that long a haul for me."

Annja nodded. "Still that means someone had plenty of time to get to her while you were fetching me."

"Maybe she got swiped by a UFO," Joey said. "That would explain the absence of tracks. They could have used one of those beams that lifts people right up into the spacecraft."

Annja smirked. "You get a lot of UFOs around these parts?"

Joey shook his head. "Unfortunately, no. This place can be a real bore sometimes."

"All right, so that means whoever grabbed her had to be extremely capable at stealthy movement."

"And strong," Joey said. "Jenny wasn't exactly light as a feather."

"For you," Annja said. "A grown man might have had an easier time of it."

Joey frowned. "I'll be grown up within two summers. It's not such a big thing."

Annja winced. She'd clearly struck a nerve with Joey. Teenaged boys only want to be men and she'd belittled that with her comment. "Joey, I'm sorry. I didn't mean to insinuate that you were weak or anything."

"No big deal." But she could see that Joey was smarting from the comment.

Annja looked around. "So what do we do now? I mean, Jenny's not here. And if we have any hope of finding her, we'll have to do it soon. I'm at a loss as to how we should proceed." She looked at him closely. "These are your woods. I'd be grateful for your advice."

Joey smiled. "Thanks."

"Well?"

Joey nodded. "Okay, we can try to search for her, but I don't know how much good it's going to do. Without a track, I'm not much use. I haven't really learned how to spirit track yet."

"What's that?"

Joey shrugged. "You'll think I'm being weird."

Annja smiled. "Did you see that sword earlier? What exactly was normal about that thing?"

"Not much."

"Exactly."

Joey sat down. "Well, spirit tracking is when you try to tune in to the person's thoughts or spirit. You use that to guide you to them. My grandfather says it's one of the ultimate tests that a true scout can undertake. Learning how to do it, you can kinda tune in on them anywhere."

"It's not limited by distance?"

"Nope. The process isn't one I'm really familiar with, though. I still need a lot of training before I can pull it off adequately."

"What about your grandfather?" Annja asked.

Joey sighed. "That guy can do anything."

"Then maybe we should get him out here to help us."

"Yeah, that would be the best thing to do, but my grandfather's not able to walk anymore. He wouldn't be able to come out here unless we drove him."

Annja frowned. "What happened to him?"

"He got hit by a car crossing the street. Paralyzed him from the waist down. He hasn't been the same since."

A stiff breeze blew across the hill, chilling Annja. Jenny was somewhere in the woods, probably still in pretty bad shape, and there wasn't a thing they could do about it. All that seemed likely was that she had a cup of pine-needle tea and little else.

"This is not how I expected to be spending my trip," Annja said.

Joey pointed to their left. "My grandfather lives about four miles that way. If we hurry, we can reach his place in a little over an hour. But it's not an easy trek. And I'm a little worried that you might not make it."

"I'm not waiting here for you," Annja said. "The last time I did that, Jenny vanished and I'm not taking the chance that whoever took her won't come back and get me, as well. That'd just make your job that much harder."

Joey shook his head. "Yeah, like if someone tried that on you, you couldn't just whip that blade out and slice them apart."

"It's not that simple," Annja said. "If they surprise me, for instance."

"Like I did?"

"Yeah, like that. Then it becomes much harder to defend yourself. Plus, I'm cold and exhausted. If you leave me here, I'll fall asleep in no time. And that would also make me vulnerable."

Joey shrugged. "Suit yourself. But you'd better be able to keep up with me. Your friend's life depends on me moving fast. If I can reach my grandfather's house and get him to spirit track Jenny, then we should be all set."

"He'll be able to tell us where she is?"

"Almost definitely."

Annja took a deep breath. "Then we'd better get going."

Joey took a moment to orient himself and then set off at a brutal pace. Annja couldn't believe how fast he moved and seemingly without getting tired. He wound his way up hills and down tight trails bordered by steep drop-offs. Streams ran parallel to their progress and, in places, the pines dipped so low that Annja had to duck repeatedly to avoid getting her eyes poked out.

Her breathing came fast and hard and, despite being bone cold earlier, the pace of the trek heated her up until she started to sweat. She could feel the rivulets running down her back and face. Her breath bellowed huge clouds of steam with every exhalation.

But still Joey kept moving.

Annja realized at some point that they weren't on the main trail any longer. Joey was using what looked like animal runs and smaller paths that would have been invisible to her eyes if she'd been here alone. But to Joey they were the back roads and side streets of the wilderness landscape. And he knew how to use them effortlessly.

"You really do know this place, huh?"

Joey nodded. "I've had the time to explore it, fortunately. But there's still plenty that I haven't seen. It keeps me excited about it."

Annja kept moving, focusing on the welfare of Jenny to keep her motivated. If they didn't manage to somehow find her, then that would weigh heavy on Annja's conscience. She just hoped that Joey's grandfather would be able to somehow tune in to Jenny's mind.

After a solid hour of travel, Joey drew himself to a halt. He took a deep breath and then seemed to smell the air. Annja came up alongside him and took the moment of rest gratefully.

"I don't think I've ever moved so fast in my life."

Joey smiled. "Quite the workout, isn't it?"

"I'll say. Are we close?"

Joey closed his eyes. "Quiet for just a moment, okay?"

"Okay."

Annja watched as Joey turned his head slowly from side to side until he locked in on one direction. He stayed quiet for two minutes and then opened his eyes. "You ready to go again?"

"Uh…sure."

"Good." Joey took off, motoring across the valley in front of them. At the base of the next hill, he leaned forward, putting all his weight onto his thighs. Annja copied his lead, and instantly her thighs screamed in protest. She was asking them to bear a lot tonight, but it was all for Jenny.

She had to keep going.

Joey crested the hill and then turned onto a new track. The number of trees seemed to be dwindling and thinning out. Annja felt a change in the air.

Civilization.

They had to be close.

Forty yards farther on, Joey stepped out of the woods onto a paved road.

"Where are we?" Annja asked.

"Close," Joey said. "Very close. This is the main road that runs from town out to the trailhead."

"I don't recognize it."

"You wouldn't have traveled this stretch coming from town."

Annja nodded. "Your grandfather lives out here by himself?"

"He's got me with him when I'm not out running around on my own."

Annja kept pace with Joey, determined not to let him wear her down entirely. "You've got a lot of freedom for someone as young as you are."

"You understand that, though, don't you? The importance of being free. Not a lot of people do. I look at some of the other guys I know and their parents are terrified that they'll get hurt so they keep them away from anything that might possibly harm them," Joey said.

"We live in a different world now," Annja replied.

"Problem is, we're cutting ourselves away from the very

earth that sustains us. No one understands nature anymore. It's tragic."

Joey stopped and pointed ahead of them. Annja could make out what looked like a small driveway.

"The house is up there," Joey said.

"I don't see it."

Joey smiled. "Wait a second."

Annja watched and then saw lights come on in one of the rooms, faintly illuminating the small home. "How?"

"He knows we're coming," Joey said. "Let's go."

7

As they approached the small house, Annja could see that the roof sagged in the middle and the gutters hung away from the roofline. The night's storm could not have been much help to the obviously aged exterior, with its gray paint flaking off in piles by the stone foundation.

A rough-hewn wooden rail led up to a planked porch. Two rain barrels set at either corner overflowed from the rainfall.

"Great place," Annja said.

Joey smirked. "You're kidding, right? It's falling apart."

"Well, yeah, but in a nice rustic way."

Joey turned and mounted the steps. Annja followed, and as she did so the front door opened, letting out a wash of light onto the porch. Backlit, Annja could just make out the form of a man in a wheelchair waving them in.

Joey bent and hugged his grandfather. "Grandpa."

"Creeping Wolf," the old man said. "I see you've been busy tonight."

Joey nodded and stepped back, letting Annja into the house. "This is Annja Creed. She needs your help."

"About the woman?"

Joey nodded.

Annja frowned. "How does he know that?"

Joey shrugged. "I told him."

"When?"

"When I took a second to contact him."

Annja frowned. "Telepathy?"

Joey's grandfather coughed and waved his hand. "You see? Everyone tries to rationalize everything. That's the problem with people these days." He motioned to Annja. "Come in and sit by the fire. You look cold."

Annja walked inside and saw that the interior was much nicer than the exterior had led her to believe. A large stone fireplace occupied the central place in the living room. Beautiful, intricate Native American tapestries hung from the walls. The floor was covered in a thick rug that looked like bearskin, although she couldn't be sure.

She chose the threadbare recliner to sit in and marveled at how comfortable it was. Her spine relaxed into it and the cushions adjusted perfectly to her frame.

Joey's grandfather smiled. "Comfy chair, ain't it?"

"Very."

The old man wheeled himself over to the fire. In the twinkling light, Annja could see the wrinkled skin that looked like aged leather. His beard was almost entirely white and hung about two inches below his chin.

He spun around then and eyed her closely. After a moment he smiled. "You may call me Dancing Deer."

Annja frowned. The name simply didn't fit, given the old man's condition. Had it been some sort of cruel joke that someone had given him that name?

Dancing Deer merely smiled. "I wasn't always like this. In my youth, I ran through the woods with the joy of a deer that has just found its strength. Even now, the soul of a mighty buck beats within my chest. Legs aside, I am still a mighty warrior."

Annja bowed her head. "I'm honored to meet you. I've heard a great deal about you from Creeping Wolf."

Dancing Deer nodded. "My grandson is a credit to his people. And he's a fine scout in his own right. He has a lot to learn still, but I can see that he has been very useful to you already."

"And I'm hoping you can be just as useful," Annja said. "I need your help to find my friend, Jenny."

Dancing Deer nodded gravely. "I can see that. The concern you have for your friend is evident on your face. It troubles your spirit greatly."

"If something should happen to her, it would be my burden," Annja said. "I do not wish for any harm to come to her."

"Very well," Dancing Deer said. "Then I must ask you to sit still and allow me to track her."

Joey sat down on the couch. "I was the last to see her, Grandpa."

Dancing Deer nodded. "Come and kneel beside me for a moment."

Annja watched as Joey got off the couch and knelt next to Dancing Deer's wheelchair. The old man placed one hand on Joey's head and then closed his eyes. Annja could see him muttering something under his breath and then it was over quickly.

Dancing Deer looked at Joey. "Bring the sage, please."

Joey ran from the room and Annja could hear him rummaging through drawers, presumably in the kitchen. When he returned, he had a large bundle of leaves in his hand. Annja recognized it as the sage Dancing Deer had requested.

"Light it and let it smolder, please."

Joey leaned in close to the fire and let the bundle catch a

kiss from one of the flames. The fire ate into the dried herbs and then Joey waved it to extinguish the flame. Smoke wafted into the room and Annja took a nice deep breath. The effect of the sage was relaxing.

Dancing Deer still had his eyes closed. "Move it around the room until we are surrounded by its essence."

Joey circled the room, letting the smoke hang in the air until it permeated everything. Finally he set the smoldering bundle in a small dish near the fire. Smoke continued to drift toward the ceiling.

Annja could feel her own eyelids getting heavy again. She desperately wanted to stay awake and watch Dancing Deer undertake the spirit track, but she wasn't sure that it was possible.

Dancing Deer looked to Joey again. "I am ready."

Joey glanced at Annja. "You need to be absolutely quiet, okay?"

She nodded.

Dancing Deer's eyes closed again, and this time he started a low chant that seemed to rumble up from somewhere deep inside his chest. As she listened to it, Annja could feel herself being carried along. A drum joined in the chant and she realized that Joey must have been drumming along in time to it.

Dancing Deer continued to chant and the drumming kept pace the entire way. Annja could feel herself starting to fall fast asleep.

She had to stay awake!

The chanting and drumming continued and now a new voice joined in. Joey was chanting along with his grandfather. How on earth were they going to be able to find Jenny? Annja desperately wanted to ask them but Joey had warned her not to make any noise. Whatever they were doing, clearly Annja saying anything would disrupt the procedure.

She relaxed and breathed deeply, inhaling and exhaling as she felt herself get lighter and lighter. The smell of sweet sage in the room drifted in and out of her lungs, and seemed to seep into every one of her muscles, making them relax even further.

The more Annja relaxed, the deeper she seemed to sink into the chair and the lighter she felt. It was an odd sort of sensation. While she'd experimented with hypnosis before, this was nothing like it. She was relaxed and deeply in some sort of state, but she simultaneously felt like she could lift right out of her chair as if she had no weight whatsoever.

The drumming and chanting seemed farther away now, as if Annja was somehow removed from it in some respects. She turned her eyes inward and saw the sword hanging in the space in her mind's eye where it always resided. She could reach out and touch it if she wanted. But somehow she knew her attention was needed elsewhere.

She looked outward and, in an instant, found herself drifting up and out of the chair toward the ceiling. Then she was carried through the house and out into the dark night again. She could hear the wind but felt none of its cold bite.

She turned toward the woods where she and Joey had come from and let herself float that way. She drifted down the trail quickly, her feet never touching the ground at all.

Annja kept breathing deeply. Somehow the sage smell still lingered in her nostrils. Somehow it still kept relaxing her, even while she was outside of the house.

The thought that she was traveling out of her body occurred to Annja and she looked back to see if there was some type of thread connecting her body as she'd often read about. She could see nothing.

Perhaps this was what it was like to die?

Annja kept traveling down the path. She rolled over the hills and down into the valleys. She could taste the air. And soon enough she found herself back where she and Joey had started.

The pine boughs still held the impression of Jenny's body. Annja rose up above the ground and looked at the area from a different perspective. Whoever had grabbed Jenny would have scared her possibly. Jenny must have felt some type of fear, even in her weakened state.

What would it be like, she wondered, to lay there so vulnerable and know that you couldn't do anything? Her heart started beating faster. Annja felt her pulse quicken at the thought of the sudden looming presence that might have carried her off.

Who was it? she wondered.

Where was she?

The fear was palpable; Annja could feel it envelop her body and her mind like some kind of blanket. She wanted to shrug it off and feel relaxed again, but a voice inside her told her this was necessary. She needed to know this fear.

Annja embraced it then, allowing herself to be swept up into the rising tide of anxiety that Jenny would have felt. And as she did so, her body shifted. She was zooming along the ground again, but no longer in control of herself. It was as if she'd stepped on a carnival ride and been whisked away from where she was.

Something was happening.

In the far distance, she could still hear the drums and chanting. It reassured her to know they were still there, but then Jenny's fear overwhelmed her again and she continued her journey.

Her body flew over the landscape to places that Annja didn't recognize. Hills too steep to climb rushed at her as she continued to move on and on, higher and higher until she felt as if she was above the treeline.

And then darkness.

It surrounded Annja. She could taste the fear in her mouth. Where was she? Who had taken her? She had no sensation of what had transported her, only that she was somewhere dark and dank.

It wasn't too cold, though. Somehow there was warmth in this place.

And then she heard the soft sound of crying in the darkness. "Jenny?"

But no one answered her. Annja frowned. Of course not. If she was still sitting in the chair in Dancing Deer's home, there'd be no way for Jenny to hear her.

Still…

"Jenny?"

There was no response. Annja frowned. "I think you're in a cave up on a mountain almost above the treeline. If you can hear me, try to get out of there and work your way down. I'll try to find you."

It felt good saying that, and as soon as that relief washed over Annja, the darkness disappeared and she was flying back down the mountain to where she'd begun her journey. Everything happened in reverse. And then Annja was back by the pine boughs.

The drumming grew louder. So did the chanting. Annja realized that her trip was over. She could smell the sage again. She could feel the heat of the living room. She wanted to be back in the chair.

She flew down the trail. Back over the hills and valleys. And then into the air.

Annja drifted back toward Dancing Deer's home and then down through the ceiling, finally coming to rest in the chair.

The drumming and chanting grew louder now as she felt herself sink into the flesh of her own body.

Annja opened her eyes and felt incredibly light and refreshed. Dancing Deer's voice trailed off. So did Joey's drumming.

After a moment, Dancing Deer opened his eyes and stared right at Annja. "Did you have a pleasant journey?"

Annja smiled. "I don't know what happened to me."

Dancing Deer nodded. "I think you do, actually. You were the one to whom your friend has the strongest connection. As such, you were the one to take the journey. Not I."

"You mean I spirit tracked her?"

"I don't know," Dancing Deer said. "Did you?"

"I'm not sure." Annja frowned. "There was a lot of darkness."

"But you know where to look now, don't you?"

Annja closed her eyes and then smiled. "Actually, I think I do."

8

Dancing Deer looked at Annja closely. "Be careful. You are still learning to trust your instincts. At this point, it can be very dangerous to be too trusting or too little trusting. Do you understand?"

Annja frowned. "I…I guess I do."

"You need only trust in the spirit that moves in all things. The Creator will guide you to what you seek."

The sage smoke had ceased billowing from the bundle and all that remained were the blackened bits of the herb in the dish. But Annja could still smell the sweet scent in the air.

Joey got up and took the dish to the kitchen. Annja could hear him washing it before he once again returned to the living room. "You ready to go?"

Annja rose from the recliner, feeling as if she'd been asleep for hours. She stretched and heard her back creak a bit. "I guess so." She smiled at Dancing Deer. "That is one comfortable chair you've got there."

Dancing Deer grinned. "And as soon as you're gone, I'm going to fall asleep in it."

Joey gave his grandfather a hug. "Thanks for your help."

Annja could see the pride in Dancing Deer's eyes as he hugged his grandson. "Don't be gone too long or I'll worry."

"You don't need to," Joey said.

"You're all I have left. I don't have a choice but to worry."

Joey stepped back and nodded. Then he turned to Annja. "Let's go."

Outside, the night sky was filled with stars not overshadowed by the brilliance of the moon in the western sky. Annja picked out several constellations and marveled at how much she could see.

"Annja?"

She looked at Joey. "Sorry, it's just so beautiful here."

"We can look at it later." Joey pointed. "We need to get going. Did you see the direction we need to head in?"

"Let's start back at where you left Jenny. I was there and then I was taken away after I tuned into her…fear, I guess."

Joey nodded. "Dancing Deer says that is one way to do it. By tuning into the emotions of the person you're trying to track, it's very easy to find them. Fear is one of the strongest. Rage and lust are others."

"Lust?"

Joey shrugged. "I don't know much about that one yet. But the things that people obsess over are stronger than just basic emotions. Pretty interesting stuff, huh?"

"Definitely."

Joey led them back down the road and into the woods again. Annja laughed. I feel as if this is the third time I've traveled this route tonight. I'm almost getting tired of seeing it again.

Joey glanced back at her. "Old hat to you now, huh?"

"I was just thinking that."

"Happened to me, too. The first time I did it."

Annja frowned. "I thought you said you didn't know how to do it. That's why we went and saw your grandfather."

"What I said was I wasn't skilled enough at leading someone else on a spirit track. I knew it would have to be you."

"You never mentioned that."

"Would you have believed me?"

"Possibly."

Joey chuckled. "I guess maybe you would have."

They wound their way back down the trail. Annja's legs knew the terrain by now and she was surprised at how relaxed she felt as she moved along. It was almost as if she was able to sense the flow of the land, to read it before she reached it and adjust her body accordingly. The result was she wasn't nearly as exhausted this time.

Joey led them back to the hill where he'd left Jenny. "Okay. Now what?"

Annja glanced around. The last time she'd been there, she'd been out of her body and tuning into Jenny's emotional state. But now, being there in the flesh, it didn't seem possible to do what she'd done back at Dancing Deer's home.

"I don't know."

"Annja."

Annja shook her head. "It doesn't look familiar. I don't know if I can do this again."

"Of course you can. You just need to stop thinking that it's different now from how it was when you were in the chair. It's not different. It's the same. It's all connected."

Annja closed her eyes. She tried to remember how she'd felt when she reached this point. She could feel her heartbeat increase as the waves of fear gripped her insides again. She was Jenny. She was feeling the approach of some kind of unseen danger. And then she was swept up.

Running.

Running.

Through the trees and across the hills and the valleys. Branches whipped past her face. She could smell the wet pines, the dampness of the rain on the air. She could hear the breezes rustling the leaves and the deadfall. She could feel her feet on the slippery mud, but somehow kept her balance just the same.

And still she could feel Jenny's fear. She knew it now like it was her own. And she saw the darkness that surrounded Jenny.

The cave.

Annja opened her eyes and nearly fell over.

She wasn't by the pine boughs where Joey had left Jenny. She was somewhere else. Far away from where they'd been. Miles away, in fact.

Joey stood nearby. He was smiling. "Hey."

"Hey, yourself. Where the hell are we?"

Joey shrugged. "I don't really know. This isn't a part of the woods that I've explored before."

"I thought you knew everywhere."

"Nope. This is a lot of land. Parts of this place are almost inaccessible. Frankly, when you took off running, I was a bit concerned I'd lose you. If you'd kept up with me like that earlier, we might have found Jenny even faster."

"Funny guy. I don't even remember moving."

Joey nodded. "Yeah, well, when you suddenly forget about keeping your body, mind and spirit together, crazy things can happen."

"I guess."

Joey glanced around. "This is some pretty steep terrain. You think Jenny's around here somewhere?"

"A cave," Annja said. She could see the darkness. "I think she's in a cave somewhere above us."

"We're almost above the treeline as it is," Joey said. "But these mountains and hills are packed with isolated areas that are almost impossible to get through. She could be in any one of them. Can you narrow it down some before we start poking our noses into every cave we come across?"

"How would I do that?"

Joey shrugged. "Close your eyes again."

"Okay."

"One thing."

Annja opened her eyes. "What?"

"This time, try to consciously move a little slower, would you? You almost had me tired out back there."

Annja grinned. "All right."

She closed her eyes and tried to focus on the darkness. If Jenny was in a cave, they would need to know where it was.

But instead of feeling like she could see the darkness, Annja found that she couldn't concentrate on the pitch-black interior any longer. For some reason, it didn't feel right.

She opened her eyes.

"Something wrong?"

"I don't know. I closed my eyes and tried to tune into Jenny again, but I don't see any darkness. I'm trying to see the cave, but it's not working for some reason."

"Weird," Joey said.

"Maybe I'm not doing it right?"

"Maybe, but a lot of this stuff is just done by gut instinct. If something feels wrong, that usually means it is."

"So you think I'm doing it wrong."

"I didn't say that. I just said if it feels wrong, then perhaps something has changed that we can't see just yet."

"Like what?"

Joey shook his head. "I don't know. Maybe Jenny's not in a cave anymore."

"You think they moved her?"

Joey frowned. "Did you say anything to her when you were spirit tracking?"

"I called her name a couple of times."

"Yeah, anything else?"

Annja frowned. "As a matter of fact, I think I told her to find a way out of the cave and that we'd find her."

"There ya go. She's probably making her way back down to us even as we stand here."

Annja looked around. "Really?"

"Why not?"

"Well, I didn't think she heard me."

"She probably didn't hear you in the way that you would if we were speaking normally. But subconsciously she might have suddenly gotten the idea to leave the cave and then done so."

Annja looked at him. "Is that how you contacted Dancing Deer when we were on our way to see him?"

"Something like that."

"Pretty incredible."

"Nah, not really. That's another problem with this stuff. When people find out, they always want to mumbo jumbo it up. Turn it into something mystical or magical when it's anything but that. The most incredible things are inherent in everyone. It's just that we forget about them or don't use them enough so that, over time, the edges get dull. And eventually we forget we have them at all. It's kind of sad, really, when you see the majority of people sort of sleepwalking through their lives. The reality of waking up to the truth is always so much more amazing than you'd think."

"Through the looking glass, right?"

Joey frowned. "Huh?"

"Never mind. So where would you suggest we look for Jenny, then? She could be anywhere."

Joey shook his head. "I say we stay right here and that she'll probably be along shortly."

"Of all the places in these woods, you think she's just going to wander down in front of us?"

"Why not?"

Annja smiled. "Methinks you've got a lot of faith."

"Just a confidence in the way the Creator works, that's all. If that's faith, then so be it. But I don't get all religious about it. Just appreciative."

"Thankful."

"Exactly."

Joey hunkered down on a nearby log and started studying the ground. Annja watched him as he ran his hands over the dirt. "Any tracks?"

Joey shrugged. "Not sure, actually. I see some depressions, but I can't tell what made them."

"Really?"

He looked up. "Well, like I said before, I'm still studying. I can't get out here every single day when school's in session. I still have to do homework."

"Sorry."

"Forget it."

Joey went back to studying the ground. "Funny thing, though, whatever made this was pretty large."

"Meaning?"

"Nothing, I guess. I'd sure like to know what track this is. There are no real impressions, just a displacement of dirt. It's weird."

"Why are you guys looking at the ground?"

Annja glanced up. Coming out of the trees in front of them was Jenny Chu.

9

Annja couldn't contain herself. She rushed up and grabbed Jenny in a bear hug. "Thank God you're alive!"

Jenny nodded and Annja let her go. "I don't know what happened exactly."

Joey frowned. "When I left you, you were passed out asleep."

Jenny smiled. "I think it was that tea you made me. It was so warm and delicious. I just about went out after a few sips of that stuff."

"Old family recipe," Joey said. "But what happened? I wouldn't have left you if I'd known you were going to up and leave like that."

Annja brought Jenny over to the side of the trail. "Are you feeling all right? Joey can make a fire if you need one."

"I'm okay, actually," Jenny said. "Getting down here helped warm me up, so that's a good thing."

Joey squatted and looked closely at Jenny. "Well, considering how bad off you were when I found you, I'd say that's definitely a good thing. You made a remarkable recovery for someone who was struggling with hypothermia. Pretty impressive."

Jenny nodded. "I feel a lot better."

"So," Annja said, "can you tell us what happened to you?"

Jenny took a deep breath. "I left the camp early this morning. I'd come because a contact of mine out here found some tracks."

"Tracks?"

"He believed they belonged to the Sasquatch."

Joey rolled his eyes and Annja resisted the urge to. Instead, she smiled. "All right, that made you launch the expedition. But what happened this morning when you left camp?"

"I was getting a feel for the lay of the land. There's something incredible about this forest. I've been to plenty of places but it's almost as if this location has some type of spirit watching over it. The trails aren't beaten down by humans. There's very little, if any, litter anywhere, and the majesty of the place can be overwhelming."

Annja glanced at Joey. "I tend to think our friend here helps keep the place looking better than average."

Joey shrugged. "Part of my duty."

Jenny smiled. "Well, you're doing a phenomenal job. But I tend to think there might be another presence here. And the footprint casts that I saw in pictures made me desperately want to come here and find out for myself."

"And drag along your skeptical friend," Annja said.

"Sure. Why wouldn't I?"

Annja nodded. "So you were out hiking this morning…"

"I hadn't planned to do much. Maybe a few miles on one of the trails. I didn't take a pack with me. I felt I needed to be out by myself, you know? Away from everyone else. I love my students, obviously, but the chatter can get annoying sometimes. I don't imagine you'd understand."

Annja frowned. "Actually, I have a pretty good idea."

"I was out for a good long time. Again, I just got caught up looking at things. I lost track of time. By late afternoon, I was heading back, but instead of the camp, I found it deserted."

"We had some nasty visitors while you were gone," Annja said. "They were very persuasive when they asked us to leave."

Jenny looked at her. "The students?"

"Safe back in town, thanks to Joey."

Jenny smiled at Joey. "That's one more I owe you, huh?"

"Added to the tab, no worries."

Jenny looked back at Annja. "And you stayed?"

"Sure, I wasn't going to desert one of my friends. Especially not one who went through so much trouble to get me to come out here in the first place."

"Thanks. I mean it. And thanks for making sure my students got taken care of. If anything happened to them—"

"Let's not think about that right now. They're safe. So are you. That's what matters." Annja glanced at Joey. "Would it be too much to ask you to make a fire? Some of that tea you made Jenny sounds really good, too. I could certainly use a cup and I'm sure Jenny would like another, as well."

Joey smiled. "Consider it done."

Annja watched him vanish into the woods to find the necessary ingredients. Annja looked back at Jenny. "All right, now what the hell is really going on here?"

"What do you mean?"

"What I mean is, you bring me out here to some camp in the middle of nowhere. I get here and instantly I'm faced with three mean dudes with guns. I have to shepherd your students back to town. Then I have a run-in with a wolf. It's been pouring buckets and you almost die from exposure. I visit some old Native American man who surreptitiously teaches me how to do something called spirit tracking and we manage to find each other." Annja took a breath. "You're sure this is all about some set of tracks?"

Jenny took a deep breath. "I don't know."

"That's not much of an answer."

Joey emerged from the brush and started making the fire pit. "I take it you want this thing kept low profile?"

Annja nodded. "The lower the better."

Joey nodded and within a few seconds had a small blaze started. Annja watched him fix several sticks together to make some sort of grill. On top of this, he placed a small container of water to boil. Where he'd managed to get the water, Annja had no idea. She wondered what else Joey had hidden away in the small pack he carried.

She glanced back at Jenny who wasn't looking nearly so happy. "Tell me about this contact of yours," Annja said.

"David? He's just a friend I met through an online site for Sasquatch aficionados. We hit it off and started comparing notes. He mentioned he was out here and that he'd come across something he thought I might find interesting."

"The tracks."

"Yes."

"And he showed them to you?"

"Via e-mail. He sent me a digital photo of them."

Joey sniffed. "Any fool with Photoshop can alter a picture and make it look like something else."

Jenny sighed. "Maybe I was naive."

"Have you seen this David guy since you've been out here?" Annja asked.

Jenny frowned. "That's the odd thing. He was supposed to meet up with me in town to discuss the search pattern we were going to run to find the creature."

"You actually thought you were going to find the Sasquatch?" Joey shook his head. "And they say kids are crazy."

"Make the tea, Joey," Annja said. She turned back to Jenny. "You really thought you might catch one?"

Jenny shook her head. "That's a bad choice of words. By *find* I meant that we would get some type of evidence on film that the creatures exist. I didn't mean that we were going to trap one and cart it off for study."

Joey sniffed again, but this time didn't say anything.

"What's the background on David? Is he local? Would Joey know him?"

Jenny shrugged. "I thought he was local. But I guess I don't really know."

Annja sighed. "For someone as intelligent as you are, Jenny, you really dropped the ball on this one. How in the world did you ever convince the university to back this expedition?"

Jenny smiled. "I used to date the head of the department of anthropology. He owed me a favor."

Annja took another breath. "So let me see if I've got this straight—you hook up with some guy on the Net. He sends you pictures. You agree to come out and meet with him and manage to convince people to give you money to do so."

"That's about it, yes."

"You realize this sounds exactly like some type of exposé on the dangers the Internet poses to children, don't you?"

Joey stirred a handful of pine needles into the boiling water. "Tea will be ready soon, everyone."

Annja frowned. She wished she had some whiskey to go along with that tea. The thought that Jenny would be so reckless, not just with her own safety but with the safety of her students, really bothered her. Annja couldn't believe it. It didn't seem like something Jenny would do, and yet here she was.

She decided to change the subject. "David never showed up, huh?"

"No."

"And just what did this guy look like?"

Jenny shrugged. "He was sort of tall. Nice face. Clean shaven. Kind of that scholarly look—you know the one I like."

Jenny had always had a thing for bookish guys.

"Yeah, I know what you like." Annja glanced around. It didn't seem as if this David had any connection to the angry gunmen. None of them fit that description. That was at least something in his favor. Still, Annja wanted to know more about this guy and why he hadn't shown up when he said he would.

"Did you have any established communication routine at all? Would he know how to get in touch with you?" she asked Jenny.

"He had my cell-phone number."

"And did he call you at any point?"

Jenny frowned. "No. He didn't."

Joey handed Jenny a cup of the tea. "Drink this. It will make you feel better. I added a few extra touches to it."

Annja accepted tea from him, as well. She could feel the heat emanating from the cup and sniffed it. "Smells good."

"It is," Joey said.

"So does this David guy sound familiar to you? You seem like the type who would know anyone in town, and this guy sounds just different enough that he might stand out in your mind."

Joey shook his head and sipped his own cup of tea. "Sorry, no. I mean, every once in a while, we get some kooks through here who think they're on the monster trail and all, but it's happened often enough that we just get bored with them. They camp out for a week or so, don't see anything and then pack it in. When the Sasquatch doesn't come out of the brush and sit in their camp, they tend to lose patience and move on."

Annja nodded. "Looks as if David is a ghost, then. If he even existed at all."

Jenny sipped her tea. "But I spoke with him."

"Online," Annja said. "There's no guarantee that it wasn't someone else on the other end feeding you a fake picture of who you thought David was."

"But why go through that trouble?"

Annja shook her head. "I don't know. But someone did apparently. Or else, there's the other option."

"What's that?"

"That David has either been kidnapped or killed."

Jenny gasped. "You're not serious."

"Why not? Missing people who don't turn up when they're supposed to? Let's not be foolish here and discount it so fast. Given the other characters I've run into since I arrived earlier today, it's not out of the realm of possibility that something bad happened."

Jenny shook her head. "I don't believe it. I think he's still around. After all, look what happened to me. I vanished and yet you found me."

"You found your way down the mountain, Jenny," Annja said. "I didn't do anything."

"You spoke to me in a dream," Jenny said. "It was very clear to me."

Joey raised his eyebrows. "Wow, pretty good for a first timer."

Annja shushed him. "You heard me?"

Jenny nodded. "When I was in the cave. It was completely dark. Couldn't see a thing. And yet, in the darkness, you spoke to me as if you were right next to me. I'd been crying softly and then it was like you were there. Pretty amazing."

Annja took another sip of tea. "You remember anything else about getting to that cave?"

"Not really. I had the distinct sensation of someone lifting me up and running with me in their arms."

"They'd have to be pretty strong to do that," Annja said. "Maybe you were just hallucinating or sleepwalking?"

Jenny shook her head. "No way. This was for real."

"And just who do you think snatched you up like that?"

Jenny took a sip of tea and then looked right at Annja. "Why, big foot, of course."

10

Joey glanced at Annja and rolled his eyes. Annja herself wasn't quite sure what to make of Jenny's statement. She seemed so utterly certain that it was almost hard to argue with her conviction.

"Big foot?"

Jenny glared at her. "I know you think I'm being crazy."

"I don't—"

"I do," Joey said. "Completely bonkers. You need serious help for that condition."

Annja frowned. "Joey…maybe we should just let her talk and get it out of her system."

"Get it out? That's not going to happen. She's completely obsessed about this stuff. Like I said earlier when I saw you on the trail."

Annja held up her hand. "Regardless, we have to let her speak her mind and tell us why she thinks that the Sasquatch had something to do with her disappearance."

"He had everything to do with it," Jenny said. "I was

almost asleep when Joey left me, just about to drop off into deep rest, when I sensed this presence around me. As if I was being enveloped by it. And then I was rushing through the forest."

Annja frowned. What Jenny said sounded similar to the experience that Annja had had when she was spirit tracking. Was it possible that the Sasquatch really did exist? Or was it something else? Something far more sinister?

"Did you see it?" she asked.

Jenny shook her head. "I was asleep, remember?"

"Yes, but if you didn't actually see it?"

Joey sighed. "What about a smell?"

"Smell?"

Joey nodded. "A lot of people who have claimed to see the Sasquatch say that it smells really awful. Some kind of body odor. But it's supposedly awful stuff. Nose-pinching quality. Did you smell anything?"

"Well, no, actually, but…" Jenny's voice trailed off.

Joey shrugged. "Seems weird that a giant ape creature could stroll in and pick you up, run you through the woods and yet you didn't think to open your eyes or take a whiff? Doesn't fly with me. I think you hallucinated the whole thing. Maybe you were sleepwalking or something. In your condition, right there on the brink of hypothermia, anything's possible."

Annja took a breath. "He might be right, Jenny."

Jenny frowned. "I didn't ask you to come all this way just so you could belittle my experiences, Annja."

"I'm not trying to belittle them. I'm just trying to play devil's advocate here. It doesn't add up. Surely you can see that?"

Jenny took a sip of her tea and then sighed. "I guess. But why did I think that it was a Sasquatch, then?"

"Maybe because that's all you think about," Joey said.

"You're so keyed up on the idea that it exists, you're filling in parts of your brain with the notion that anything even slightly unexplainable is due to something Sasquatch related."

Annja cocked an eyebrow. "That was awfully insightful, Joey."

"Thanks."

Jenny shook her head. "Well, I don't know what to make of what happened. But if you guys won't believe me, then I suppose there's no sense arguing about it. I'll just chalk it up as unexplained and leave it at that."

Annja helped her to stand. "And how are you feeling otherwise? Still cold and shivering?"

"No. Joey's fire saw to that. And the tea. I'm much better now. I think I just needed to recharge the battery."

Joey watched her. "You should be careful all the same. Ideally, you should sleep and let your body restore its balance. What about if we pitch camp here and get some rest?"

Annja glanced around. "Can we bushwhack off the trail some? I don't like the thought of those guys roving around the hills looking for us."

"As far as they know, we all went back to town," Joey said.

Annja nodded. "Just the same, I don't want us easily found. Can you make us a camp that's nice and concealed?"

Joey shrugged. "Take me a bit of time, but yeah. How far off the trail should it be?"

Annja looked around. It was still quite dark. The sun would start coming up in a few hours, however. "Far enough so we can't be seen. For that matter, it should be far enough that we can't be heard, either. Talking's going to be a no-no until we get this figured out."

Joey erased all signs of a fire pit and then stood. "All

right, follow me." He led them up the hill and into the dense vegetation.

Annja made sure to keep Jenny between them. She had to watch her step. In this part of the woods, the trees grew thick together, their trunks entwined like snakes oozing all over the soft pine needle carpet.

Joey led them for the better part of half an hour. Annja was lost in thought. There were still a lot of questions to ask and she wanted answers.

But would Jenny be in any shape to answer them? Or would she even answer them honestly? Annja didn't necessarily think that Jenny would deliberately mislead her, but she also knew that big foot was an all-consuming passion of hers. Back in school, Jenny had forsaken an active social life for her studies. She devoured everything she could get her hands on on the legends of big foot. Not just the sightings in the United States, but also the reports from China and the Himalayas.

Jenny had even gone so far as to undertake an expedition to Nepal as part of her work on her graduate thesis. She'd endured an amazing amount of adversity only to come home with very little to show for it.

Annja admired her resolve and her perseverance, but when it came right down to it, part of her wished that her friend would give up the ghost chase and get on with studying something much more concrete in origin.

Annja sighed. But then again, what would people say about her if they knew the half of what she herself had been through, including her own trip to Nepal and her encounter with what some people would claim was the infamous yeti?

They'd think I'm a nut, Annja admitted to herself, and they might be justified.

Annja grinned.

As they walked on, Annja pressed closer to Jenny, trying to keep her voice quiet. "So tell me about David's disappearance."

"What about it?"

"I'm sorry to keep bringing it up, but do you think we should contact the sheriff?"

Jenny shrugged. "Would it do any good?"

"I don't know. Would it?"

Jenny stopped and turned. "Are you driving at something here?"

Annja shook her head. "I'm trying to figure out what the hell is going on, like why we have three armed men roving around, warning you off an expedition to prove the existence of big foot. Doesn't that strike you as slightly out of the ordinary?"

"Of course it does. Don't insinuate that it doesn't."

"And David? What's his role in all of this? Did you two have an understanding? Was there something there?"

"Like something romantic?" Jenny asked angrily.

Annja nodded. "A lot of people hook up on the Internet. It's no big thing. I'm just wondering if there was a spark between you two. Maybe something that led you out here, even if the promise of discovering some real evidence wasn't as convincing as it could have been."

"Now you're questioning my motives. That's nice. You think I deliberately defrauded the university so I could come on the trip? What, that I'm too poor to come out on my own if I wanted to?" Jenny turned and stormed away.

"That didn't come out right," Annja said.

"It didn't sound good, that's for sure."

Annja rushed ahead. "Jenny, neither of us come from money. But I didn't mean to imply that you're financially hard up."

"No, just that I would willingly lie to my superiors so they could bankroll this little camping trip. What's worse? I wonder."

Annja sighed. Jenny picked up speed and Annja let her catch up with Joey, who was navigating his way over a tangle of fallen logs. Overhead, the moon peeked out from behind a cloud and showed a fair expanse of the forest.

Annja could make out the lay of the land. Joey seemed to be leading them uphill on a very slight slope. Probably he would make camp someplace where they were surrounded by trees. Annja knew the best hidden campsites always took advantage of natural surroundings to blend in. And she was sure that Joey would know how to make best use of the environment to guarantee that they wouldn't be disturbed.

After they'd rested and gotten some much-needed sleep, they could trek into town and see the sheriff. Annja wanted to ask him some questions and get his take on this David guy. She still didn't trust the story. It seemed far too strange to believe, even if Jenny was determined to do so. She'd obviously lost all sense of objectivity on the situation.

And then there was the matter of the three riflemen. The sheriff definitely needed to know that he had those guys prowling around, looking to scare folks off for some unknown reason.

Joey stopped up ahead. He gestured that this was where they would make camp, and Jenny immediately sank down onto a log, resting her head in her hands.

Annja came up next to her. "Look, I'm sorry, okay? Not necessarily for what I said but for how I said it. I should have waited until you felt better to explain how I was thinking things through."

Jenny looked up at her. "You've always been somewhat impatient."

Annja smirked. "No argument there. Time, I've found, is a pretty crazy thing. I don't like to waste it."

"And sometimes—"

Annja nodded. "Sometimes it gets in the way of my good manners. Absolutely."

Jenny nodded. "All right. I don't agree with you, per se, but I appreciate the apology."

"We've known each other too long to let this come between us."

"Fair enough."

Joey came back into the small clearing carrying armloads of pine boughs. He dropped them into a big pile and then left to go for more.

"I could sleep for a day," Annja said. "I've been all over this forest for the past day."

"Me, too," Jenny said. "I don't think I'll ever look at pine trees in the same way again."

Joey came back twice more and combined the piles until he had a good area large enough for all of them to sleep on. He added some leaf litter, tested the bed and declared it suitable for sleeping.

Jenny collapsed onto it immediately. Annja followed and then sat up when she saw Joey going out again.

"Aren't you sleeping?"

Joey nodded overhead. "Remember where you are? The Pacific Northwest? See that cloud? It's going to rain."

Jenny groaned. "Not again."

Joey smiled. "I'll get some branches and more boughs so we can have a waterproof roof over us. Once that's done, I'll get a small fire going to warm the shelter. In an hour we'll all be asleep."

Annja turned as the first of Jenny's light snores reached her ears. "Looks like someone's already out."

"Good," Joey said. "I'll be back soon."

Annja watched him go and then turned to look at Jenny. She wondered what her friend had gotten mixed up in. Jenny was exhausted and she'd almost died tonight, and yet she seemed determined to continue her quest, regardless of the threat to her safety.

Annja knew she'd go along. There was no way she could turn her back on her friend, not knowing what she did about the situation. Even if it was precious little.

Jenny would need protecting. If not from the external threats like the mysterious gunmen, then from herself. Annja had seen obsession kill other people and knew that Jenny could easily fall prey to the same fate.

I won't let her die, she thought.

Joey came back into the camp dragging branches behind him. "She still out?"

"Yeah."

"Good. I don't want her hearing this."

Annja frowned. "Hearing what?"

Behind Joey, Annja could hear a low howl of some sort. It sounded like a cross between a coyote and a banshee. She looked at Joey. "What the heck is that?"

Joey busied himself with thatching a roof together. "I don't know. Now if you'll help me make this roof, we can get to bed and hopefully forget we ever heard that. Because it's not something I've ever heard before."

"Ever?"

"Never," Joey said. "But whatever it is, it sounds like it's coming this way."

11

Joey and Annja thatched a roof together more quickly than she would have thought possible. But Joey was a master at building shelters, and Annja had done more than her fair share of roughing it, so he got her squared away as he laid down the branches and boughs. He stood outside the shelter, even as the howling sounds grew louder.

Behind Annja, Jenny stirred and then woke up. "What's that noise?"

Annja shushed her. "Joey's making sure that the shelter can't be seen from outside."

"He'd better hurry—it sounds like the source of the noise is close by."

As if on cue, Joey's feet emerged into the shelter itself. Joey wriggled his body into the narrow entranceway and then he reached behind him to pull the last bit of pine boughs over the small opening.

Annja started to whisper something, but Joey put his hand over her mouth and gestured slowly outside.

It was close.

Annja held her breath and thought she could feel Jenny's body shaking nearby. She'd better keep it together, Annja thought. Otherwise, whatever is out there will know we're in here.

Annja closed her eyes and checked to make sure she could get the sword. As many times as she'd done so and knew it was usually available, it still felt good to double-check. There'd been a few instances in her past when she hadn't been able to use it for one reason or another.

Joey leaned forward and tried peering through the branches and boughs to see what was outside. Annja strained her ears and thought she could hear something rustling around on the fringes of the camp area.

Maybe it would simply pass through and leave them alone.

She glanced at Jenny and saw her friend's eyes were wide with fright, and at the same time she could detect the curiosity that drove any true adventurer. As terrified as Jenny might be, there was a part of her that desperately wanted to creep out of the shelter and see for herself if the source of the noise just might be a real Sasquatch.

Annja was curious, as well. Could this be the real thing? She almost laughed at the idea, but at that moment she heard what sounded like a heavy footstep come down on a branch that couldn't have been more than ten feet from the shelter.

Joey's body seemed tensed. He had claimed to know most of this forest, but even he with all of his skill and knowledge was concerned about the creature outside of their shelter.

Annja thought about Cheehawk and wondered if the wolf might be prowling around the area. Would it protect them? Could Joey call him in some way like he'd supposedly contacted his grandfather?

She could imagine the great wolf leaping through the forest until it could launch an attack upon the beast outside.

At that point, Annja could stand and draw her sword. The distraction would give her the necessary time to decide if she should simply kill the creature or not.

Another howl erupted a few feet away and sounded so utterly dreadful that Jenny clapped her hands over her ears and choked off a scream.

Annja's eyes blazed and ran with tears, and in that second she caught a whiff of the most horrible scent she'd ever smelled in her life. Hadn't Joey mentioned something about that with regards to previous big-foot sightings? Was this the real deal just outside? Could it smell them? Would it attack?

Legends of the Sasquatch came down from the Native American tribes that used to live around these parts, and Annja tried to remember what little bit she knew. Supposedly it stood at least seven feet tall and would easily weigh more than three hundred pounds. Hair or fur covered its entire body.

Joey wouldn't necessarily have grown up with the legends since his tribe had migrated from the Southwest of the United States.

Another branch snapped outside the shelter. Annja's heart thundered in her chest. Maybe she should just leap up and try to rush it.

It was still quite dark outside and she couldn't see through any of the boughs that Joey had laid over them unless she suddenly felt like compromising their position. It was infuriating to think that she might easily know with one simple glance if the Sasquatch truly did exist or not.

Another branch snapped.

Annja tensed. Was that sound closer than before? Was the creature nearer to them now?

It would be able to smell them soon. Annja certainly hadn't been out in the forest long enough to lose her smell from the city. It would cling to her like a musk that she felt certain any type of creature like a Sasquatch would easily smell.

Jenny herself hadn't been out that long, either, and Annja knew that Jenny liked using scented soaps.

That could be trouble.

Despite his youth, Joey looked as if he was ready for a fight. Annja knew that even though he'd insisted otherwise earlier, he would fight if need be. But she also knew that Joey wouldn't purposefully look to harm something that lived in the woods around these parts. Joey considered himself a caretaker and protector. If the creature did indeed live here, then Joey would rightfully assume it had every right to protect its territory.

Just like Cheehawk.

A sudden scrape on the outside of the shelter made them all jump. It was like a heavy pawing at the structure. At first, nothing much happened, but then the scraping continued. It was trying to get inside the shelter.

Jenny backed up until she was against the trunk of the tree that Joey had built the shelter next to. Her hand gripped Annja's arm.

Joey glanced back at Annja and made a doublehanded grip.

Annja frowned. Joey wanted her to use the sword.

Great.

It was bad enough that he knew about it. But Annja wasn't crazy about pulling the sword out in front of Jenny. For one thing, it would be one more person who knew her secret.

And it might galvanize Jenny's belief that the Sasquatch did indeed exist.

Although, at just that moment, even Annja herself was considering revising her previous hard-line stance against the creature's existence.

Bits of branches and boughs came away from the shelter.

The noises and scrapes were accompanied by a low whining howl. The volume was less than it had been before.

But the fear still kept them all frozen in place.

Joey nudged Annja.

He showed her the small knife he carried and Annja knew that it would do no good if it came down to defending them against whatever was outside.

It would be up to Annja to save them.

How was she going to do this? The shelter was cramped and at close quarters. From past experience, she knew that drawing the sword required a minimum amount of space. If things were too tight, it simply wouldn't materialize.

But one way or another, she was going to have do something soon. More branches and boughs came away from the shelter.

Joey frowned and then whispered, "Annja."

Annja nodded. "I need some space."

The howling grew louder, as if the creature outside had heard them speak. The scraping sounds of more branches and boughs coming away increased to a frenzy. A constant assault on their position was under way and Annja knew that she would have to literally go through the roof.

She figured she would have about three seconds to break out and draw the blade. She would need to be quick or she'd be completely vulnerable to attack.

But what other choice was there?

She turned to Joey and mouthed, "On three."

Joey nodded.

Annja closed her eyes. This had better work or else it was going to get ugly really quick.

Joey tapped Annja's arm.

One, two, three!

Annja jumped up and crashed through the mass of pine branches and boughs that they had just thatched together a few minutes before. There was a ripping sound as the branches tore away from the top of the structure. Annja's arms went through first, followed by the rest of her upper torso.

As she went through the roof, Annja closed her eyes and saw the sword in front of her in her mind's eye.

She reached for it and felt the hilt settle into her hands.

Annja opened her eyes.

The outside of the shelter was a horrible mess. She hadn't realized how much work Joey had put into making it. Branches and boughs lay scattered at the base of the shelter.

And there in front of her lay the creature.

Cheehawk.

"No!"

Annja let her arms come down and released the sword. It disappeared in an instant. "Oh, my God, no."

Joey poked his head out. "What's the matter?"

"It's Cheehawk."

Joey crashed through the remainder of the shelter not seeming to care about keeping it intact any longer. Annja could see the sorrow in his eyes the moment he saw the wolf.

Cheehawk's entire left side looked as though it had almost been torn wide open. Bloody chunks of flesh clung to his fur and Annja could even see bits of white bone protruding through his flesh at odd angles.

No wonder the sound had been so horrifying. Cheehawk was in absolute agony and had been dragging himself through the woods looking for Joey.

Joey pressed his face into Cheehawk's neck and stroked the wolf. "Who did this to you?"

Cheehawk's whine reduced to a whimper as he struggled to lay flat on the ground to rest. Behind them, Jenny came out of the shelter and cried out in shock when she saw the damage to the wolf.

"Who would do such a thing?"

Annja frowned. There were three people she thought might be likely candidates for such brutality.

Joey looked at Annja. "It was them. They did this to him."

Annja didn't say anything. Her heart felt heavy, watching the extreme agony that Cheehawk must have endured on his journey. He was such a beautiful animal and the reality of the situation hit her hard. Cheehawk would not survive his wounds.

As soon as she thought it, the wolf lifted its head and stared at her. Annja felt like his eyes were peering into her soul.

She shook her head. "No."

Joey looked at her. After a moment he seemed to understand. "Annja."

Annja kept shaking her head. "I won't do it."

"You must."

"No."

"He's asking you to. Would you deny him the right to be free of his pain and suffering?"

"Of course not, but—"

Joey frowned. "There's no but. Those bastards didn't show him any mercy. They just did this and then left him to suffer. The cruelty and indignity of it is horrible."

Annja felt her throat go dry. "I don't know if I can."

Joey nodded. "You have to. He has asked."

Annja walked behind the shelter and summoned the sword. She stared at it for a long moment and knew it was the right thing to do.

Jenny gasped when she saw the sword Annja held. "Where the hell did that come from?"

"Long story," Annja said. And then, as if she was in a dream, she felt herself walking toward Cheehawk. She knelt next to him and stroked his fur.

The wolf looked at her. Annja could see the plaintive look and knew it would have to be done. She glanced at Joey.

"Are you sure?"

"Yes."

"Is he sure?"

"Search your heart, Annja. You know it's the right thing to do."

Annja took a calming breath. "I know." She stood and gripped the sword.

Joey whispered something into Cheehawk's ear and then nuzzled him one last time. The wolf lay its head on the ground as if it knew just how to position itself.

Joey stepped back.

"Annja," Jenny said, "what in the world are you going to do to that poor wounded animal?"

Annja shook her head. "Not now, Jenny. Not now."

Annja raised the sword over her head. She closed her eyes. Forgive me for this. And may it release you from your suffering.

She cut down.

12

Joey managed to find a branch suitable for scraping a hole out of the muddy earth and got to work making a burial plot large enough for Cheehawk's body. When he'd finished digging it out, he laid a bed of fresh pine boughs, and then with Annja's help they carefully laid the mighty wolf in the ground.

"I'm sorry," Annja said.

Joey nodded. "He's one with the spirit that moves within us all. At least he's not suffering."

Annja sighed. She felt terrible about what she'd done. It didn't ease her mind that Cheehawk had been badly mauled and was dying, anyway. She was the one who killed him.

"You did a good thing," Joey said quietly. "And I know that he appreciated your mercy."

Annja's eyes welled up. "Whoever did that to him... Such cruelty. Why would they harm him like that?"

"Because they didn't understand him. And they had no wish to." Joey scooped handfuls of earth into the hole. In a short time, he had covered Cheehawk's body. He kept working until the burial plot was indistinguishable from the rest of the area.

Annja watched him finish and turned away. Jenny stood a short distance from them, leaning against a tree. As Annja approached, she looked up.

"You want to tell me where you found a sword like that?"

"Not particularly."

Jenny frowned. "You always liked keeping secrets, huh?"

"Don't be jealous, Jenny."

Jenny shook her head. "What is with you? You think I'm jealous of everything you have? You've got a sword. Big whoop."

"And the TV show. I haven't forgotten that bugged the hell out of you when it happened."

Jenny shrugged. "I'm over it."

"Are you?"

"Last I checked, neither one of us had a man."

Annja smiled. "So if I had a boyfriend, then you'd be even more upset with me?"

"Definitely," Jenny said with a slight smile.

Annja leaned against the tree. "I don't need some guy in my life to feel complete. Besides, the more I learn about the male species, the more I realize that truly good men are almost impossible to find."

"I'd take a half-decent guy," Jenny said. "I haven't been on a date in almost a year."

"Dry spell, huh?"

Jenny cracked a grin. "Mojave Desert, Annja. David was supposed to bring on the rainy season and now he's gone and vanished."

"What if we head into town and see if we can talk to the local sheriff about finding him?"

Jenny nodded. "I guess."

"We'll need to be careful. Dawn will be breaking soon.

And that means those goons we ran into yesterday will be back patrolling the woods." Annja faced Jenny. "Are you sure you don't know why they'd be out here?"

"Nope."

"All right, then. We'll just have to make sure we don't run into them. I don't think they'll be as understanding as they were yesterday if they find me still out here."

Joey started dismantling what was left of the improvised shelter. Annja frowned. "Don't we still need that?"

Joey scattered a bunch of branches and looked at her. "I don't know how long Cheehawk's body will remain buried."

Jenny frowned. "What's that mean?"

"Predators and scavengers will smell the decomposition starting. They'll come around and dig it up. I don't want to be here when that happens."

Annja sighed. "It can't be helped, I suppose."

"It's the way of the natural cycle," Joey said. "But it doesn't mean I have to be here when it goes down. And besides, we each have our own agendas now."

Annja turned. "Each?"

Joey nodded. "I'll lead you out to the road so you can find your way back into town. That way you can take care of finding the sheriff and stuff like that. Maybe find that David dude."

"And what will you be doing?"

Joey looked up from throwing more branches into the scrub. "I need to find the men who chased us out of here yesterday."

There was something in his voice that disturbed Annja. It was cold. And the edge to the words made her heart jump. "You can't take them on by yourself, Joey. They've got guns. Let us get the sheriff out here and he'll know what to do. And he has a gun, too."

"I don't care about whether they have guns or not," Joey said.

Annja shook her head. "You may not care but the fact that

they do have them could make your life a thing of the past. Is that what you want?"

"They killed my friend," Joey said.

"I know they did. And believe me, I want them to pay for that just as badly as you do. But chasing after them by yourself isn't the smartest thing to do right now."

"Why? Because I'm a kid? You think I don't know how to handle myself?"

"I think anyone would have a hard time handling themselves against three men armed with rifles."

Joey glared at her. "Cheehawk didn't deserve to die."

Annja nodded. "We know that. But you rushing off on some suicide mission isn't the way to honor the memory of his spirit."

"What would you know about honoring the spirit of the dead?" Joey muttered.

"You think you're the only one who's ever lost someone or something precious to them?" Annja shook her head. "You're not. It just seems like you are because of what has happened. Tragedy is always like that. It feels as if there's no one else in the world who understands the pain and the grief you have swelling in your heart. But everyone knows about tragedy. No one goes through life without feeling pain at some point. That's just the way it is."

"Then you know that I have to do this."

"I know you have to do something. And I want to help you get justice. But not this way. You go charging after these guys and they'll just kill you. I don't think they'd even care that you're fourteen years old. Your life wouldn't mean a damn thing to them."

"If it's my time to die in battle, then so be it."

"Don't dishonor your grandfather with that kind of talk," Annja said. "You think he spent all those years teaching you how to become one with the woods, how to stalk and track,

entrusting the secrets of your people to you, just so you could run off recklessly and get killed?"

Joey fell silent. Annja could see the rage coursing through him and she felt awful that someone so young should have to battle the conflicting emotions he must have been feeling.

"Annja," Jenny said. "Maybe we should just let him go."

"Are you nuts? He'll get killed."

Jenny nodded. "Perhaps. But maybe he's made up his mind. Maybe he won't listen to reason."

"He's just a child—"

"I am not a child," Joey said. "I'm growing into manhood."

Annja glanced at him. "Not by doing something stupid, you aren't. You run off now and do what you want to do, you'll just die some stupid kid. Sorry to have to say that to you, Joey. I have a lot of respect for you and your skills, but show me that you've got a mind upstairs. Show me you can *think* like a man. Show me you know there will be a time and a place to get justice for Cheehawk."

Joey looked at her for a moment and Annja could see the tears starting to flow. He looked away and busied himself with scattering more of the shelter.

Annja gave him his space and turned back to Jenny. "That wasn't a very smart thing to say," she said angrily.

"Who's to say what our individual destinies are? Maybe it's his to die out here in the woods with his wolf."

"I'd like to think that whoever's in charge upstairs had a grander plan than letting such a gifted young man run off to die needlessly."

"Tell that to everyone who's known the death of a child. Or the death of someone lost in a useless war."

"Now you're getting political."

"Nah, I'm just showing my cynical side."

Annja shook her head. "We can be as cynical as we want to be. But I won't see Joey go off to die if I can help it."

"And just how do you think you're going to prevent that from happening? He's not some baby you can stow on your back and take with you. He knows his way around here better than either of us."

"I was hoping to use reason to get through to him."

Jenny smirked. "Sometimes I think you're even more naive than I am."

"Who's being naive?"

"You are, girl. You think you can use reason to get through to Joey? That's being naive."

"Why so? He's an intelligent kid."

Jenny shook her head. "Doesn't matter if he's intelligent. You're forgetting he's also a teenager. That means reason takes a backseat to raging hormones and overwrought emotions."

Annja sighed. "Regardless, there's no way I'm going to simply let him walk off into the woods on some vendetta mission."

"So he takes us out to the main road and then leaves."

"He's not leaving," Annja insisted.

"And just how do you propose to stop him?"

Annja chewed her lip. Through the trees, she could see the first streaks of light starting to break over the horizon. Pale colors began to show themselves as the last of the storm clouds faded away. It might be a nice day, after all.

"I guess we'll handle that when we get there."

"I suppose."

Annja turned around. Joey had done a remarkable job of scattering the shelter. It was difficult for Annja to even tell where they'd been holed up forty minutes earlier.

Near Cheehawk's burial plot she saw a pile of stones. Annja walked over and knelt down near it.

Jenny came over, as well. "What is that?"

"I think it's a cairn. But I'm not sure what it's supposed to mean."

"Maybe it's a burial marker? You know, so Joey remembers where he buried Cheehawk?"

Annja frowned. The pile of smooth stones branched off to the right. She glanced in that direction and saw something else near the base of a large oak tree. "Over there."

She and Jenny rose and walked to the tree. Jenny squatted. "Another cairn?"

"Looks to be, yeah. But what's it mean?"

Jenny shrugged. "I don't know. Why don't you ask Joey to explain it to us?"

Annja nodded. "Joey?"

A breeze blew through the woods. Joey didn't respond. Annja raised her voice a little louder. "Joey!"

But she heard nothing in response. And Annja got a bad feeling.

Jenny came up next to her. "Looks like the kid has made his decision."

Annja nodded. "I just hope it isn't his last."

13

"Well, that's just great," Annja said. "Our guide has gone and deserted us, leaving us alone in these woods."

Jenny sighed. "We probably shouldn't have been talking about him like we were, huh?"

Annja glanced around. "He wouldn't have just left us. That would be cruel. And it wouldn't be in his spirit to do something like that. Those piles of stones must mean something. We just have to figure it out. And then, hopefully, we can get the hell out of here."

Jenny pointed out into the woods. "We're not going after him?"

Annja shook her head. "You know your way around here?"

"Not really."

"Me, neither. In fact, I'd go so far as to say that if we took off to find him, we'd end up getting even more lost than we are right now."

"We're lost?"

Annja sighed. "Hopefully not."

"But what about Joey?"

Annja looked into the woods. He had a head start on them. And knowing what he knew, he could be a mile away already. Joey knew how to vanish into the shadows, and he was driven to do whatever it was he was going to do.

"We can't go after him. Our best bet right now is to figure out the stones and then go for help. If we find the sheriff, we can get him out here, and that's how we'll help Joey. Otherwise, it's not going to be good."

"It's just that after what you said a few minutes ago, I thought you'd be a lot more driven to search for him."

Annja looked at her. "Jenny, I am driven. But I'm also a realist. We don't know which way is up around here. Hell, Joey led me around this place a few hours back when we were looking for you and I still don't know if I could find my way around without him. The fact of the matter is I'm worried about Joey and hope he doesn't do anything stupid. But that can't be helped right now."

"So instead we try to get back to town?"

"Yes. We find the sheriff and explain it to him. Maybe he'll be able to help us out. And he might even have a cute deputy for you to swoon over."

Jenny perked up. "You think?"

Annja turned back to the stone cairn and studied it. "I don't know. I don't really care, to be honest. Just help me with this and let's get going."

Jenny knelt next to her. "I never studied cairns. Did you?"

"Not really, I'm ashamed to say. Here we are, both archaeologists, and yet something as simple as this is a bit befuddling."

Jenny looked at her. "Befuddling?"

"What?"

"You just sounded like my old aunt there for a second."

Annja frowned. "Sorry. Maybe my age is starting to show."

"Either that or the age of that sword you're carrying around with you. It's pretty old, isn't it?"

"What makes you say that?"

"I took a course on European weapons one time. If I recall correctly, the sword you have looks like something made around five to six hundred years ago."

Annja shrugged. "I guess that's about right."

"Really?"

Annja shook her head. "Can we study the rocks, please? Trust me, there are times when the sword is much more of a pain in the ass than an asset."

"But where did it come from and where did it go? How do you do that?"

Annja took a breath. "Jenny, I really don't know everything about it or why it came to me. I'd rather not talk about the sword right now. We have more important things to worry about."

"Okay, okay, I'm just amazed by it, is all."

"More amazed than your hunt for big foot?"

"Well…"

"All right, then." Annja turned back to the stone cairn. "The one over by the burial mound seemed to point this way because of how the rocks were stacked. This one seems to point over to the left there, which would make it sort of a southerly direction. You think?"

Jenny followed where Annja pointed and nodded. "Seems to be. The sun's coming up from over in that direction, so, yeah, south it is."

Annja got up. "Good." She kicked over the cairn.

"What are you doing now?"

"Making sure that whoever those guys are we don't leave them a clear trail to follow us. I don't want to have to think about them being behind us as we try to find our way out of here."

"But what about Joey?"

Annja looked into the woods. He had a head start on them. And knowing what he knew, he could be a mile away already. Joey knew how to vanish into the shadows, and he was driven to do whatever it was he was going to do.

"We can't go after him. Our best bet right now is to figure out the stones and then go for help. If we find the sheriff, we can get him out here, and that's how we'll help Joey. Otherwise, it's not going to be good."

"It's just that after what you said a few minutes ago, I thought you'd be a lot more driven to search for him."

Annja looked at her. "Jenny, I am driven. But I'm also a realist. We don't know which way is up around here. Hell, Joey led me around this place a few hours back when we were looking for you and I still don't know if I could find my way around without him. The fact of the matter is I'm worried about Joey and hope he doesn't do anything stupid. But that can't be helped right now."

"So instead we try to get back to town?"

"Yes. We find the sheriff and explain it to him. Maybe he'll be able to help us out. And he might even have a cute deputy for you to swoon over."

Jenny perked up. "You think?"

Annja turned back to the stone cairn and studied it. "I don't know. I don't really care, to be honest. Just help me with this and let's get going."

Jenny knelt next to her. "I never studied cairns. Did you?"

"Not really, I'm ashamed to say. Here we are, both archaeologists, and yet something as simple as this is a bit befuddling."

Jenny looked at her. "Befuddling?"

"What?"

"You just sounded like my old aunt there for a second."

Annja frowned. "Sorry. Maybe my age is starting to show."

"Either that or the age of that sword you're carrying around with you. It's pretty old, isn't it?"

"What makes you say that?"

"I took a course on European weapons one time. If I recall correctly, the sword you have looks like something made around five to six hundred years ago."

Annja shrugged. "I guess that's about right."

"Really?"

Annja shook her head. "Can we study the rocks, please? Trust me, there are times when the sword is much more of a pain in the ass than an asset."

"But where did it come from and where did it go? How do you do that?"

Annja took a breath. "Jenny, I really don't know everything about it or why it came to me. I'd rather not talk about the sword right now. We have more important things to worry about."

"Okay, okay, I'm just amazed by it, is all."

"More amazed than your hunt for big foot?"

"Well…"

"All right, then." Annja turned back to the stone cairn. "The one over by the burial mound seemed to point this way because of how the rocks were stacked. This one seems to point over to the left there, which would make it sort of a southerly direction. You think?"

Jenny followed where Annja pointed and nodded. "Seems to be. The sun's coming up from over in that direction, so, yeah, south it is."

Annja got up. "Good." She kicked over the cairn.

"What are you doing now?"

"Making sure that whoever those guys are we don't leave them a clear trail to follow us. I don't want to have to think about them being behind us as we try to find our way out of here."

does it simply lie dormant until something triggers it all over again?

"Annja?"

She glanced back at Jenny. "What?"

"You okay?"

"Yeah, why?"

"Because I just asked you a question and you ignored me."

Annja smiled. "Sorry, I got a little lost inside myself for a moment. It happens sometimes. I didn't mean to ignore you."

"Okay."

Annja kept walking. "So what was your question?"

"When did you first get that sword of yours and where is it now?"

Annja groaned. "I thought we agreed not to talk about it?"

"I never agreed to that. I simply let you get on with figuring out what direction we were going. Now it's open season on you and that big hunk of metal you somehow heft."

"You're not going to let me out of answering your questions this time, are you?"

"Not a chance, sister. Now start dishing."

Annja stooped to avoid a low pine branch. "It was back in France. Several years ago. And ever since I got the sword, it's always with me."

"I don't get it. Where is it?"

Annja decided the truth was the only way to go, even if Jenny had a hard time with it. "I don't honestly know. It's as if it's in some other plane of existence. I can summon the sword and I can put it back there again."

"What are you talking about? Like an out-of-body experience?"

Annja didn't feel like getting into this or the spirit walk

she'd supposedly made with Joey's grandfather. "I guess so. Maybe."

"How weird."

"It's most definitely weird. And since I'm not entirely sure how all of it works, it's even stranger to discuss, you know? I mean, I know that you want answers to your questions. But you've got to understand that I don't necessarily have any answers to give."

"You've got questions of your own, huh?"

"You can say that again. The sword comes with a host of stuff that I can't even begin to talk about, let alone try to make you comprehend. I was chosen to have the sword for some reason, and that's all I know. For the time being, I have to accept that. Until I'm made aware of my destiny, if there even is one, then I guess I just keep doing what I know how to do."

"In any event," Jenny said, "it makes for something to talk about on a long walk back to town."

Annja stopped. "Maybe not so long."

"What?"

Annja pointed. "Look."

Through the trees, they could see what looked like the black asphalt of a road. They'd made it out of the woods.

14

Annja stepped out onto the well-worn asphalt of the main road. Small puddles of water from the overnight storm acted like moats between the woods and civilization. Annja glanced one way and then the other before looking at Jenny.

"What do you think?"

"About what?"

"Which way do we go? Left or right?"

Jenny looked right and then left. "I think left. That was the direction we headed initially when we drove in."

Annja nodded. Her gut instinct was to head left, as well. What had Joey said in the darkness? That the distance was a few miles? They could cover that in under an hour if they were lucky.

"Let's go."

Jenny fell in step beside her. "I should apologize."

"For what?"

"Getting you involved in all of this. I never meant for it to be such a headache. I just wanted you to see what David had promised to show me."

Annja smiled. "You dragged me out here without even knowing what it was first?"

"I guess so." Jenny shook her head. "I wasn't thinking very clearly. So am I forgiven?"

Annja shrugged, listening to her boots roll over bits of loose stone on the road. "You show me some definitive proof that big foot exists and I might think about it."

Jenny smiled. "I knew you were a closet believer."

"I never said that."

"Didn't have to. I know you'd be thrilled if it turns out that David has something truly amazing to show us. Who wouldn't be?"

"Of course I would, but I'm still skeptical as hell. I just can't accept the idea that something like a Sasquatch could survive in the wilderness what with all our technology and encroachment."

"Joey disappeared on us when we were less than ten feet away from him."

"We were distracted."

"He built those cairns without us even realizing it. I'd say that was pretty impressive."

"So what? You think that makes him a relative to the Sasquatch or something?" Annja frowned. "That's crazy."

"I'm not suggesting that at all. I'm simply saying that if Joey can be that stealthy with us so close and we knew he was there, then why is it so difficult for you to consider the possibility that a creature who knows these woods like the back of his hand could evade any attempt to find him?"

"Because a Sasquatch isn't a Joey."

"How do you know how intelligent they are? They could be more evolved than us. You never know."

Annja sighed. She had to admit that for a moment before she saw Cheehawk clawing at their structure, she had briefly wondered whether they were being attacked by the likes of big foot or not. She'd stood, fully expecting to be confronted by a giant ape-man covered in long coarse hair and fur.

"Well, let's wait to see what amazing evidence this David guy has and then I'll make up my mind. You know, because I'm a scientist and I'm supposed to say things like that."

Jenny smirked. "It isn't all facts. It's the burning questions that drive us to explore and discover things, not the reinforcement of factual information. If that's what drove me, then I'd be a pretty dull woman."

"You're saying I'm dull now?"

Jenny shook her head. "Nope. But maybe you've forgotten the wonder of all that we do. Maybe it's become stale for you in the wake of finding out you have to carry that sword around with you."

"Not the sword again."

"Well, can you blame me for wondering about you? The last time we were together, you were much more happy-go-lucky. Now you're much more a cynic. You frown a lot more than you used to, and I wonder what happened to the Annja Creed I used to know."

"You sound like the mother I never had."

"Don't dodge the question, Annja."

Annja walked another few steps and took a deep breath. "I've seen a lot of bad stuff since I got this sword. Maybe it's having an effect on me that I haven't realized until now."

"What kinds of bad stuff?"

"A lot of death. And I've been the cause of some of it. Justifiable, of course, but it's death just the same. "

"You've killed people?"

"Yes."

Jenny fell silent for a moment. "That's a lot of bad karma you're hauling there."

"Tell me about it."

"And here I thought my man troubles were plenty bad."

"I don't have time to think about men. Well, not much, anyway."

Jenny laughed. "I knew the old Annja was still in there somewhere. Remember that time in Virginia Beach at that bar with the Navy guys?"

"Don't even bring that up."

"So you do remember."

"How in the world could I ever forget? I never heard someone sing in quite that way before. It was horrifying and hilarious at the same time."

"You saying I shouldn't try out for *American Idol* anytime soon, huh?"

"You'd be better off sticking with big foot," Annja said.

They kept walking and, for Annja, the sound of the footsteps was in some small way comforting. The rhythm of their pace as they continued to trek down the road with the forest on either side helped refresh her spirit. As different as she and Jenny were, there was a comfort in being with her. The sense of the familiar. It was something Annja realized was missing from her life in a big way.

Maybe this globe-trotting stuff was getting old. Maybe the whole *Chasing History's Monsters* thing was getting old, too. She could always stop, she supposed. Settle down somewhere and teach. She'd had job offers from universities before. Who wouldn't want to hire a former television personality? Her classes would be enormously popular.

But could she stop? Could she quench her desire to explore and discover? And if she managed to quell the sense of curiosity that had been driving her for years, what would happen to the sword? Would it go away and find another home? Would it stay with her and continue to be a presence in her life?

And what about the death she'd dealt?

"You okay?" Jenny asked.

Annja nodded. "Yeah, just thinking."

"About what?"

"About everything. It isn't often I find myself able to devote so much time to my thoughts about my life and work. Most of the time people are shooting guns at me or trying to stab me to death or some other really bad stuff."

"That sounds awfully dramatic, Annja."

"It's just the way things are for me these days," Annja said quietly.

"Why don't you stop?"

Annja glanced at her. "I've thought about it. I don't know if I can stop."

"Why? Because you don't want to?"

"That's part of it."

"Because the sword won't let you?"

Annja shrugged. "I don't know. I'm not sure if I have to ask or what. Maybe I can just stop. Maybe I'm meant for something greater than what I can understand at this moment in time."

"Your role in this may not even be determined yet."

Annja nodded. "I've thought about that, as well. Doesn't make any of this any easier to take, let me tell you."

"I think you'll probably keep going."

Annja smiled. "Maybe so. But you'd better find a nice man and settle down so I can at least pretend I know what a grounded, stable life is all about."

"I'm trying, I'm trying." Jenny laughed. "It's good to have you around again, Annja."

"Likewise."

From behind them, Annja heard a low rumbling sound. She stopped and stepped closer to the edge of the road. "You hear that? This could be our ticket into town."

Jenny smiled. "I was always told not to hitchhike. Are you saying I should go back on my pledge?"

"Flash your legs if you need to, but I'm tired of walking and wasting time. We need to get out of these woods."

The sound of the engine grew louder and Annja figured it was the steady throttle of a pickup truck.

Jenny started primping. "If the driver's cute, I call shotgun."

Annja sighed. "Fine. I'll sit in the back, for all I care. My legs are tired and I can use the rest."

The sound grew even louder. Annja pulled Jenny closer to her. "He sounds as if he's going at a fairly good clip. Better stand over here so we don't get hit."

"It's coming," Jenny said.

Annja saw the front of the truck emerge from around the corner about three hundred yards down the road. It was a dark pickup with its headlights still on.

"They won't miss us," Jenny said. She started waving her hands, trying to flag down the truck.

"Think it's the sheriff out patroling?"

Jenny shrugged. "Who cares? It's a vehicle and we can ride into town instead of walking. As long as they're not cannibals interested in stripping off our flesh, I don't care who they are."

Annja frowned. "Lovely thought."

"I'm just kidding."

The truck rumbled closer and Annja could see it was starting to slow down as it approached.

"They see us," Jenny said. "We're in!"

Annja stepped out onto the road and waved with Jenny. The truck eased to a stop about twenty yards away. Jenny ran to the truck cab and Annja had to follow after her. "Wait up."

Jenny climbed into the truck.

Annja came abreast of the cab and looked in the open door, half expecting to see someone dangerous staring back at her.

Instead, she saw Jenny beaming. Next to her was a handsome man with dark brown hair and the brightest blue eyes

Annja had ever seen. Even though he was sitting, Annja could tell that he was tall and extremely fit.

She looked at Jenny. "Happy?"

"Annja, this is *David*. The guy I told you about."

Annja looked at him, seeing the brass star on his chest for the first time. "You never mentioned he was the sheriff."

"I didn't know."

The sheriff held out his hand. "Climb in. You two look as if you've had quite the adventure."

Annja climbed into the truck and stared back at the woods. I hope we can find Joey in time, she thought.

15

David glanced over at Annja. "All set?"

Annja nodded and risked a look at Jenny, who looked positively ecstatic to be squeezed in next to David. "You okay?"

Jenny winked at her. "Perfect."

David slid the truck into gear and they rolled off down the main road. The truck bucked as it went over a pothole in the road. David rested his hands on the steering wheel.

"You guys were walking back to town?"

Annja nodded. "It's been a rough night."

"Has it?"

Jenny looked at him. "What in the world happened to you? Why weren't you at the hotel like you said you were going to be?"

David looked a little sheepish. "I got called out of town unexpectedly. I tried to get in touch, but the cell-phone reception is absolutely terrible up in these parts. I'm really sorry."

"Well, as long as nothing happened to you." Jenny squeezed herself over a little more, prompting David to chuckle.

"I need to drive, Jenny."

"Sorry," she said, sounding miffed.

Annja watched the road for a moment. "What called you out of town?"

"Pardon?"

"The errand you had to run? What was it?"

David shrugged. "Just some police stuff. I was about twenty miles up north, is all. I'd tell you about it, but it's really boring. I wouldn't want you guys to fall asleep on me."

Annja felt uneasy. Something didn't feel right. How could Jenny not know that David was the sheriff up here? Was that the truth? And why was David so evasive about why he'd been out of town?

"Jenny tells me you've got some amazing big-foot evidence to show her?"

David nodded. "In town. We'll go past the station so I can get some stuff, and then I'll show you."

"What is it exactly?"

David shook his head. "I don't want to spoil the surprise."

"Annja," Jenny said, "just be a little patient."

"We need to get some help when we get back to town," she said to David.

"Oh?"

"Do you have deputies or anything like that? Guys you can call on for help? Maybe the State Police?"

"Why would I need to do a thing like that?"

"Because you've got a roving trio of gun-toting guys up in the woods who scared off Jenny's students yesterday."

David frowned. "So they were telling the truth?"

"What's that supposed to mean?"

"Ellen, the lady who handles the calls at the station, got me on the radio late yesterday and said that a group of kids came into the station claiming they'd been run out of the woods by a bunch of psychos. Ellen didn't put much credence in what they said, and since I was out of town there wasn't much she could do about it."

Annja frowned. "I guess that answers my question about the deputies."

David shook his head. "Can't afford 'em. The town, I mean. We're a backwater place. Barely got enough funds for me and Ellen."

The truck rolled over another pothole, bouncing them in the interior of the cab. Annja knocked the top of her head against the roof. "Or enough for road work, apparently."

"Exactly," David said. "We're working on it, though. A wealthy industrialist recently moved to the outskirts of town and set up shop. His property taxes alone should be enough to at least get another part-timer on the force. That would help me out a lot."

"Who's the guy that moved in?" Annja asked.

"Made his money in mineral mining down in South America," David said. "Name's something like Bettancourt."

Annja frowned. "I've heard of him. I think he was in the news for something, a mine collapse down in Venezuela or something like that."

David nodded. "That's him. He was in a lot of hot water, but he's a nice guy. Invited me up for a chat one afternoon recently. He's really taken with the area, loves going for hikes, that sort of thing."

"Better warn him not to go out there while those nuts are stalking around."

David nodded. "We'll take care of those guys, don't worry about it."

"Well, we'll need to hurry up because there's a fourteen-year-old boy who's determined to wreak vengeance on them for killing his wolf," Annja said.

David slammed on the brakes and looked at Annja. "Joey?"

Annja nodded. "Yep."

David took a breath. "Cripes. What in the world is he thinking?"

"He's not. That's the problem."

Jenny shook her head. "They killed his wolf. It was terrible. The poor thing came to us and died."

"Cheehawk." David was quiet for a moment. "It was a beautiful creature, wasn't it?"

"Yes."

"And Joey's out there now?"

Annja nodded. "Yes."

"Well, one thing's for sure—whoever killed Cheehawk, they're going to have their hands full with Joey."

Annja raised her eyebrows. "Are you kidding?"

"What?"

"That's all you can say? Joey's just a boy. He can't handle those guys alone. They'll kill him."

"I highly doubt that."

"You doubt that?"

David held up his hand. "Hang on a second, Annja. We'll get out there, trust me. I know his grandfather very well and I promised him I'd always look out for Joey, but you should know that Joey's a pretty accomplished woodsman. His grandfather taught him a fair lot of stuff. Joey knows those woods like no one else in the area and can disappear anytime he wants."

"That's not going to help him when they shoot him dead for being a pain in the ass. What happens to your promise to his grandfather then?"

"Joey knows how to handle himself. I'm honestly not that concerned. I've seen him fight before."

"Joey?"

David nodded. "We had a guy come through here about a year or so back. Got drunk at the bar and started some crap.

I was on my way there when Joey happened to stop by the bar, dropping off some stuff for Mr. Crowe, the owner. The drunk guy saw that Joey was Native American and started hassling him. According to Mr. Crowe, Joey held out as long as any reasonable man might be expected to. Then he leveled the guy. Threw him out of the bar just as I was pulling up."

"Was the man armed?" Annja asked.

"Had a knife about as long as my arm," David said. "Didn't matter to Joey. He just handled him. Never saw the guy again."

David started driving again. "I asked Crowe if he wanted to press any charges, but most folks around these parts are happy if trouble just leaves them alone. I'm inclined to agree with the sentiment. People leave us alone and we can keep on with our lives."

"What if they don't leave you alone?"

"Then we take them over to the State Police barracks about an hour from here. They lock 'em up and prosecute them, if need be. But that's only happened once, long before my time as sheriff."

Annja sighed. "I'm still worried. I met Joey's grandfather last night and, after everything he's taught Joey, I can't imagine he'd be thrilled if he knew his only male heir was out in the woods facing down three armed guys."

"You don't know his grandfather, then," David said. "He'll eat this up and ask for seconds."

Jenny glanced at Annja and then back at David. "David, maybe we should try to get out into the woods as soon as we can. I mean, I know you think Joey can handle himself and he probably can, but wouldn't it be better to make sure those guys, whoever they are, are taken care of before we look at the evidence you've got?"

David shrugged. "Sure, no problem. But we still need to go back to the station. I'll need my rifle." He glanced at Annja. "You shoot?"

Annja shrugged. "Do I have to?"

"I don't know. You saw these guys. Are they skilled?"

"From what I know about guns, they looked as if they knew what they were doing."

"Okay. I'll give you both a crash course in handling the rifles."

Jenny's eyes opened wide. "You want me to take a gun, too?"

"Any dumb ass can shoot a gun," David said. "And apparently there are three of them out in the woods right now. You'll be okay, trust me."

Annja wasn't happy about the situation. She glanced at David. Just what the hell was going on around here? He didn't seem the least bit concerned about Joey. And he wasn't too concerned about the guys in the woods, either. Why did everyone seem to think she was overreacting?

She didn't detect any real threat from David aside from a general sense of apathy, and yet she felt extremely uneasy.

Jenny seemed absolutely content.

Maybe I'm overthinking things, she thought. Maybe this is all just the product of stress. After all, I haven't had any sleep since I arrived. The lack of rest could be affecting my decision-making ability.

She remembered reading that lack of sleep could produce feelings of paranoia, hallucinations and worse. Maybe this was a textbook case of that.

Maybe.

David agreed to get them to town as quickly as possible and accelerated the truck. The road was twisting and they took several curves faster than seemed safe. Annja decided there was nothing she could do but hang on and enjoy the ride.

She closed her eyes and thought about the sword. Instantly, she could see it hovering in front of her. She was feeling calm and clearheaded. She'd go after Joey on her own if she had to.

She was completely unprepared for an explosion.

She opened her eyes as the entire body of the truck flew into the air, and then they were rolling, turning and flipping over and over again as the truck came down with a screeching gnash of metal.

Jenny screamed.

Annja felt the truck hit the ground and blackness rushed over her.

16

Annja had the distinct impression that she was flying through the air. And she found herself experiencing the worry that eventually she would have to come back to earth, thanks to the effects of gravity.

And yet she did not crash into the ground at all.

After a moment, she felt the hardness of the ground around her body, but she had no idea how she'd gotten there. She couldn't see anything, just the same blackness that had rushed at her when her world had suddenly exploded into an intense flash and concussive roar that made her ears ring.

Slowly, her senses started to return. She could taste acrid smoke in her mouth. It seemed to have singed the interior of her nostrils, as well. Something was burning and she hoped that it wasn't her flesh.

Aches suddenly invaded her joints and her bones. The back of her neck seemed to have seized up, and Annja found it difficult to move her head or neck at all.

Am I paralyzed? She tried to wiggle her toes, but she couldn't feel anything down there, either.

This is bad, she thought. What the hell happened?

Annja felt as if she'd been used to scrape barnacles off the hull of a tramp steamer. She tried to take an internal assessment of her injuries, but found she simply couldn't concentrate enough to draw her awareness throughout her body.

The blackness that surrounded her seemed absolute. She thought about the sword and imagined reaching her hands out for it in the otherwhere.

She took a breath and felt the stabbing of a thousand needles in her lungs. It felt as if shards of hot metal had lanced her through. Fragmentation? She couldn't be sure. She wondered if she was in some sort of catatonic limbo where she couldn't die and yet wasn't quite alive.

I need help, she thought. I've got to get some help. But how?

She tried to move her arms. Nothing.

Her legs refused to even twitch.

She took another breath, trying to draw some strength out of the air itself. If she could just get enough power, she might be able to shake off the darkness and get out of wherever she was.

It was no use. Her body simply wouldn't respond to her commands.

Her heart was solidly pumping. Annja willed herself to stay relaxed and calm. Panic would rob her of whatever little bit of energy she could manage to muster.

And she needed every ounce of it.

She kept breathing, concentrating on just counting her breaths over and over again all the way up to fifty and then starting back at one again. Breathe, relax, breathe, relax, she told herself.

The darkness lightened. Annja could see a bit of light flashing in her eyes.

"Annja?"

That voice. She'd heard it before. But where?

"Annja?"

She opened her eyes. The wrecked corpse of a truck loomed over her, twisted and gnarled almost beyond recognition. She looked down and saw part of the front end was pinning her down.

She was trapped.

No wonder I couldn't feel anything down there, she thought. Still, it didn't look good, not one bit. She might have extensive damage to her limbs.

"She's awake."

Jenny's face came into blurry view. Annja had to blink several times to clear the picture.

She smiled at Annja. "Nice to have you back with us."

"Wh-what happened?"

Jenny shook her head. Annja cold see the streaks of dirt and grease across Jenny's face. "Some sort of explosion. It tossed the truck through the air and we came down pretty hard."

"You're okay?" Annja asked as everything came flooding back to her.

Jenny nodded. "Probably got a sprain or two, but nothing too serious."

"David?"

"He's okay, thank God. He's a pretty hardy guy. Got some cuts but nothing beyond that."

Annja frowned. "Looks as if I drew the short straw this time out, huh?"

"David says he's got a jack that must have gone flying when we exploded or whatever it was that happened. He thinks he can crank this off you and we'll be able to pull you out."

"Does it look bad from your angle?"

Jenny glanced down and then back at Annja. "I can't see your legs, so I'm not going to speculate on what it looks like."

Annja frowned. "I can't feel anything down there."

Jenny shook her head. "That doesn't mean anything. You could have no circulation right now. Sort of a pins-and-needles thing, you know? Once David gets the truck off you, we'll be in a better position to see the extent of the damage."

Annja nodded.

The darkness had vanished.

She heard movement around her and opened her eyes again. David smiled at her. "Hey."

"Hey, yourself."

"Found the jack. I'm going to try to get this rig off you. Don't try to move until I tell Jenny to start pulling, okay? I want to make sure you're all…connected down there before we try to move you. Understand?"

"Yeah."

David nodded. "Good. Just stay with me while I do this and we'll have you out in no time flat."

Jenny came around and took Annja's hands in hers. "I think I'll just hold on to your hands here in case I need to tug you out fast."

Annja smiled and looked around. "We're not still on the road?"

"Partially. We're also on the dirt."

Annja frowned. "Where's he setting up the jack?"

"On the asphalt," David called out. "Don't worry. It wouldn't do you much good if I set it up on the dirt and gravel, would it?"

Annja smiled. "Guess not."

"Here we go."

Annja closed her eyes and let the gray mist envelop her. She calmed herself down and relaxed her breathing even as she heard David start cranking the jack. She wondered if there would be a sudden onslaught of pain once the truck was lifted. Would she scream out in agony?

Her heart started beating faster but she kept focusing on her breathing. I just need to stay relaxed, she told herself. And the gray mist that enveloped her seemed to soothe her.

Annja had the sensation of a sudden release of pressure.

Jenny's voice was quiet in her ear. "It's up."

David came around. Annja kept her eyes closed. She was afraid. The prospect of losing her legs was terrifying.

"Well, that's interesting," David said.

Jenny started to giggle.

Annja opened her eyes.

"If you two are through mocking my situation here..."

Jenny pointed and Annja glanced down as much as the pain in her neck let her.

She could see her legs. They were completely bare.

"Looks like you lost your pants, Annja," David said.

Annja flexed her toes. They responded. She slumped back. "Thank God they're all right."

"The truck wasn't actually on your legs. Your legs were pushed into the dirt but the angle of the rig was resting more on the asphalt." David got to his feet and went behind Annja. "You are really lucky."

"My neck hurts."

"I'm not surprised," David said. He looped his arms under Annja's armpits. "I've got to move you before the truck actually does come down. You okay with that?"

"Do it."

David tightened his grip and then pulled Annja out from under the truck. She felt a wave of pain lance through her upper back and neck. "Ow!"

David laid her down some feet away from the crumpled heap. "You okay?"

"Back's killing me."

David ran his hands under Annja's back. "I can't be sure, of course, but it doesn't feel like there's anything broken."

Annja frowned. "I could get up and walk two steps and sever my own spinal cord, though."

"That's true."

Jenny frowned. "That's not going to happen."

Annja smiled. "Optimist."

David looked around. "I'll see if I can find your pants. Kinda cold to be lying out here in your skivvies like that."

"Thanks." Annja watched him move off and then turned to Jenny, wincing as she did. "Seems like a nice enough guy."

"He is, isn't he?"

She glanced at Jenny. "It's okay. I'm fine now." She struggled to sit up.

David came back around the side of the truck holding a pair of pants. Annja could see there were burns on the fabric. He saw Annja and stopped short.

"You shouldn't be sitting."

Annja shook her head. "I'm all right."

"We should really wait to get a medical opinion on that from someone more qualified. Like maybe after you've had an X-ray?"

"No time," Annja said. "I'll take my pants, please."

David handed them over and Annja struggled into them. Her body felt sore but she was certain there was no real damage. That was a lucky break, she thought. If the truck had landed on her, it might have spelled the end of her adventurous ways.

17

"We need to get out of here," Annja said, glancing into the woods.

David shook his head. "Are you kidding me? I've got to stay and figure out what happened. In case you didn't notice, my truck exploded."

"Of course I noticed," Annja said. "I was just pinned under it."

"What's going on, Annja?" Jenny asked.

"Don't you think that explosion happened for a reason? Like maybe to target someone?"

"Me?" David shrugged. "Why would anyone want to see me dead?"

"I don't know," Annja said. "Maybe we could start with what you supposedly know about the existence of the Sasquatch."

David fell silent. Annja pressed her attack. "Maybe someone thinks you know a few things that you shouldn't. Rather than shoot you, they could just blow you up."

"That would be as obvious as shooting him, though," Jenny said. "It would still be a homicide."

"Maybe not," Annja said. "It really depends on what blew up. Was it a road mine or some type of improvised explosive device? Or was it something faulty in the mechanics of the truck itself?"

David leaned against a nearby tree. "You really think someone wants to see me dead?"

Annja shrugged. "Look, this is what I know. There are armed men in those woods who seem determined to run off everyone in this area. I have no idea what their game is. All I know is they've been making life hell. And this explosion seems to fit in with their plans."

Jenny stood close to David. "So what do we do?"

"Right now? I'd suggest we vanish. I think that explosion will probably act like chum for these guys and we can count on them making an appearance sooner than later," Annja replied.

David unholstered his gun. "In that case, I can arrest them."

Annja shook her head. "They'd kill you before you got the chance. There are three of them, remember? And I don't think they'll come out nice and neat for you to order them to drop the guns and put their hands up."

David frowned. "I suppose you're right."

"We need to regroup. Find our way into town and call for backup. That's the best thing to do right now."

David nodded. "Let's do it. We aren't much more than a mile or two from town. We were cruising along pretty quick when we blew up."

Annja wiped her hands on her pants and then carefully stood. She took a few steps and decided she felt fine, all things considered. "We need to go now."

David started walking down the road but Annja stopped

him. "Is there a path we can use through the woods? Staying on the road probably isn't the smartest thing to do right now. Those guys will be looking for us here."

David pointed. "There's a footpath that runs alongside a stream and tracks back to town. But do you think you can do it?"

"I'm good," Annja said.

David led them into the woods on the opposite side of the road. He kept his gun out, which Annja appreciated. No telling if those three goons would make a sudden appearance. Better safe than sorry.

They followed the footpath, and the stream that flowed to their right ran brisk with cold water coming down from the mountains that surrounded the area. Tall pines stretched up toward the sky, their branches extending to the warm rays just beginning to reach down from the sun.

As hard as she tried to wrap her head around it, Annja couldn't quite fathom the explosion. Why take a chance that someone else would trigger the bomb? If it even was a bomb at all. Was it mechanical failure? Had they sabotaged David's fuel tank?

She frowned. "Is your truck usually in good condition, David?"

He glanced back with a grin. "Not currently."

"Before the explosion."

He nodded. "Absolutely. Not much good being the sheriff if your vehicle isn't in top condition. I took care of that thing like it was my baby."

"Poor truck," Jenny said.

Annja rolled her eyes. "So do you think this was an actual bomb in the road?"

David shrugged. "Who knows? I'm not exactly a forensic specialist. I can call one of the state crime lab guys to come down and take a look at the wreckage. They can get swabs and send them to the lab for analysis. That should give us an idea of what we're dealing with."

"That'll take a long time," Annja said.

"Probably."

"Was that the route you drove every single day?"

"Any day I was working, which is...yeah, every day."

"That's the main road into town, right?"

"Yep." David stopped and checked on Jenny before looking back at Annja. "There's a couple of other ways to get into town by back roads and whatnot, but the road is what we all use."

Annja frowned. "How many people in town?"

"Only about two hundred. We're small. We like it that way. Everyone knows one another. Even folks who leave somehow seem to find their way back after a few years. There's about a thousand more people scattered around the area that I have jurisdiction over."

David moved off again and they followed him. Annja could feel the sun's rays starting to warm her through her shirt. The day promised to be rather hot, which in contrast to the cold of the night before, was a welcome change.

The stream bubbled along beside them, running over moss-slicked rocks. Annja could smell the water and the sweet fragrance of the pines around her. She inhaled deeply and felt her body relax as the beauty of the surrounding woods enveloped her.

I'd almost failed to notice how beautiful it is here, she thought. All this stuff with bombs and guns and big foot completely took my awareness away.

She stopped and squatted near the stream, watching bits of leaf debris flow quickly past her. By the edge of the stream, the mud glistened in the moisture. She spotted rabbit tracks and what looked like those of a fox. Had the rabbit escaped the fox or wound up being a meal? She smiled at the flow of life and how it continued, oblivious to the machinations of mankind. In a way, it was almost reassuring. Whatever they were going through, nature took little heed of it and continued doing what it did best.

"Annja?"

She glanced up. Jenny and David were staring at her.

"Sorry. I just got caught up being here. For the first time, actually. It's kind of nice forgetting for a minute that there are dangerous people out there looking for us."

David smiled. "We get this stuff all settled, I'll take you two to some really amazing vistas around here. You won't believe your eyes."

Annja smiled. "Sounds great."

"It's a date," Jenny said, squeezing David's arm.

"Let's keep going. We shouldn't be much more than ten minutes away from town," he said.

The footpath widened and Annja walked next to Jenny behind David. Jenny smiled at her. "It is nice here, isn't it?"

"Definitely."

"Makes all the rest of the world seem, I don't know, somehow unimportant, doesn't it?"

Annja knew what she was getting at. The thought of leaving the stress behind and just hiding out in a place like this that seemed immune from all the chaos of the modern world was very appealing. The problem was, could Annja ever do that? Could she ever escape?

With my luck, she thought, I'd move out to someplace like this, only to have the chaos follow me.

"Maybe someday," Annja said.

"Someday what?"

"Maybe someday a place like this will be possible. But for now, I don't belong here. I've got other things to do first."

Jenny frowned. "Is that you talking or the sword?"

"Both," Annja said. "I don't think I can separate myself from it if I tried."

Jenny shook her head. "I don't envy you."

David stopped. "What's this about a sword?"

Jenny glanced quickly at Annja. "Nothing. Just two history fanatics talking about our past digs."

"That archaeology stuff?"

"Yeah."

David nodded. "We're almost there."

Annja looked up ahead and could see small breaks in the trees. The footpath itself seemed a lot more worn, as well. There was evidence of more human traffic than animal. But the stream kept bubbling along next to them.

Jenny pointed. "Look at the bridge."

David nodded. "We had it built. It's not much, but a few of us got together and put it up, figuring it would make for a nice place to walk with that special someone." He smiled. "You like it?"

"Definitely," she said.

"We cross that bridge and we're in town."

Annja looked at the bridge as they approached. Rough-hewn beams created a neat archway and they'd covered it like the old-style bridges. It was just wide enough for two people to walk through abreast.

"Nice work," Annja said.

David nodded. "We have many craftsmen in town. The kind of people who take a lot of pride in their work."

On the other side of the bridge, the footpath changed to gravel and then a bit of asphalt led up to the main road. The three of them stepped out onto the street.

About a dozen buildings lined the street on both sides. She spotted four cars in total and there were even a few places where you could tie up a horse if you had ridden into town.

"You weren't kidding. This place is a bit old-fashioned."

David pointed. "My office is over there."

They crossed the street and headed toward the police building. Annja felt a twinge in her gut and decided that a hot cup of coffee would be just the thing to make her feel worlds better.

David held the door open for them. "Come on in."

Annja and Jenny stepped into the station and David came in behind them. "Coffee?"

"That's the magic word," Jenny said.

"Annja?"

"Please."

A side door opened and a trim woman in her forties walked out. She smiled at David. "I wondered when you might be in."

David grinned. "That's it?"

"What?"

"That's all you have to say?"

The woman eyed him up and down. "Well, you look like hell, if that's what you're angling for."

David smiled. "Annja, Jenny, this is Ellen. She helps me out on the admin side."

"And dispatch, and occasionally I strap on a pistol and back him up. But you know, don't let that keep him from making me seem like his personal secretary."

David held up his hands. "Hey, we've got guests. Is the coffee hot?"

"Scalding. I burned my tongue on it."

"Great. You guys help yourselves."

Ellen stopped him. "Speaking of guests, you've got some waiting in your office."

"Really?"

Ellen nodded. "They seemed anxious to see you."

"All right," David said. "In the meantime, can you raise the State Police in Southville? Someone tried to blow us up on the way in this morning."

Ellen's eyebrows jumped. "You're serious?"

"Absolutely."

Ellen busied herself with the phone while David winked

at Jenny. "This shouldn't take too long. You guys relax and I'll be out soon." He stepped into his office and, as he did so, Annja caught a glimpse of the two men sitting there.

One of them looked exactly like the lead gunman who'd terrorized the camp.

18

Jenny stirred some creamer into her coffee. She looked up as Annja approached. "You want some of this?"

Annja shook her head. "Those guys David is meeting with—you recognize any of them?"

Jenny tried to look over Annja's shoulder. "Blinds are drawn on his office windows. I can't tell who is in there."

Annja frowned. "Well, I do."

"You do?"

"Yeah, one of them is the guy who ran us off your campsite yesterday and has been presumably prowling the woods, looking for trouble."

Jenny sipped the coffee and yanked her lips away. "Ellen wasn't kidding, this stuff is boiling."

"Jenny, I'm being serious here. If that guy is in David's office, what if it means that David is one of them?"

Jenny frowned. "You're joking, right? David? Annja, unless I'm seriously mistaken and I'm not, you were just riding in the truck that blew up with all of us in it. Remember?"

"Vividly. But still—"

"And you say I have a crazy imagination. Tell me, why on earth would David rig his own truck to explode? He could have killed himself."

Annja glanced around the office. Ellen seemed absorbed in the file she was poring over. "I don't know. There are plenty of skilled people who can rig an explosion so it blows a certain way."

"Annja, the truck somersaulted about a half dozen times before coming to rest. David could have been seriously injured. We all could have been killed. I don't see the likelihood of him doing something like that. It just seems absolutely crazy to me."

Annja sighed. "Yeah, I know it does sound insane. But why on earth is that guy in his office?"

Jenny shrugged. "I have no idea. Maybe David doesn't know he's a bad guy."

Annja sat down on the bench across from Ellen's desk. "Have they been waiting long to see the sheriff?"

Ellen looked up. "Sorry?"

"The men in his office. They've been waiting a long time?"

"They were here when I arrived about an hour ago. They smell like smoke. Probably been camping the past few days. Got that kind of funk to them. You know, sort of like how you and Jenny smell."

Annja laughed. "We could do with hot showers."

Ellen smiled and looked back at her report. Annja leaned forward. "Have you seen them before? Around here, I mean."

Ellen frowned. "You ask a lot of questions, don't you?"

"I'm curious by nature," Annja said.

"Nope. I've never seen them around these parts before. Of course, that doesn't mean much. We have a lot of folks who live sorta off the grid, so to speak. They make their own way in life and every once in a while turn up. Could be these guys are like that, too."

Annja took a breath. "I doubt that."

Jenny sat down next to her. "So what do you want to do? Barge in and confront them?"

"Well, they did hold a gun on me yesterday," Annja said. She stood.

Jenny grabbed her arm. "You're not serious."

"Why not? No time like the present to figure out exactly what the hell is going on around here."

Jenny shook her head. "Annja, you can't just barge in there. What if—"

"What if what?" Annja jerked her arm free. "I'm tired of wandering through the woods. You've got big-foot fever. I've had guns held on me. You nearly died from exposure. A fourteen-year-old kid who can communicate with wolves is off on his own. I took some sort of weird spirit trip."

"You did?"

"Don't ask." Annja shook her head. "No, I want to know what is going on and I want to know now."

Ellen looked up. "Everything okay with you two?"

Annja smiled at Ellen. "Does David's office door have a lock on it?"

Ellen frowned. "What would make you ask a thing like that?"

Annja shook her head. "Never mind. I'll find out."

She walked across the office and kicked David's door open.

The door banged against the inside wall and the blinds rattled. David and the two men jumped out of their seats as Annja blocked the doorway. "Hi, guys. I've got some questions I'd like answered."

David started to stand behind his desk. "Annja, what the hell do you think you're doing?"

She kept herself in the doorway. While the gunman had initially jumped at her entrance, he had regained his composure and sat staring at Annja with an expression of mild amusement.

Annja glared at him and then looked back at David. "That guy's the one who came into Jenny's camp yesterday and made us all leave at gunpoint."

David frowned. "Annja."

"And now you're sitting here with him in your office and I don't particularly like it. I see this and I have to think that's something is rotten in Denmark. And I want to know exactly what it is."

The gunman cleared his throat. "Perhaps we should leave, Sheriff."

David held up his hand. "No one's going anywhere. Stay put." He looked at Annja. "You shouldn't have come in here, Annja. This doesn't concern you."

"Gun-toting jerks always seem to concern me," Annja said. "And I'll be damned if I don't say something about this."

The gunman shifted in his chair. "I told you this would be a problem."

David shook his head. "You're wrong. It's containable. Just let me handle it, okay?"

"Sure, sure." The man started picking his teeth with a small toothpick Annja hadn't noticed earlier.

David took a deep breath and then let it out slowly. "Annja, you've sort of stumbled onto something here that I wish you hadn't."

"What have we stumbled onto?" Jenny asked, suddenly appearing behind Annja in the doorway.

David shrugged. "These men are not what they seem."

"They're not nasty pieces of work?" Annja said. "Could have fooled me."

The men didn't even bristle from the insult. Annja frowned. Something had changed about the gunman's demeanor. The look of a redneck seemed to be slowly peeling away. Something far more sinister replaced it.

David turned to Jenny. "I asked you out here for a reason."

"What was that?" she asked.

"Your expertise. I did find something that I wanted you to take a look at. Something I think proves the existence of the Sasquatch."

"Well, where is it?"

"We have it," the gunman said.

"And why on earth would you have it?" Annja asked.

The man stared at David and then at Annja. "Because the government happens to be interested in it," he said coldly.

Annja chewed her lip. That's why he seems so different. He works for the Feds, she thought. She had interacted with enough government agents to recognize one when she saw one. This guy definitely fit the bill. Albeit in a scummy way.

"What agency do you work for?" she asked.

He shook his head. "You don't need to know that."

Annja pointed at David. "I take it they showed you some identification?"

"Of course they did. I don't just take people at their word, you know," the sheriff stated angrily.

"Naturally." Annja looked behind her at Jenny. "Nice to see what we've gotten mixed up in, huh?"

Annja looked back at the Fed. "So what are you doing here, Agent...?"

"Simpson. You can call me Simpson. This is Baker." The silent man sitting next to him inclined his head only vaguely in their direction.

Annja groaned. "What was wrong with the names Smith and Jones, were they already being used?" She took a moment to calm her anger. "So some government operatives wander up here into the dense forests of Oregon because a local sheriff finds something that he thinks proves the existence of big foot. Is that what you're trying to tell me?"

"So far, so good," Simpson said. "Oh, and Jones had to head back to D.C."

"Which means the suits back in Washington must think there's something to this stuff if they sent you guys."

Simpson only smiled.

"Either that," Annja said, "or you two are buffoons and they wanted you out of their hair for a good long time. Something I can actually see happening on a fairly frequent basis."

Simpson's jaw tightened. "You might remember that we have jurisdiction in this area, Ms. Creed."

"How do you know my name?"

Simpson smirked. "We know all about you. And the e-mail Ms. Chu sent to you. We've known everything about this trip since you started making arrangements to come here. It's one way we stay on top of things so we don't have...surprises."

"Must be that good ol' Patriot Act in action again, huh?"

Simpson put his hand over his heart. "The safety and security of our great nation is our highest priority."

Before Annja could retort, David cleared his throat. "They don't actually have jurisdiction over my command, just over the forests for right now. And unfortunately I have to yield to their federal powers. I don't necessarily like it, but I play by the rules."

"Or else what?" Annja asked. "You don't get federal funds for some road repair project?"

Simpson smiled. "Or this little piece of paradise might just be in the way of a brand-new interstate and that old eminent domain clause might mean its very downfall."

"You wouldn't," Annja said.

Simpson shrugged. "Wouldn't be the first time. Believe me when I tell you that Uncle Sam does not take kindly to people who get in his way where matters of national security are involved."

"National security?" Jenny shook her head. "How in the world could this have anything to do with national security?"

Baker cleared his throat and spoke for the first time.

"When we hear reports about the possibility of a giant ape-man wandering the forests of our country, able to travel from here to Canada and back without ever so much as attracting the attention of any of our border patrols, or tripping any of the rather elaborate monitoring systems currently deployed in this sector, we get a little nervous."

Annja rolled her eyes. "After all, if a giant missing-link creature can do it, what's to stop an al Qaeda operative from doing the same."

"Exactly," Baker said without a hint of humor.

Annja shook her head. "So which one of you dolts dreamed up that ludicrous scenario?"

"It's not ludicrous," Simpson said. "It's a very real concern to those in power back in Washington."

"I can't believe the President would fall for such a stupid line of thinking as that," Annja said. "I don't see it."

"And since when do you believe that the White House has any real power in such matters?" Simpson said.

Annja frowned. "Since my naiveté hasn't yet been shattered by the hammer of some black-book operative like yourself."

Simpson chuckled. "Well put. But, unfortunately, there are other people who wield much more power and they've decided that it's time to lay this matter to rest. That's why we're here."

"By doing what?" Annja asked.

"Yeah," Jenny said. "Are you guys going to interview the Sasquatch and ask him how he does it?"

Annja smiled. "That'd be a sight."

Simpson stood and Baker followed. "You're not far off the mark, ladies." Simpson nodded at David. "We'll be in touch."

Annja stopped him at the door. "What exactly do you mean by that—not far off?"

"Very simply," Simpson said, "we're here to capture the ape."

19

Annja burst out laughing. "Capture it? You think there haven't been other intrepid adventurers over the years who thought they'd try the same exact thing? You guys are crazy!"

Simpson shrugged. "I don't care one bit what other people might have attempted in the past. What matters is that Baker and I will succeed this time around. Failure simply isn't an option for us."

Baker nodded. "He's right. We don't expect to fail."

Jenny sighed. "Can we just agree not to call this an ape? The Sasquatch may be just as far removed from the primate family as we are."

Simpson rolled his eyes. "He's tall and hairy. Looks like an ape to me and that's what I'll call him. The exact genus of the creature isn't for us to figure out. I'm here for one thing only."

"So you're a hired hand," Annja said. "Just a mercenary, in effect."

Simpson smirked. "I enjoy your feeble attempts at baiting me, Annja. Truly, I do. But in this case, there's only one thing you need to remember."

"And what's that?"

"If you get in my way, I have the authority to use deadly force."

"Whose authority?"

Simpson smiled. "The only one that counts—Washington's."

Annja glanced at David. "You're going to put up with this without a fight?"

David shrugged. "Not a whole lot I can do, Annja. I can file an appeal that my jurisdiction shouldn't be undermined, but who would listen? And in the post-9/11 world, my chances of superceding Simpson's command are slim to none."

Annja felt the heat rising in her face. Something about Simpson's demeanor really irked her, but she knew David was right. As long as Simpson had Washington power backing him, he was untouchable.

Simpson offered a hand to David. "Well, we have to get going. Good seeing you again, sheriff. I'll be in touch if we need your assistance with anything…such as annoying saboteurs or the like." He turned to Annja. "Remember what I said."

Annja eyed him. "How could I possibly forget? There's yet another untouchable scumbag from Washington prowling the woods, hoping to disrupt a delicate ecosystem all for the sake of someone's paranoia."

Baker moved past Annja. "He's really not all that bad," he said.

Annja raised an eyebrow. "You're kidding, right? He's a complete jackass."

Baker grinned. "Guess that makes me the jackass in tow, huh?"

Annja frowned. "You said it, not me."

Jenny stopped him. "You can't imagine it's going to be easy capturing the Sasquatch, do you?"

Baker shrugged. "That's the directive. We do what we're

told. It wasn't exactly open to discussion back in D.C., if you get my meaning."

Annja glanced over her shoulder as Simpson slid on his jacket. "By the way, I saw a sample of your work last night," she said bitterly.

Simpson stopped. "What are you talking about?"

"The wolf you shot. His name was Cheehawk. That poor animal struggled to find its way back to friends before it finally died."

Simpson shook his head. "I don't know what you're talking about. Baker, we've got to get going."

"You know it was in agony the entire time it limped back to us? And yet somehow it managed to get to people who loved and respected it. You've got to admire that kind of resolve even in the face of blatant cowardice."

Simpson's face turned red. "As I said before, I don't know what you're talking about. No one in my command shot a wolf last night. And they wouldn't be permitted to unless their life was in immediate danger."

"I'll bet."

David stood. "I hope I don't have to send you packing for doing anything excessive like that, Simpson. Because if I find out you were responsible for the death of that animal, I will kick you out of my jurisdiction and risk the wrath your superiors can heave down on me. But before that, I'll call every media outlet around and let them know exactly what's going on."

Simpson walked toward the outside door. "Need I remind you that this is a national security issue? You could go to jail for talking to anyone from the media."

Annja smiled. "Touchy, touchy. Guess Washington wouldn't be too crazy about the masses knowing they wasted taxpayer dollars hunting down big foot because of border-security issues."

"Everyone is barred from talking about it," Simpson said. "And I can have the state police and FBI here in a few hours to haul you all off to jail if I feel like it."

Jenny frowned. "Have fun hunting down your ape, you big idiot."

Simpson backed out of the office and Annja watched as he and Baker left, slamming the front door behind them. In seconds, she heard the motor of a truck turn over and then they were gone.

She looked back at David who only held up his hands. "Annja, I don't know what to tell you. There's not a damn thing I can do. He's got the right paperwork, and he's got the identification that proves he is who he says he is. I've got a phone call into the number on the paperwork, but I fully expect that everything will check out. There's really nothing more I can do."

"He killed Cheehawk. You know that."

David sighed. "Yeah, probably he did. But what do you want me to do about it? Even if I dig up Cheehawk's body and send it to a lab to run a ballistics report on the slug, that would take too long and cost the town too much. Plus, it would dishonor the grave site. And I don't think our friend Creeping Wolf would like that very much."

"Speaking of him," Annja said. "I wonder where he is. We haven't seen him for a few hours."

"You won't, either," David said. "He can disappear at will and stay hidden for days. He's exactly like his namesake. His grandfather taught him the kind of secrets that people never knew existed. If he wants to cause havoc for Simpson and Baker and anyone else they have out there, he knows how to do it. I almost feel sorry for them. Almost."

"I don't," Annja said. "Simpson's the worst kind of government bureaucrat. He's little more than a psychopath."

"Well, right now, he's a psychopath with the proper paperwork, so I can't arrest him. Much as I'd like to."

Jenny crossed her arms and sat down on the bench outside David's office. "So what was this thing you wanted to show me? You know, the only reason you dragged me out here in the first place before getting mixed up with all this government nonsense."

David glanced at Annja. But she only shrugged. "I'll let you two handle this. I'm getting some coffee."

David sat down next to Jenny and started talking to her in hushed tones. Annja took a final glimpse at them and then turned to Ellen. "Somehow I think this needs to play out without any involvement from me."

Ellen cocked her head and peered around Annja. "Looks that way."

"There anyplace around here to get some breakfast?"

Ellen nodded. "End of the street. Milton's Hotel has a little café on the first floor. Tell Sheila I sent you and she'll do up a breakfast like you've never had before."

Annja smiled. "That sounds perfect. They have hot water in the rooms?"

"Like maybe a shower?"

"I was thinking a hot bath to get all this grunge off me."

Ellen grinned. "You may just find heaven there."

Annja slid her coat back on. "Thanks."

Outside the police station, she looked around. A few people meandered down the street, but the population seemed scarce. Annja figured most people were working someplace else and only a few would wander into town on any given day.

In the dirt in front of the police station, she could see the deep cuts made by Simpson's truck. He was clearly angry, judging by how he'd dug up bits of gravel and sand prior to getting back on the asphalt.

What a jerk, she thought.

Annja walked down the street. A small curio shop looked dark until she pressed her face against the glass and saw a small lamp on inside. Maybe after breakfast and a bath she'd come back and see if the place had anything special. She'd lost count of how many times in the past these types of little stores had yielded something incredibly interesting in the midst of the bric-a-brac.

The hotel was at the end of the street in one of those old brick buildings that seemed to dot the majority of the Midwest. It looked a little out of place here in the Pacific Northwest, but the multistory facade was a welcome sight. It had an old hand-carved sign dangling out front, weathered from years of wind, sun and rain. But something about it felt homey and Annja pushed in the door eagerly.

A stout woman approached immediately. "Annja?"

"Yes," she said, startled.

The woman smiled. "I'm Sheila. Ellen called and said you'd be coming down. Looking for a good meal and a bath, I think?"

Annja grinned. "Could I have them both at the same time?"

Sheila laughed. "Been out in the woods, have you? I know that feeling. Tell you what. Why not go up to your room and have a soak? As soon as Ellen called, I got one of the rooms ready for you, so the tub should just be about filled."

"You're kidding."

Sheila shook her head. "Not at all. We take the comfort of our guests here very seriously." She handed Annja a key. "It's number fifteen on the third floor. You get yourself squared away, and when you come down I'll have Tom set you out a great spread."

"Tom?"

Sheila indicated over her beefy shoulder. "Husband. He works the grill in back. Not much of a front-counter man, but he can cook like no one's business. Really knows how to make you a good eat."

"Awesome."

Sheila pointed. "Up two flights, around the corner. Call me when you're coming down."

Annja started toward the steps and then stopped. "Say, Sheila?"

"Yep?"

Annja ran her hands over her clothes. "You don't, by any chance—"

"There's a robe upstairs that should do while I get your clothes washed. Just bring them down when you're coming to eat and I'll have them done for you by the end of your meal."

Annja smiled. "I can't tell you how much I appreciate this."

"Got your credit card with you?"

Annja laughed. "Yes."

"All the thanks I need," Sheila said. "It's been a bit slow around here of late. Business is always appreciated."

"I'll bring it down with my dirty clothes."

"Enjoy."

Annja walked up the stairs, marveling at the craftsmanship in the banisters and spindles of the railing. Clearly, whoever had designed this building had put a lot of time and skill into its construction. She frowned. From the outside, the place didn't look like much, but inside the rich dark mahogany was polished to a brilliant gleam.

Photographs of the surrounding forest decorated the walls as she took the stairs to the third floor. Either Sheila or Tom must have taken them. From what she could see, they had a good eye for detail. And even Annja, with her limited knowledge of the area, could pick out a few places that looked familiar from her roaming the previous day and night.

Annja crested the third floor and turned to her right. Around the corner, she found the heavy wooden door with the old-style lock on it. She slid the key in and opened the door. It opened soundlessly, again reflecting the care that Sheila and Tom must have put into the place.

In front of her, a double bed piled high with blankets and pillows looked like the most luxurious pile of comfort she'd ever seen. On the edge of the bed, she spotted the thick white terry-cloth robe emblazoned with the initials MH for Milton's Hotel.

Annja heard the water rushing into the tub and turned the spigot off. Thick clouds of steam billowed out of the bathroom as she began to undress. Bits of leaves, wet twigs and dirt sprinkled the floor as she removed her clothes.

"Gross," she said. "I must reek."

Sheila had taken the liberty of adding some type of bubble bath to the tub. Mountains of bubbles boiled over the edge and the scent of lavender hung in the air.

Annja dipped a foot into the steaming water and instantly felt herself starting to relax. She eased into the tub and slid down until the water came up to her neck.

"Thank God for the small comforts," she said.

She closed her eyes and drifted. Thoughts ran together in a melted swirl of images and words. Simpson was trouble. And Annja would have to deal with him before too long.

What's really going on here?

20

By the time Annja emerged from the bathtub, she felt like several layers of gunk had melted off her body. The terry-cloth robe felt like a thick blanket wrapped around her body, and Sheila had even included a pair of slippers Annja hadn't seen until she lifted the robe.

Downstairs, Sheila got her squared away at a corner booth. She smiled as she handed Annja a simple menu. "Feeling better?"

"Almost human, actually. And thanks for the slippers."

Sheila nodded. "Well, your hiking boots don't really go with the robe, and I couldn't have you wandering around here without anything on your feet."

"They feel as nice as the robe."

Sheila winked at her. "I stole them from some big ritzy hotel in Vegas when Tom and I were there a few years back."

"You mean I'm staying with criminals? I'm horrified."

Sheila laughed and pointed at the menu. "See anything you like?"

"One of everything, please. I didn't realize how hungry I was until I got out of the bath. It's as if I haven't eaten in a week."

"The combination of fresh air and the water in the bath will do that to you. Anyway, I'll tell Tom to make you up something great. Any allergies I should know about?"

"Uh…no."

"Good. You wouldn't believe the tourists who stop here from time to time with a whole laundry list of things we can't put in their food. The times certainly have changed from when I grew up."

Annja smiled. "I guess they have."

"I mean, what's wrong with an egg yolk every once in a while? Or a few slices of bacon? It's not going to kill you, is it?"

Annja licked her lips. "You're making my mouth water with all this talk of eggs and bacon."

Sheila nodded. "Okay, okay, I'm off. By the way, your friend is upstairs, too. I set her up across the hall from your room. She should be down soon, although she didn't look as if she was in a very good mood."

"She didn't?"

Sheila shook her head. "She came in looking all glum. I tried to get her to smile but she wasn't having any of it. No idea what's got her so upset."

"An affair of the heart, I'd expect," Annja said. "She came to town looking for one thing and found out that she was here for something else. I think that's got her a little bit down."

"She gets any lower and she can be an anchor." Sheila headed back toward the kitchen and left Annja alone in the dining room. Ten tables sat around the room, scattered in a fashion that wouldn't have anyone sitting right on top of their neighbors. Annja appreciated the fact that Sheila had obviously set up the place for private conversations, if need be.

In most of the restaurants Annja had been to lately, the tables were so close together that confidential talk was impossible.

Sheila came back out wielding a coffee pot and a mug. She set the mug down in front of Annja. "This should help wake you up. You look as if you could use about a year of sleep, though."

"I could." Annja sniffed the wafting steam and sighed. "Nice."

Sheila nodded. "Nothing like a stiff cup of java. I wonder if I should call up to your friend and see what's keeping her?"

Annja shook her head. "I wouldn't bother. The only thing that took Jenny longer than getting ready for anything back in college was trying to get her to stop talking about her latest crush."

"One of them, huh?"

Annja smiled. "She's good people, Sheila. Just a little lovelorn and lonely."

"Aren't we all," Sheila muttered as she walked away again.

Jenny managed to make her way down faster than Annja expected. She wore a similar terry-cloth robe and slippers. Annja wondered which Vegas hotel Sheila and Tom had knocked off to get that set.

Jenny sat down. "Hi."

"Feeling any better after the bath?"

Jenny glanced around. "Yeah, I guess so. It's nice not to be so dirty anymore. My water was pretty filthy."

"Mine, too." Annja looked at her. "You okay?"

"No."

"David?"

"Yeah."

Annja sighed. "Jenny, you've got to look at it from his perspective. He needed your help. Maybe he thought you wouldn't come out unless he offered you something enticing, like some type of supposed evidence."

Jenny looked up. "I would have come out for just the evidence. He didn't need to lead me on like he did."

"Well, you know guys. They don't always think things through so well. Maybe that was just his twisted logic."

Jenny frowned. "I don't think he even likes me."

Annja sipped her coffee. "What's not to like? You're gorgeous."

"I'm old."

Annja stopped drinking. "Hold on a second. If you're old, then that makes me old, as well. And I don't feel old, so I would like to ask you to please stop saying that you're old, okay?"

"I'm almost thirty, Annja. Do you know what the odds are for a single woman in her thirties to find true love and marriage? Very slim."

"You're really a bundle of joy today, aren't you?"

"Sorry."

Annja leaned forward. "Look, so what if things didn't work out with David? There are tons of other guys around. You know that. You'll find someone, I know you will. And when you do, that guy will be the luckiest dude around. You're too good not to have someone recognize that."

"You think so?"

"Know so."

Jenny managed a smile. "Thanks for the pep talk. I appreciate it even if you don't necessarily mean it."

"Huh?"

"Well, just look at you. You're my age and no prospects in sight for you, either. I know you're just as depressed as I am but you're keeping up a strong front for me. I appreciate that."

Annja leaned back. "Jenny, I am not depressed. Nor am I putting up some sort of front for you. I'm trying to help you as my friend."

"You're not lonely?"

Annja snorted. "I'm too busy running around the world to be lonely."

Jenny eyed her. "That's a convenient excuse. Are you sure you're not just using that to avoid the issue?"

Annja sighed. "There's no issue. I've had plenty of guys in my life but nothing really has a chance to develop. It's the price I pay for doing what I do. I've made my peace with it. Anytime I think my heart's needs outweigh my professional aspirations, I'll simply stop."

"You think it will be that easy? To stop, I mean."

"I don't know. I've never really tried." And with the sword, there's no telling if I'd even be able to, Annja thought.

"And what about the whole love thing? You think that will just happen easily, too?"

"What I think," Annja said, "is that if we put our minds to it, there's nothing we can't do."

Jenny smiled. "I guess. It's just hard. I mean, I'm a college professor. I see truckloads of good-looking young boys all day long. And all I want is a man to call my own."

Annja leveled a finger at her. "You'd better keep your hands off those college boys. You wouldn't want to add unemployment to your list of woes."

"I know it. But we all want someone at the end of the day. That's what I'm saying."

"So let's see if we can find someone for you."

"Huh?"

Annja grinned. "I'll bet that guy Simpson is available."

"Please."

"What about Baker? Did you see that receding hairline? Hot."

Jenny shook her head. "What the hell, I'll just invite them both back at the same time."

"There you go. Give 'em the thrill of a lifetime."

Jenny giggled. "Probably be over in thirty seconds and then I'd be no better off than I was at the start."

"Probably."

Sheila came over to the table with two plates piled high with food. "Did I just hear laughter?"

Annja nodded. "I think she'll be okay."

Sheila smiled. "Well, maybe, but I'd be willing to bet a plate of Tom's breakfast would help the cause even more." She glanced at Jenny. "I didn't get you a menu, dear, but I thought I'd just have Tom double it all up and you could pick and choose what you like."

"Are those hash browns?" Jenny said happily.

Sheila nodded. "Of course."

Jenny tore into her plate. Annja looked at Sheila. "Looks like you made a good decision."

"Refills on the coffee?"

"I could use one," Annja said. "And if you've got some fruit juice?"

"Two glasses coming up," Sheila said. She turned and rushed back into the kitchen.

"She seems nice," Jenny said around a mouthful of food.

"Very," Annja agreed. "Now what are we going to do about our situation?"

"What situation is that?"

Annja took a forkful of eggs and chewed. "The way I see it, we've got a few things to tackle here."

"Such as?"

"Well, first and foremost, you brought me out here to help you find the Sasquatch."

"Or evidence of its existence."

"Okay. Next, we've got to deal with a couple of idiots from Washington who think they're going to kidnap the creature without getting themselves killed in the process."

"I don't see that venture being very successful."

"Neither do I," Annja said. She swallowed some of the hash browns. "God, these are good."

"I know."

"And then there's the last thing."

Jenny looked up. "What's the last thing?"

"Your relationship with super sheriff David."

Jenny shook her head. "That's a lost cause. We can forget about that right here and now."

"Why should we do that?"

"He's not interested in me. He said so."

Annja frowned. "Maybe he just said that to keep you from getting distracted. You know how you get when there's a cute guy around."

"How do I get?"

"Loopy."

Jenny frowned. "Yeah, I guess."

"David could have seen that and simply decided he wanted you focused on the evidence he was going to show you and not on him. I guess that means he might be really driven to prove this thing exists."

"Is that a good thing?"

"Well, not exactly for you right now, but overall? Maybe."

Sheila came back with two glasses of orange juice. "Fresh squeezed, girls. But there's not a lot of pulp. We got a lot of complaints about that before so we strain it more now."

Annja took a sip. "It's delicious."

Sheila hauled a chair over and plopped herself down. "So Ellen didn't say anything, but I thought I'd just go ahead and ask."

"Ask what?"

"What brings a pair of you out this way?"

Annja nodded at Jenny. "She dragged me here."

"Oh? And for what?"

Jenny smiled. "You'll laugh."

Sheila leaned back. "What? No, I won't."

"I want to prove that big foot exists."

Sheila's eyebrows jumped. "Big foot, you say. Sasquatch? Why on earth would you want to find that thing?"

"I don't want to find it, per se, just prove it's out here."

Sheila frowned. "Oh, it's out here all right."

Annja looked at her. "You know this for a fact?"

Sheila nodded. "Of course I do. I've seen it with my own eyes."

21

Jenny stopped chewing. "Are you serious?"

Sheila shrugged. "Sure. But what's the big deal?"

Annja took a sip of coffee. "You don't think it's unusual for some giant apelike creature to be roaming around the forest?"

Sheila smiled. "We just accept it, I guess. One of those things. You know, like maybe how your neighbor likes to play loud music or something. We happen to live in a town near big foot."

"That's awfully nonchalant of you," Jenny said. "Would you mind telling me about your experience?"

Sheila shrugged. "Not much to tell. Tom and me were hiking one day and I got sidetracked by some blueberry bushes—they grow thick in parts of the woods out there— and I squatted down to pick them, thinking about how they'd make for some good pancakes. I popped a few in my mouth and happened to look up. That's when I saw it."

"Where? Was it far away from you?"

Sheila laughed. "Oh, my Lord, no. It was about as close as we are right now. Apparently, I wasn't the only one who liked blueberries. It had a mouthful of them with little bits all around its hairy chin. It looked as surprised as I was. Neither of us did anything, but then it sort of just walked off."

"You didn't scream?"

Sheila shook her head. "You know, I think I was just more shocked than anything else. We'd heard about the sightings, of course. Everyone around here does. Just part of life. Anyway, it didn't give me any cause to be afraid. Aside from the fact that it must have been more than seven feet tall."

"You're sure about that?" Jenny asked.

Sheila nodded. "It was huge. Anyway, I found my way back to Tom and told him what happened. And Tom, being Tom, well, he just nodded and we continued our hike. It really wasn't a big deal. Most folks around this area just consider it part of the landscape. It's obviously got a life to lead just like we do. No sense upsetting the balance, if you will."

"Have you seen it at any other times?"

Sheila shook her head. "Nope. Once was all I needed to convince me it was real enough."

"What about Tom?"

"Nope. But he believes me so I know he thinks it's real."

Jenny sighed. "Incredible. I'm jealous."

Sheila smiled. "Now, honey, there's no sense being jealous. If you're out there enough, chances are you'll run into it, as well."

Jenny slapped her hand down onto the table. "Well, that settles it. I'm leaving right away."

Annja smirked. "Not without a change of clothes, you're not."

Sheila stood. "I'll check on them and see if they're ready for the dryer yet."

Annja watched her go and then leaned closer to Jenny. "You don't buy that story, do you?"

"Why wouldn't I?"

Annja shrugged. "Isn't it possible that she might have had a few fermented berries and they went to her head? She could have seen anything out there and thought it was big foot."

Jenny frowned. "I see we haven't lost Miss Skeptical yet."

"Miss Skeptical has kept me alive for a long time. I don't fall for every person who can cook up a story."

"You think I do?"

"We've been over this already, Jenny. I'm just saying that, as scientists, we're supposed to use logic and facts to help us prove a theory, not the emotional memories of a person who may or may not be trustworthy."

"She seems trustworthy to me."

"We just met her barely an hour ago."

Jenny sighed. "Humor me here, would you? I'm having a bad couple of days. I nearly died from hypothermia. My love interest either doesn't like me or is pretending not to like me so I can concentrate on this big-foot thing. And now you think I'm too gullible."

Annja smiled. "Hey, the food's good."

"Small consolation."

Sheila came back out. "Your clothes are going to need more time. The rinse cycle just ended."

Annja stretched her arms over her head. "That's fine. I could use a nap, anyway."

"That does sound good," Jenny said. "But is a nap enough? I feel like I might sleep for days."

"I probably could," Annja said with a yawn.

Sheila held up her hands. "You two had better stop that stuff or else I'm going to pass out right along with you. Nothing like a good siesta to keep one on top of the world. You two wander upstairs and I'll make sure you get your clothes back when they're finished drying."

Annja pushed back from the table and looked at Jenny. "Do you have any plans for later?"

"What—like meeting up with David?"

"Yeah. Doesn't he have something he wants to show you?"

"I guess. He told me to call him when we got settled here. Maybe that means he'll take me out tonight."

Sheila stood quietly by with a vague frown on her face. But as soon as Annja saw it, Sheila made it disappear. What was that about? she wondered. Did Sheila know something about David that they didn't? And if there was something else to know about the small-town sheriff, what was it?

"Why don't you head on up, Jenny. I'll help Sheila clear the dishes. No sense not helping out after all she's done for us."

"I can help, too," Jenny said. She grabbed a handful of dishes and walked them over to the plastic tub set out for clearing the tables. Annja looked at Sheila, who busied herself with the plates.

"There's no need to help, girls. I've got this. You two go on upstairs and get some rest. By the look of it, you need it. And if you're here to find big foot, then you might need even more than you think."

Jenny looked at Annja ,who shrugged. "You're sure?"

"Absolutely."

"All right, then. Thanks."

"Have a good nap."

Annja and Jenny walked upstairs. "That was a little weird," Jenny said. "Did you say something to upset her?"

"Me? What could I have possibly said? You were with me the entire time."

Jenny nodded. "I know. Just seems strange. Like one moment she was all fine and jovial and the next she was a little…wary."

"Yeah, I got that, too."

"Did you notice when she changed?"

Annja frowned. "Right about when we started talking about David."

"Damn," Jenny said. "I was hoping I was wrong about that. But, yeah, she did get a bit odd after that, huh?"

"Yep."

Jenny stopped. "What do you think it means?"

Annja shook her head. "I don't know. But I do know that we should probably be on our most alert around him. With crazy nuts like Simpson and Baker running around, combined with the Sasquatch, and then this whole thing with the sheriff, we've got to watch out for each other."

"Okay."

They crested the third floor and Jenny waved. "Sleep well."

"You, too." Annja watched her go and then turned toward her own room. She opened the door and stepped inside, locking the door behind her.

The lavender scent from the bath still lingered. Annja took a deep breath and exhaled, feeling a wave of relaxation wash over her. The bed looked incredibly comfortable and she couldn't believe she hadn't even tested it.

I would have fallen fast asleep if I had, she thought with a grin.

She took off her robe and jumped into bed, snuggling under the thick blankets. It wasn't cold outside, but somehow the feeling of thick blankets on top of her made her feel like a child again, back when the world didn't seem quite so big and scary.

How that impression has changed, she thought. Nowadays, everyone seemed to have an agenda and oftentimes that agenda clashed with Annja's, resulting in a lot of people who weren't particularly crazy about her continued insistence on breathing.

She burped quietly. Breakfast or lunch or whatever it was had been fantastic. Sheila hadn't lied about Tom being a great cook. He'd obviously come up around other chefs if he could make a typical breakfast like that taste as good as it had.

Or else Annja had simply been famished beyond belief.

She smiled. Anything was possible.

She shifted the pillow around until her shoulder felt comfortable on the mattress. It was a little firmer than she usually liked, but then again, she didn't think her body would complain given how she'd been battered for the previous day or so.

Her thoughts drifted. Sheila's reaction to big foot seemed weird to Annja, but she hadn't had the encounter. Who knew how people would respond to things until it actually happened? Sheila might just be one of those people who seem to cruise through life without getting excited about very much at all.

Or she could be lying about seeing big foot in order to feed into Jenny's fantasy.

But for what purpose?

And if Sheila didn't get upset about stuff, then why had she been so visibly disturbed, even for a moment, when David had entered into the conversation? What did she know about him that set her on edge?

It didn't make any sense.

Annja shifted again. Her stomach gurgled a bit and she wondered if she'd maybe had too much to eat. Annja didn't normally stuff herself, preferring to equate food with gasoline. You don't overfill the tank, but keep enough in there to keep the car running in top condition.

Still…

It wasn't the food. Annja found herself sinking in toward her subconscious. Wave after wave of drowsiness washed over her and she briefly worried that the food might have been drugged.

But no. Annja had been drugged before and this felt nothing like it. This was her body telling her that it needed to relax.

No sense fighting it, she supposed. She took a deep breath and exhaled, willing herself to let go of her hold on staying awake, to give in to the temptation to drift off to sleep.

And then she felt herself jerked back up toward her waking self.

Little sounds dripped and dribbled down to her subconscious, slipping into places where her logical mind could process them.

The result disturbed her.

Someone was coming into her room.

Annja felt herself moving toward being fully awake. Part of her resisted. She was so tired. And yet the adrenaline that had started coursing through her system fought off that sluggishness and forced her awareness back to peak.

Whoever was coming in would have needed a key. Jenny didn't have a key. And that pretty much meant that this person would have to be considered a threat,

She could hear it now.

Coming closer.

Annja steeled herself. In a second, she'd toss the covers and confront the person. Get them to talk.

But then she heard a familiar voice.

"Annja?"

Annja opened her eyes.

Sheila stared back at her.

"We need to talk."

22

Annja sat up in bed with the covers wrapped around her. "Why couldn't you just tell me downstairs when we were eating?"

Sheila glanced around. "I never know who's listening. And it's better up here, anyway. No one can see me talking to you."

Annja frowned. Beams of sunlight cut through the drapes in front of the window, giving the room a much brighter look than Sheila's demeanor. "You're talking like someone doesn't want us to know what's going on here."

"Someone doesn't," Sheila said. "You're absolutely right."

"And why not tell us this when Jenny was around?"

Sheila shrugged. "I don't know, really. I mean, how much do you trust your friend?"

"Jenny?" Annja grinned. "I trust her completely. We've known each other for years. We haven't been in constant contact, of course, but overall…" She stopped. "Look, there's nothing unsavory about Jenny no matter how weird she might seem. I'd stake my life on it."

"You might have to," Sheila said. "You don't have any idea what's going on here and that fact could get you killed."

"So why don't you go ahead and tell me, then?" Annja stretched her legs. "I'm finding this whole adventure rather strange."

"You can't trust the sheriff."

"David? Why not? I mean, he wasn't going to be a close confidant or anything, but what reason do you have that we shouldn't trust him?"

"He hasn't been himself lately."

Annja sighed. "Look, Sheila, I don't mean to be rude here or anything, but I'm really tired. So if we could just skip the 'you give me one line and I have to pry more out of you' thing, that'd be great."

"Dave is an imposter. He isn't the real Dave."

Annja eyed Sheila. "Okay, now I'm lost. What do you mean he's not the real David?"

"I mean he looks the same as he used to, but he's all different now. Everyone knows it. He changed when he got back after going hiking a few months back. Friday evening he set out to spend some time tracking. Monday he came back looking…strange."

"Maybe he ran into the Sasquatch."

Sheila waved her hand. "That was a load of hooey. I told that story because I could see your friend needed to hear it."

"You lied?"

"For her sake, yes. Tell me she isn't feeling a bit more excited now that she thinks I ran into the thing."

"Well, of course she is. But now she wants to go out and find it for herself. You heard her. She's jealous of you!"

Sheila shook her head. "Whatever you do, you've got to keep her out of the woods. Do not go in there again unless you have a means of arming yourself."

Annja thought about her sword. "Yeah, well, why shouldn't we go back there?"

"I know about those guys."

"Simpson and Baker?"

"Yes. Ellen keeps me in the loop. She was the first person to notice the change in Dave."

"And what exactly do you think happened to him?"

Sheila glanced away. "It's too ridiculous to talk about."

Annja smiled. "You'd be surprised at how many crazy stories I've heard in my life. Why don't you try me?"

"About four months back—a month before Dave went camping—there was a meteor shower. It came upon us suddenly but the show was incredible. For two nights, we watched the fireworks in the sky. Brilliant flashes and streaks cut across the heavens at night. Wondrous stuff."

Annja nodded. "I've seen some amazing displays in my time."

"Well, one of the shooting stars seemed to touch down out there." She pointed to the window. "Somewhere in the woods, one of those meteors landed. And somewhere out there, something happened."

"And you think that David stumbled across the meteor, perhaps?"

"Maybe."

"And then what?" Annja frowned. "It would seem unlikely that he came into contact with an extraterrestrial race who then turned him into a mindless zombie that they could control with strange thought beams and stuff like that."

Sheila eyed her. "You're mocking me, Annja. I don't appreciate that."

"Well, try to see it from my perspective. It sounds like another load of BS."

"It's not bullshit."

"So you say, right after you tell me that you just lied to my good friend about seeing big foot."

Sheila sighed. "Look, they're not related. I told a white lie and now I'm telling you the truth."

Annja took a deep breath. "So what exactly are we supposed to do, then?"

"Wait until your clothes are dry and then leave this place. While you still can."

"While we still can? What does that mean?"

"Haven't you noticed the lack of people in town? The lack of activity? Folks are starting to disappear."

Annja nodded. "Things do seem a bit quiet, but I chalked that up to people not needing to come into town all that often."

"Before Dave changed, this place was much busier."

"And you're saying he's directly responsible for the people going missing?"

Sheila nodded. "He knows he can't get rid of everyone without raising the alarm, so he went after the people living farthest away first. Eventually, he'll get to the rest of us. Those of us who live here in town."

"Why don't you leave?"

Sheila shook her head. "Not everyone is convinced."

"You don't say."

"They think I'm crazy. Just because I had a nervous breakdown a few years back and had to spend some time resting. They think I'm out of my mind. Sure, they're all nice to my face but I know how they talk behind my back."

"And Ellen thinks this is the case, too?"

"Ellen's my best friend. She's the only friend I have here in town aside from my husband. She's the only one who lets me know what's going on, but she spends most of her days in abject terror of what Dave has become."

Annja frowned. Ellen hadn't seemed particularly upset or

concerned back at the station. "And what does Ellen think you should be doing?"

"We need help."

Someone does, Annja thought. "And?"

"We're hoping you might help us."

"How in the world could I ever do that?"

"You and Jenny, you could let the outside world know what's going on here. You could get help for us."

Annja shook her head. "Look, Sheila, you're talking like you're trapped here. I don't see any gates or fences keeping you in town. I'm sure you could easily hop into your car and drive far away from this place. Both you and Ellen for that matter. If you're as concerned about this as you seem to be, then maybe that's exactly what you should be doing."

"You don't believe me." Sheila stood. "I knew this was a mistake. I told Ellen there was no way you'd believe me but she insisted. And now you think I'm just as crazy as everyone else in town does. Don't you?"

Annja shook her head. "I don't think you're crazy, Sheila. But honestly, this is all a bit much for me to handle right now. I'm exhausted. I'm supposed to be looking for big foot. And all this extra stuff keeps popping up, turning my world upside down. Truthfully, I don't know what to think about your story."

"Will you at least do me a favor and think about what I've told you?"

Annja nodded. "Absolutely. I promise."

Sheila grinned. "Thanks. I really appreciate that." She started for the door and then turned around, her body bathed in a sunbeam. "I'll bring your clothes up when they're finished. I'm sorry I disturbed your sleep."

"It's okay."

Sheila nodded once, turned and let herself out of the room

again. Annja heard the lock engage and then slumped back down onto the mattress.

Good grief.

David was apparently an alien of some type or at least under the control of evil beings from another planet. She smirked. This was one for the books. Somewhere out in the woods there was potentially a Sasquatch or a family of them. Joey was still out there, as well, doing who knew what. Probably he was going to make Simpson's and Baker's lives a living hell.

Simpson and Baker. Annja frowned. What were they really doing in this area? Surely they didn't think they were actually going to trap big foot and bring it to some laboratory, did they?

And if they didn't, then why were they here?

I need a computer and Internet access, she thought. She could at least investigate the meteor shower. And if that was confirmed, then perhaps there might be some shred of truth to Sheila's story that David was somehow different now.

Not that Annja believed for one moment that he was under the control of aliens. But perhaps Simpson and Baker were exerting more control than they'd let on earlier. And perhaps it had something more to do with the meteors and less to do with big foot.

What a mess.

Annja took a deep breath and tried to relax. But the images and thoughts swirling through her mind made that difficult. She rolled over and tried to focus on the soft drapes hanging in front of the windows.

The day outside was bright and sunny, contrasting with the mood of how she felt. She wondered if Jenny was sound asleep. Probably. And her dreams were most likely filled with visions of David in very little clothing.

Annja grinned. That was one of the things she loved about her friend. Jenny had two passions—her work and men. She couldn't fault her for it, either. And if she was being completely honest, Jenny might have hit a little too close to home earlier when she asked if Annja was lonely.

It seemed odd to admit, but there were times when Annja wanted nothing more than to snuggle with someone.

Or at least something other than a mysterious sword.

She wondered where Roux and Garin might be at this moment. They were the only two people in the world who understood what Annja's life had become since she gained possession of the sword. They had as much at stake with the sword as she did since they'd been searching for it and piecing it together for five hundred years. Garin had a way of showing up in strange places that happened to coincide with Annja being there. Part of her wondered if the sword enabled both men to know where she was to some extent.

But she also knew they both had untold sums of money that could buy them any information in the world that they desired. More than likely that was how they kept tabs on her.

As strange as it sounded, Annja would have welcomed their advice on this situation. Knowing them both, they would probably advocate taking the bull by the proverbial horns and beating the truth out of everyone involved.

Of course, they would also expect that Annja would use her sword, regardless of the consequences.

And she didn't agree with that approach.

Annja took another deep breath and tried to still her mind. She needed sleep in the worst way.

Her inner eye drew her back inside of herself, melting her thoughts into a spiraling swirl that sucked her back toward the blackness. She let herself get pulled under into the unseen riptide of her subconscious.

Annja felt sleep finally coming for her, and with the hornet's nest of questions buzzing around her head, she mercifully gave herself over to unconsciousness.

23

By the time Annja woke, she felt as if she'd started to recover the level of energy she normally had. Shadows drew long across the room and the rapidly fading sunlight told her that she'd slept more than she'd intended to. But at the same time, she felt rested and that would be important given what she had to deal with.

She almost slid her legs out of bed when something stopped her. A sudden warning from her subconscious, and there in the corner she saw why.

"Hey."

Annja shook her head. "Do you always show up so unexpectedly like that?"

Joey smiled. "Not my fault you didn't sense me until it was almost too late."

"Yeah, well, you didn't happen to see my clothes anywhere nearby, did you? Sheila promised she'd bring them up when they were done."

"I didn't happen to pass by Sheila," Joey said.

Annja frowned. "Then how the hell did you get into my room?"

Joey shrugged. "The window was unlocked."

Annja glanced at the window. It would have been about thirty feet to the ground. "We're three stories up."

"There's a fire escape on the back of the building that leads all the way up."

"I didn't hear you."

Joey grinned again. "Of course you didn't."

"I also didn't sense you."

Joey got up from the small chair and walked to the window. "My grandfather taught me how to disguise my presence, not just physically but on other levels, as well. It helps from time to time to be able to come and go as I please with no one noticing me being around."

Annja wrapped the covers around her. So much for door locks. "Where have you been? We've all been worried about you."

"Who is we?"

"Jenny. Me. The sheriff."

Joey glanced at her. "Dave? He knew I was out there?"

"We ran into him on the main road leading into town after you got the idea to run off on some vengeance mission." Annja narrowed her eyes. "How did that work out for you, by the way?"

"Their camp was abandoned. But I destroyed it, anyway. I figured they'd come into town so that's why I'm here. I had to stop and get cleaned up first. No sense walking into town all camouflaged. Makes people nervous."

"The few people that are left, huh?"

Joey frowned. "Does seem a little less active than usual. Did Sheila mention something about it?"

"She mentioned meteors in the area. Did you happen to see anything like that a few months back?"

"Oh, sure. Lots of them in the sky. Nothing too unusual, except there seemed to be more of them than last year."

"Sheila thought one of them might have actually landed out in the forest. Did you see anything in your travels to suggest she might be right?"

Joey sat on the edge of the bed. "Sheila's a little…strange sometimes, Annja. She has a tendency to say things that aren't always true. I'd be careful of what you choose to believe if it's coming from her."

Annja nodded. "She did seem a bit odd."

"She told you her conspiracy theory yet? That Dave is somehow different? That he's the puppet of aliens or something like that?"

Annja looked at him. "Actually, she did."

Joey smirked. "I thought so. She's been telling anyone who will listen that Dave is changed since the camping accident."

"Accident?"

Joey nodded. "He went out by himself. Not the wisest thing to do unless you're truly skilled. Dave's not bad, but he hasn't been trained like some of us. Anyway, he fell and bumped his head. Probably had a minor concussion or something, and when he came back, it took him a little while to get himself right again."

"And this was after the meteor showers?"

"Yeah, but I don't think they're connected. According to Dave, he fell down a gravel slope by one of the streams when his feet slipped out from under him and he got a gash on the back of his head. Knocked him a little loopy, is all. Nothing to be so concerned about. I think that Sheila's just anxious for someone else to take the role of town weirdo."

Annja smiled. "Well, that clears up that. What about the guys in the woods you were going after? How do they fit in with all of this?"

"They killed Cheehawk. I don't much care what they're here for. They'll pay for killing my friend."

Annja held up a hand. "Their names are Simpson and Baker. Apparently, they're with the government."

"Feds? Why?"

"They claim they're going to trap the Sasquatch and take it to a laboratory."

Joey shook his head. "What the hell would they do that for?"

"The reason they gave me is because they think that the creature can bypass border security and they view that as a threat to national security. They need to plug the leak, so to speak."

Joey sighed. "So that's why they're out there?"

"According to them. Whether or not they're telling the truth remains to be seen."

"Yeah, well, I don't suppose they told you why they saw fit to kill Cheehawk, did they?"

"They claimed they didn't do it."

"Of course they did. Cowards. I swear, it sometimes seems that people need protecting *from* the government, not *by* the government. Biggest bunch of reckless psychos, I tell you."

"I don't necessarily disagree with you," Annja said. "But for right now, we've got to figure out what to do about them. I've already got one obsessive person to deal with. I don't need a couple of gun-toting government lackeys obsessing over a mythical creature, as well."

Joey stood and walked to Annja's door and opened it. Outside was a neat pile of clean clothes. He stooped and brought them over to Annja. "You should get dressed, first of all. I'll go and knock on Jenny's door."

"How do you know which room she's staying in?"

Joey smirked. "You two are the only guests here. Shouldn't

be too hard to find her and, knowing Sheila, she probably put her across the hall."

Annja smiled. "Okay, I'll see you downstairs in five?"

"Good."

Joey slipped out of her room, closing the door without making a sound. Annja smirked and then quickly got dressed before Joey somehow managed to get back into her room and grab a quick eyeful of her birthday suit.

She walked toward the window. Through a gap in the curtains she could see the sun sinking toward the horizon. She took a deep breath, sucking in the last tendrils of lavender and then opened the door to the hall.

Downstairs, she found Joey sitting at a table talking with Sheila. Sheila looked up as Annja approached. "Sleep well?"

"Eventually, yes. The bed's incredibly comfortable."

Sheila smiled. "Hungry?"

Annja shrugged. "You know, not just yet. I think Jenny, Joey and I are going to take a walk around town. We'll be back later on."

Sheila nodded. "Door stays open until ten o'clock."

Jenny appeared behind Annja. "Wow, did I need that. I feel like a new woman."

Joey smiled. "You look pretty good, too."

"Thanks."

Annja stretched and yawned. "We all set?"

They left the hotel and wandered down the main street. Jenny walked alongside Annja. "So what's the plan?"

"The plan is to find David and see exactly what it is he has to show you. May as well see the reason for him dragging you out here and then you dragging me out here."

"What's he got?" Joey asked.

"Supposedly, evidence of the Sasquatch," Annja said.

"Is that so?" Joey chuckled. "This ought to be good."

Jenny glanced at him. "You don't believe him?"

Joey shook his head. "Never said that. A lot of people have thought they've found evidence over the years. As long as I've been around I've heard stories about people who claim to have found tracks and hairs and even scat. Nothing ever pans out as being authentic."

"Well, maybe David found something real this time," Jenny said defensively.

"Maybe he did," Joey said. "And if so, then good for him. I just hope it doesn't provoke an onslaught into this town and to these woods. I've sort of adopted them as my own and that makes me something of a caretaker."

"Did your grandfather teach you that, too?" Annja asked.

Joey nodded. "All woodlands are sacred. The flow of life continues even in the face of death. Cheehawk's spirit now roams those same woods as he did in life. The cycle always continues."

"And as a caretaker you do what?"

"I make sure nothing upsets the balance and harmony of the place. It's my job to ensure nothing threatens the creatures that live there."

They stopped outside the police station. Annja looked at Jenny. "You okay with doing this?"

"Why wouldn't I be?"

Annja shrugged. "What we talked about earlier. David's reaction to you. That kind of thing."

Jenny frowned. "He just doesn't realize how great I am yet. The trick is to make him see."

"I suggest subtlety," Annja said. "Don't be so overt about it."

"I can be subtle," Jenny said, and she marched up the steps into the office.

Annja glanced at Joey. "She's never been subtle."

Joey smirked. "Now there's something I never would have guessed."

Inside, Jenny was already deep in conversation with

David, who sat on the bench outside his office drinking a cup of coffee. Annja studied him and found it tough to imagine that he was anything like how Sheila had described him.

Glancing at Ellen, who laughed from time to time as the flow of conversation slowly progressed, Annja doubted that she was in any way distressed by her boss. Like Joey had warned her, Sheila might have been a few sandwiches shy of a picnic. She was a great hostess, but still a bit crazy.

David called out to her. "Jenny tells me you guys found the hotel okay."

Annja nodded. "Nothing like a hot bath and a nap to make you feel almost human again."

"I'll bet." David got up and washed his coffee mug in the sink.

Annja looked at Ellen. "You and Sheila must be pretty tight, huh?"

Ellen shrugged. "I don't really talk to her that much. She had some issues a few years back, and as a result of that she pretty much keeps to herself."

"Well, thanks for calling her earlier to let her know we were coming."

Ellen shook her head. "I never called her."

Annja frowned. "She said you called her. Told her we would be looking for rooms."

Ellen shook her head. "Nope. Soon as you left, I was on the horn with the state police. Been busy playing phone tag ever since. I haven't had time to take my lunch break, let alone call down to Sheila."

Annja looked at Jenny. "Well, that's odd."

Ellen sighed. "I wouldn't put much stock in what she says. She just hasn't been right since the breakdown. People round these parts think she's a bit loony."

"That's not a nice thing to say," David said as he dried the mug. "Everyone's got their own troubles to deal with."

"It might not be nice," Ellen said, "but it's a fair shade more accurate than pooh-poohing it away as if she's perfectly fine. She's not."

David nodded. "Well, let's just hope you never go through the same thing and have to endure all the teasing she has."

"No one teases her," Ellen said. "She makes all that stuff up just to feel better. Honestly."

David shrugged and then turned to Joey. "I see you're back."

"Safe and sound as always," Joey said. "I suppose Annja told you why I was out there."

David nodded. "I'm sorry about Cheehawk. Can we do a ceremony sometime?"

Joey nodded. "They killed him, sheriff. I know they did. He was in terrible pain when he died. Well, before Annja helped out, that is."

David looked up. "Oh? And how did she help?"

Annja spoke up hurriedly. "I just helped ease him over to the other side, that's all. Nothing special."

David looked at her for a moment and then nodded. "So why don't we go and see why I asked Jenny to come out here. I suppose that's what you're anxious to do, huh?"

Annja nodded. "Absolutely."

David smiled. "Fine, let's all take a drive."

24

Outside, David led Annja, Jenny and Joey around the back of the police station to a new black Chevy Tahoe.

Annja whistled as they approached. "Well, this certainly is a step up from the truck you were driving earlier this morning. Did you hit the lottery right after we exploded or what?"

David grinned. "Simpson and Baker left it behind for me, actually. They'd been using my truck for some of their backwoods tracking so they felt bad about what happened to it."

Joey frowned. "That's a bit like sleeping with the enemy, don't you think?"

"They're not the enemy," David said. "They have a job to do like everyone else in the world. They're simply looking for a little cooperation, is all. And I suggest we give it to them."

"Suggest all you want," Jenny said. "But I'm not cooperating with those bastards at any point in the near future."

David smiled. "Not even if I asked you nicely?"

"Not even," she said, grinning.

David sighed. "All right, then. Climb in, everyone. Let's get going. It'll be a slower ride in the dark as it is."

Annja took a look at the sky. Unlike the previous night, there didn't seem to be any clouds looming overhead, ready to open up on them at any second. Instead, pinpoints of light dotted the heavens in every direction, producing quite a bit of ambient light. It's really beautiful here, she thought.

"Annja, you ready?"

She looked back at Jenny, who was already in the back-seat. "Sorry. Just got caught up looking at the sky."

Annja belted herself in as David threw the truck into gear and rolled quietly out of the back lot. Gravel crunched underneath the tires as they hit the asphalt. David steered them onto the main road and then drove out of town.

"You're not taking us back to where we nearly died this morning, are you?" Annja asked. "I really hate revisiting the scene of near tragedies."

"Not at all, but we do roll past there. We're going to my home up in the mountains. It won't take us much more than ten minutes to get there. We can eat, then I'll show you the evidence I have that proves that big foot exists."

"I prefer you call him Sasquatch," Joey said. "It's a Native American thing."

"Sorry."

Joey shrugged. "Forget it. So what is it you have, anyway? A plaster cast of a footprint?"

David shook his head. "I'm not telling. Not yet, at least."

Jenny elbowed Annja. "I'm getting bored with this teasing bit."

"So am I."

Joey kept guessing. "Piles of old poop?"

David laughed. "You'll have to be patient."

Joey leaned back into the seat and sighed. "Well, what's for dinner, then? Can you at least tell us that?"

"Sure. Barbecued chicken and potato salad. You guys okay with that? I've got the grill out and can get it fired up in no time."

"It's a little dark to be grilling, don't you think?" Jenny said.

David shook his head. "Porch lights will help. Besides, we'll need them on for later."

Annja looked at Jenny. Why would they need porch lights? That didn't make any sense, unless what David had to show them was outside. But what could he possibly have as evidence that had to be kept outside?

"So where are Simpson and Baker now?" she asked. "I'm assuming you know where their camp is."

David shook his head. "They don't need to check in with me, unfortunately, so I don't know where they are. All they have to do is let me know what they're up to and that's about it. They really have free reign of the place."

"Must be nice," Joey said. "All that power. Not having to answer for any crimes. Must be very nice."

David eyed him. "You driving at something, Joey?"

Joey shrugged. "Nope. Just saying that no one is untouchable. Even those who think they've got the best position can sometimes be unseated unexpectedly."

David held up a finger. "Joey, I'm going to have to tell you not to disturb those guys. They aren't going to fool around with you. You know what they can do if they're provoked."

"How would I provoke them?"

"I know some of what you're capable of."

Joey sighed. "It's not my fault if the laws of nature decide to move against them. I can't be held responsible for that."

"You can be if you're the tool of their justice. You know I'd have to arrest you. And even though you're still a juvenile, you'd still get into a lot of trouble for interfering. I have no doubt that these guys can make your life pretty miserable. They might even be able to make you disappear."

"I'm not a magic trick," Joey said.

"Nope, you're not. But you are a fourteen-year-old boy who can do things most adults can't do. Surely your grandfather has taught you that with power comes great responsibility. And that responsibility is yours to ignore or abide by."

"He might have said something like that."

"Then I hope you'll honor his wise words by following them. To ignore them would be foolish and dangerous."

Joey lapsed into silence as the trees flew past the windows. David's headlights cut through the night, and the road in front of them was reduced to two beams of yellow that just enabled him to navigate the twists and turns.

"Where do you live, David?" Annja asked.

"We're almost there," he said. "Just another half mile. Then there's the turnoff and a steep grade to climb, but we'll be at the house."

"You live alone?"

"Except for Missy."

Jenny tensed up. "Who is Missy?"

"A calico cat who keeps me company. I've had her for about ten years now. Mostly she sleeps, gets up to eat and then finds another place to sleep. She's got quite the busy schedule."

Jenny relaxed and went back to looking out the window. Annja watched her and sighed. Jenny needed to get over whatever it was she felt for David. Annja still wasn't sure how much she even trusted him.

"We're here."

David turned the steering wheel and abruptly the truck seemed to rear back on its wheels as the front treads bit into the steep incline and churned to gain purchase. They eased up the driveway and then leveled off.

David put the truck into Park and then switched off the ignition. "Home sweet home."

Annja stepped out of the truck and instantly felt the bite of the night air sweep over her. They were up a bit higher in elevation and she could feel the cold air settling in.

Jenny stepped out and shivered. "Wow, it's colder up here."

David waved them inside the ranch house. "It'll be warmer inside once I get the lights on and stuff. Come on in."

Joey crept out of the truck and took a look around. Annja saw him stooping and studying the ground. "Everything okay?"

Joey looked up. "Huh? Yeah. I guess."

"What's that supposed to mean?"

Joey shrugged. "Nothing. I'm tired, I guess. And he's right. As much as I want to hurt the guys who killed Cheehawk, I really can't. How would I care for this place if I was in jail? As much as they deserve it, sometimes the toughest part of being powerful is knowing when the universe has to dish out the justice and not you."

Annja smiled. "You say some pretty wise things for a kid."

Joey grinned. "I'm not a kid anymore. Not after Cheehawk died. And not after I saw who killed him." He walked inside, leaving Annja alone in the darkness.

Lights flickered on inside the house and Annja could see more of it as it became illuminated from within. It was a modified ranch that looked as though there was an upstairs. Bits of wooden porch furniture sat near the entrance and Annja could see that David had a nice view of the valley below.

This must be something in the daylight, she thought.

"Annja?" David's voice called out from inside. "You want a beer?"

Annja grinned in spite of herself. "Yeah, great, thanks."

The sheriff appeared on the porch with a bottle. He handed it to her and then pointed toward the valley. "Pretty nice, huh?"

Annja took a sip and swallowed. "I'd probably be in a better position to make that call when I can actually see it, but, yeah, it looks pretty nice."

David smiled and moved closer to her. "I'm glad you're here."

Annja frowned. "Really?" She took another sip from the bottle, watching David as he smiled at her.

"Yes."

She could feel the shift in energy. Oh, great, she thought. Not this on top of everything else that's going on. She put up a hand as David moved in even closer. "Please don't," she said.

"What?"

"You know what."

David moved in again. "What? I shouldn't try to kiss you?"

She put up her hand to stop him. "You'd better not."

David shook his head. "I can't help myself. I'm really attracted to you. What's the harm in letting that show?"

"The harm," Annja said, "is that my friend is nuts about you and she's deeply hurt that you're not interested in her."

David took a deep breath. "Look, I've got a confession to make. The only reason I asked her to come out here was because I knew she was friends with you. And I hoped you'd follow her."

Annja frowned. "How the hell did you know we're friends?"

"Jenny wrote something in one of her e-mails that mentioned you had been close in college. I took a chance that if she came out here to solve the Sasquatch mystery she might include you. And obviously it paid off."

Annja held the beer bottle in front of her. This was both-ering her more and more. "Look, David, don't take this the wrong way, but I'm not into you. At least not like that."

"You might be if you let me kiss you." David leaned in again.

Annja backed away. "Come any closer and I will put you down on the ground painfully," she said.

"Technically, you'd be guilty of assaulting a police of-ficer."

Annja frowned. "Don't play that petty power bullshit with me, *Sheriff*. I've tangled with guys a lot meaner than you before. And they all lost. Every last one of them."

David stepped back. "I'm not like the other guys, Annja. You'd know that if you'd just let me do what I need to do."

Annja pointed at the door. "Right now, you need to take yourself back inside that house and get dinner grilling. Or else you're going to have a lot of explaining to do to Jenny."

"The hell with her."

Annja gripped the bottle tighter. "You're talking about my friend, David. One I happen to care about very much."

"Then you should kiss me."

"Why on earth would I do that?"

David smiled but there was nothing pleasant about it. "To keep me from telling her how you've thrown yourself at me," he said.

"What? I've done no such thing."

"You really think she'd believe you? After all, you said yourself how crazy she is for me. You think she's in the right frame of mind to tell who's lying and who isn't? I don't think she is. And jealousy is a real pain the ass for friends to deal with. But, hey, you go ahead and try it if you want." He leaned back on the porch railing and crossed his arms.

Annja looked at him. What a jerk, she thought. But she would have to play this just right. Jenny was fragile enough not to believe her if David really ran with this. Just how much did Jenny trust Annja? How jealous was she?

The door swung open and Jenny walked out. "What's going on, guys?"

Annja eyed David, who cocked an eyebrow and mouthed the word *later* to her. She frowned but quickly looked back at Jenny. "Nothing. David was just telling me how nice it is up here during the daytime. The view is spectacular, apparently."

Jenny nodded. "David, Joey says to tell you that the chicken is almost finished and he's starving."

David laughed. "All right, I'm going. I'm going." He walked inside and left Annja alone with Jenny.

Jenny looked at her. "You okay? You don't look so good."

Do I tell her? Annja frowned and tried to work all the scenarios through in her head. How would Jenny take it if she knew David had a thing for Annja instead of her? Not well.

And Annja had no way of knowing what Jenny's reaction might be. This whole thing was spiraling out of control far too quickly for Annja to keep up. Somehow she'd have to get to grips with it all and fast.

David would want a kiss before too long, and if Annja didn't have a solution for his looming libido Jenny would be hurt badly. And Annja was determined to make sure that didn't happen.

She took another swig of the beer, which now tasted stale to her. "Nothing's wrong. I'm hungry, is all. Let's get inside and see if David is at all talented in the kitchen."

Jenny smiled. "Sounds good to me. But I really want to see whatever it is he says he has to prove that big foot exists."

"Yeah," Annja said. "That should be interesting."

25

As disgusted as Annja was with David, even she had to admit that he could whip up some pretty tasty grub. The barbecued chicken had a slick coating of thick sauce that made her mouth water. The potato salad had an interesting mix of mayonnaise and mustard that gave it a yellow hue and delivered just the slightest tang. Combined with the cold beer, Annja was in culinary heaven.

She wiped her mouth. "Food's good, David."

He smirked. "Finger-licking good, huh?"

Annja grew serious. "So when are we going to get to this evidence of the Sasquatch? I don't know about anyone else, but I'm anxious to see it."

Joey nodded. "I agree. Let's see it."

David held up his sauce-stained hand. "First we enjoy the meal and then we can get to business." He glanced at Jenny. "Food okay, Jenny?"

She nodded. "You're quite the chef."

"I grew up with a family of cooks. My mother and grandmother made sure that I knew how to work a kitchen. Maybe they thought they'd better do it because no woman could ever stand to be with me for too long. If they didn't teach me to cook, I'd starve to death."

Annja grimaced. If only they knew how right they were, she thought. She glanced at Jenny and grinned. Jenny smiled back.

Joey finished his chicken and wiped his mouth. "I'm done."

David smiled. "Joey, I've got a nice chocolate cake for dessert. Just try to be patient, would you?"

Joey slumped back into his chair.

David checked his watch. "Besides, we're still too early."

"Early for what?" Annja asked.

"The evidence," David said.

"You don't have it here?"

Dave shook his head. "It's coming, though. Probably even as we speak."

Annja's radar was on full alert. What was he talking about? If he didn't have the evidence, then who did? And why wasn't it here already? She sighed and took another sip of her beer. "This just keeps getting better and better."

"What's that?" David asked.

"Nothing," she muttered.

David eyed her and then went back to his chicken. Joey, however, stared at him and frowned.

"Seriously, Sheriff, what the hell is going on here? What do you mean you don't have the evidence but it's on its way? What's that about? It's mobile?"

David grinned. "Very mobile."

"You've got someone helping you?" Annja asked.

David shrugged. "I guess you could say that."

Joey shook his head. "I hate riddles like this. They're a waste of time. Better to just come out and say what you mean, rather than dick around with this useless teasing crap."

"You need to learn some patience, Joey," David said sharply. "There's something to be said for creating an atmosphere."

"There's also something to be said for getting back to the hotel for some much-needed sleep," Annja said. "Just how much longer are we going to be waiting for your evidence to show up?"

"Maybe twenty minutes. Long enough for a piece of cake."

Jenny pushed her plate away. "I'm stuffed. I don't know if I can handle a slab of cake right now."

Joey nodded. "Yeah, I'm not into the cake, either. Maybe later, huh?"

David shook his head. "No. You have to have the cake. It won't taste as good once it cools. Fresh out of the oven is the best time to eat it."

Annja shook her head. "Fine. Whatever. Just dish out the cake and let us eat it and then we can get to the reason we're all here."

David stood and collected the plates. "You guys relax and I'll be right back with dessert."

Annja watched him leave the dining room and then looked at Joey and Jenny. "Anyone else think this is getting a little strange?"

Joey nodded. "He's different. This isn't how he normally is. He seems obsessed about that cake for some reason."

"And what was up with the evidence not being here yet?"

"Beats me."

Annja looked at Jenny. "You okay? You haven't said much."

Jenny looked at her. "What were you guys doing out on the porch for so long before I came outside?"

Annja swallowed. "You want the truth?"

"Of course."

Annja frowned. "Your would-be suitor made a pass at me."

Jenny jerked back. "Cut it out."

Annja shook her head. "I hate having to tell you this, but it's true. He tried a few times to kiss me."

"Did you?"

Annja leaned forward. "No, Jenny, I did not. In fact, I told him that you were crazy for him and that he should really open his eyes to the great woman he has in front of him."

"You said that?"

"Something like that."

"What did he say?"

Annja sighed. "I don't think he's interested, Jenny. He went so far as to suggest that the reason he got you out here was because he knew you'd contact me and I'd come out, too."

Jenny frowned. "He didn't say that."

"Unfortunately, he did."

"I don't believe you."

Annja put her hands on the table. "And why would I lie? I'm not even attracted to him."

"That's why. Because you don't like him."

"Whether or not I like him has nothing to do with this. If it was up to me, I'd force him to like you just so you could stop whining about not having a boyfriend."

Jenny stopped short and pulled back.

Annja took a breath.

Joey shook his head. "Wow, you guys really have some issues to work out, huh?"

"Shut up, Joey," Annja said. "This doesn't concern you."

"Fortunately," he said.

Annja leaned across the table. "Jenny, I just want you to be happy. That's all. I don't want David for myself. Honestly. I even debated telling you the truth because I knew you might take it badly."

"Maybe I should leave," Jenny said.

Annja put a hand on hers. "Don't. That would be a mistake."

"Cake's ready." David appeared in the doorway and looked at the scene. "Everything okay?"

Joey shrugged. "Female issues, apparently."

Annja frowned again. "Shut up, Joey."

"Yeah, yeah, whatever." Joey grabbed a plate of the cake. "May as well try this incredible cake and see what the big deal is." He ate a forkful and chewed slowly until a big smile spread across his face. "Holy cow, this is some great stuff."

David smiled. "See?" He put plates down in front of Annja and Jenny. "Ladies, enjoy."

Annja picked up her fork and took a bite. She chewed slowly and then felt the burst of flavor in her mouth. David must have used a particularly rich vein of dark chocolate in the baking because it tasted almost like warm pudding.

"Wow."

Even Jenny couldn't stop eating it. "It's really delicious, David."

"I'm glad you think so. It's an old recipe passed down to me from my grandmother. No one else in the family can make it as well as I do."

Annja kept chewing. "You have a big family, David?"

"Actually, no. Well, not anymore."

Jenny smiled sadly at him. "Sorry to hear that."

David bit into his own cake. "Well, we can't stop the clock, can we? Everyone dies eventually."

Joey polished off his cake. "That was great. Thanks for insisting we have it."

"The dark chocolate in the cake helps settle the stomach after a meal. Plus, it contains antioxidants. Important these days, I think."

Annja looked at David's plate. "You're not eating yours?"

"I think I might have had a bit too much potato salad. But I did try it. Pretty good if I do say so myself."

Joey reached across the table. "I'll finish yours off, then."

David tried to stop him. "Joey, don't—"

But Joey grabbed the plate and started eating. Annja watched him put a big forkful in his mouth and chew. After a few seconds, he frowned. "Hey."

David got up from the table. "Everyone finished?" He collected the plates, including Joey's, and took them out of the room.

"Something wrong, Joey?" Annja asked.

Joey finished chewing and swallowed. "His cake wasn't warm."

Jenny sighed. "What are you talking about now?"

"His cake. It wasn't hot. Like it hadn't been in the oven."

"How is that possible?" Jenny said. "We were all eating the same cake, silly."

Annja felt thirsty and reached for her beer. After she took a swig, she put the bottle down. "Actually, we never saw him cut the cake. He brought us out plates of it, remember?"

Jenny frowned. "So you're saying he gave us different pieces? Why would he do a thing like that?"

"Maybe he's drugging us," Joey said.

Annja took another sip of beer. "The cake didn't taste as if it had anything in it. Just rich and full of chocolate."

Joey got up from his chair. "I don't feel any different, do you?"

Annja shook her head. "Nope. And I've been drugged enough times to know what it feels like."

"There's a surprise," Jenny said.

"What's that supposed to mean?" Annja whirled around. "If you've got something to say, you'd better just say it."

"What—you're taking offense at the fact that you're always off trying to save the world? No wonder you're alone all the time. You've got an ego the size of Texas keeping you from landing anyone around you as a potential mate. Meanwhile, I work my ass off and have little to show for it. But you, Miss TV Hotshot, you've got guys you don't even know luring you across the globe, trying to get in your pants. Must be nice, must be really nice."

Annja stared at her. "Is that what you think? Is that what you actually believe?"

Jenny got out of her chair. "I'm going to use the bathroom."

Annja watched her go and then looked at Joey. "It's not like that. Really."

Joey put up his hands. "Annja, I haven't known you all that long but if you even think that I'm getting anywhere near this thing, you're out of your mind. I'm keeping my nose out of it. All I want to do is see this supposed evidence and then get the hell out of here. No wonder I always feel so much better in the woods."

Annja sighed. "You're right."

David came back into the room. "Where's Jenny?"

"Bathroom," Annja said. "We had a little misunderstanding."

David put a hand on his chest. "Not over me, I hope."

"Shut up, David."

Joey smirked. "She's been saying that a lot tonight."

"Well, I hope she comes back soon. The evidence should be here any minute and I don't want any of you to miss it," David said.

"Miss it?" Annja frowned. "How would we miss it?"

"Let's go outside. You'll be able to understand better out there."

"What about Jenny?"

"She'll be along, I'm sure. She's a big girl. She can figure out where we're at." David waved them out of the dining room. "Now, come on and see."

Joey glanced at Annja and shrugged. "Guess we find out what the big deal is, huh?"

"I guess."

Annja blinked. She still didn't trust David and this whole thing might be some elaborate setup. It had certainly happened to her enough times in the past.

She walked through the kitchen on the way to the back door. As she passed the counter and the sink, she saw the dishes stacked inside it.

"Annja?"

She turned. David stood in front of her. "Yeah?"

"You all set?"

"Yeah."

David grinned. "Then let's go."

Annja took a final glimpse at the sink, noting as she did so that there were two cake knives and two pans in among the dishes.

Two knives.

Two cakes.

She frowned, but then walked outside after David.

26

The darkness beyond the glow of the porch lights seemed to spread off in the distance forever, an endless horizon of impenetrable shadow. Annja tried to adjust her breathing so she was more relaxed and hopefully more in tune with her surroundings. At the same time, she switched from trying to focus on everything and allowed her vision to become softer, knowing that at night this was the better way to see in the dark.

"It shouldn't be long now," David said. He stood right behind Annja. His presence was so close it made her feel uncomfortable. She wished Jenny would see how aggressive he was and how Annja was not encouraging him in the slightest.

She sighed. "Get away from me, David."

Joey glanced at her and grinned, but then went back to watching the woods. "What exactly are we waiting for here, Sheriff?"

"Just keep your voice down and be still. If it hears you, it won't come out of the woods."

"It?" Jenny said as she approached them. "You don't actually mean the Sasquatch is going to come here, do you?"

"I certainly do."

Annja shook her head. "There'd better be a good explanation for how you managed to achieve that miracle."

"Simple. A few months back, I noticed some obscure tracks on the periphery of my property. They weren't like anything I'd ever seen before. Of course, my skills aren't nearly what Joey's are so I couldn't be sure of anything, really."

Joey frowned. "Well, you certainly could have asked me."

David shrugged. "I guess I wanted this to be my discovery and mine only. I wasn't ready to ask for any help. I just wanted to make sure this was what I thought it was and not some big mistake."

"So what did you do?" Annja asked.

"I set up small feeding stations around the edge of the woods back there. And then I started sitting out all night long, making notes of when the creature came in and for how long. What it liked to eat, what spooked it, that sort of thing."

"That's pretty intriguing," Jenny said. "Did you think to set up a night-vision camera or some other method of actually capturing this thing on film for the rest of the world to see?"

"No. I didn't want to spook it before I was ready to, at long last, unveil this to friends. That's you guys."

Joey sighed. "I don't buy it."

Annja smiled. "Me, either. How did you keep this to yourself? Most people would have busted at the seams with the urge to tell the world they'd discovered the truth about the Sasquatch. And yet you kept it quiet. Why?"

David shrugged. "Guess I'm just better at keeping secrets than other people."

Annja nodded. "Sure seem to be."

Jenny looked at her watch. "Well, when does the nightly entertainment start around here?"

"Should be right about now," David said. "If it keeps to its normal patterns and comes by. Of course, it could also be spooked by the presence of you guys."

"But it's fine with you seeing it?" Annja asked.

"Well, sure. By now it's gotten used to my scent being here. I'm not a threat anymore."

"And we are."

David frowned. "Annja, if you were a creature like this who had survived for so long by being so careful, then wouldn't you feel a little threatened if you smelled someone you hadn't before? Even someone who smells as lovely as you?"

Joey groaned. "Dude, please."

Jenny's voice grew terse. "So what exactly are we supposed to be looking at, then?"

"The outer border of the lights. Sometimes you can see it moving just beyond the glow."

"And you think it will be here tonight?" Jenny asked.

"I refilled the feed bags earlier today."

Annja glanced at David. "What in the world did you use as bait?"

"Venison."

Joey groaned. "You killed a deer?"

"I found a dead deer by the side of the road. It was still fresh. Someone must have hit it and kept going. It wasn't spoiled and it seemed a shame to waste it. So I used it. I thought you'd be proud of me for not wasting it."

Joey frowned. "It wouldn't have been wasted, anyway. It would have been food for the other creatures in the forest."

"And it is," David said. "It just so happens that the creature in question is a bit larger than the scavengers that would normally get to the deer first."

"You've done this before, then," Annja said.

"Yes."

"Each time with deer?"

David shook his head. "No, it was a very interesting trial-and-error system. I tried berries for a while and they didn't work. It just left them untouched. I tried leaves and plants, testing to see if it was an herbivore. Not so much."

"So what beyond the venison actually worked?" Jenny asked.

"Honey."

Jenny nodded. "I can see that. Sweets are always a good way to break down barriers with animals and people alike."

Annja went back to watching the darkness. Her eyes couldn't pierce the cloaked environs beyond the reach of the lights, but somewhere deep down inside her she felt something moving out there.

Slowly.

"What time is it?" she asked.

David checked his watch. "It's about that time."

Annja nodded. "I think it's out there."

"Are you sure?" Jenny moved closer to her. "I don't see anything."

Annja smiled at her. "Too much time in the classroom. Let your eyes go out of focus and deepen your breathing until you're more relaxed. Sense the rhythm of the woods and then you'll start to hear and see things."

Jenny took a breath and released it slowly, exhaling in one smooth stream. "I feel like I'm meditating."

"You are, sort of," Annja said. "Now just let your awareness expand outward in concentric circles, almost like radar."

Annja went back to watching the woods. Her senses were heightened. There was definitely something moving out there. She shivered. Having something like the Sasquatch lurking on her property would have made her distinctly uneasy at night. She wondered how David the lothario fared.

Joey leaned his head forward, and his voice, when he spoke, was the vaguest whisper. "It's here."

David snaked his head in next to Annja and Jenny. "I told you it would be here. Do you believe me now?"

"I can sense something out there," Annja said. "But I haven't seen anything yet that proves it exists. I'll withhold judgment until I do."

"That shouldn't be long," David said.

"I still can't see anything," Jenny said.

David smiled. "Want to get closer?"

Annja looked at him. "Are you crazy?"

"We're not in danger," David said. "And I really want Jenny to see what this thing is that I've been dying to tell her about all this time."

"When you weren't luring me out here," Annja said.

"We can discuss that later," David said. He looked at Jenny. "What do you say? Shall we get closer?"

Jenny nodded. "I'm in."

Annja frowned. "Well, there's no way you two are going without an escort. Joey and I will come with you."

"Great," Joey said. "This better not turn out like the last horror movie I saw."

David led them off the porch and onto the grass. Tall weeds reached up, threatening to entangle their shoes, but David took them on a route that spared them from the largest plants.

Annja's senses were on high alert and she could hear vague snaps of twigs and branches as whatever lurked beyond the clearing moved smoothly through the woods at a slow pace.

This doesn't feel right, she thought. We ought to be back on the porch where we can see. In the darkness, anything can happen.

Joey stalked through the grass next to her and she mar-

...ape appeared, partially
...es and a tall shrub. Was this the Sas-

Jenny froze in her tracks and then glanced back at Annja, her eyes wide. "Oh, my God, Annja. That's it."

But Annja couldn't see any detail, just a shape and that bothered her. I need to get closer, she thought.

Next to her, Joey held her arm. "What are you doing?"

"Getting a better look. All I see is a vague shape. That's not enough for me to become a true believer."

Joey sighed. "You're on your own, then."

Annja nodded and stalked farther on, past David and Jenny. Behind her she could hear Jenny whispering at her to come back and not be a fool. But Annja hadn't gotten to where she was in life by being afraid to take a chance. Or many chances. And this time was no different. She needed to know. She needed to see.

She approached the edge of the woods. Still, the shape kept moving, and Annja could see something hanging from a tree close by. That must be one of the feeding stations, she thought.

Was it eating?

I just need to get a solid look, she thought. That's it. If I can actually see the creature, I'll go back and leave it alone.

quarich
obscured by branches

-er.
On the edge of the woods, a large sh
saw it before the others did and she froze.
David stopped moving and pointed ahead of him. Annja

develop similar techniques, geographically, could sometimes de-
ent cultures, isolated movements in martial
arts training. She was always fascinated by the way differ-
Annja nodded. She'd seen similar technique.
and whispered to her. "Old stalking technique."
moving through the water in search of fish. He glanced ove-
his legs came up out of the grass and back into it like a sto-
veled at how silent he was. He was half crouched over

never

get my own

of the

creature.

Annja plunged into the

The sounds ahead of her sto

re wasn't eating anymore.

Annja heard a soft whiff of air. And then she felt something pierce her skin just below her heart. She looked down and then brushed her hand down the front of her shirt.

She came away holding a tranquilizer dart.

Since when does the Sasquatch use tranquilizer darts? she wondered as she slipped into unconsciousness.

27

Annja groaned as she became aware of the painful throbbing in her head. She tasted something in her mouth, something faintly sweet, and wondered just what drug had been used to take her down.

"Ugh."

She opened her eyes and looked around. She was in a cave of some sort, but exactly where she had no idea. She could hear the steady *drip-drip-drip* of water falling from the cavern ceiling to the floor below. Combined with the ache in her head, the dripping water seemed to echo her pain.

The area where the dart had struck her felt a little tender, but the wound was nothing too serious. I've probably got a nice welt there, she thought. It wasn't the first time she'd been struck with a drugged dart. It probably wouldn't be the last, either. Annja almost grinned at the thought of how ridiculous that sounded.

Her hands were bound tightly behind her and movement was difficult. But at least the ropes flexed some when she moved her hands. She'd been in handcuffs before and that was far worse.

The ambient light in the cave seemed to be coming from somewhere else. She wondered if there was a way to get to the outside and, if so, was sunlight somehow penetrating the cavern? She couldn't be sure, but it felt as if she'd been out for the better part of several hours. That would make it coming up close to dawn.

From behind her, she heard something shift and Annja tensed, expecting the worst. Instead, when she turned around, she saw Joey and Jenny. They were tied up, as well. Jenny was trying to sit up, but was clearly not used to being bound.

"Are you all right?" Annja asked.

Jenny nodded as she finally succeeded in righting herself. "I think so, aside from one hell of a bruised ego."

"David?" Annja asked.

Jenny nodded. "The bastard conned me, Annja. And he did such a great job on me that I was distracted and I never even noticed he was setting us up."

Annja shrugged. "I got conned, too. It happens."

"What happened to you? We saw you go into the bushes and then it sounded as if you'd fallen."

"As soon as I stepped in, someone shot me with a dart. I didn't see a damn thing," Annja said.

Jenny smirked. "I did. Don't worry, you didn't miss much. It was just a guy dressed in some kind of special suit I've seen soldiers wearing before. It covered him from head to foot in strips of burlap and stuff like that."

"He wore a gillie suit?"

Jenny nodded. "That's what they call it. Thanks. Yeah, he was in one of those. He came walking out, raised his gun and shot Joey first. Then he nailed me. As I went down, I heard David telling him what a great shot it was. Jerk."

Annja frowned. "I wonder exactly who David is working with. And why the hell has he fabricated the entire existence of big foot?"

"I thought we were calling it Sasquatch," Joey said, opening his eyes for the first time."

"You okay?" Annja asked him.

Joey nodded. "Yeah. My stomach hurts a lot, though."

Annja grinned. "Did you get shot in the stomach?"

"Yeah."

"It's the localized pain from the dart hitting you. Sort of feels like you got punched real hard."

"Yeah."

Annja smiled. "It wears off in time. The important thing is you're okay and back with us."

Joey flexed his hands. "Whoever tied these ropes did a good job. There doesn't seem to be any give to them."

"Agreed," Annja said. "Which leaves us with the questions that have been plaguing us for the past day or so. Namely, what the devil is going on around here?"

"Well, Dave hasn't succeeded in luring the Sasquatch to his backyard, that's for sure," Joey said. "He did, however, succeed in suckering us something silly. Speaking for myself, as a fourteen-year-old, I'm not happy. But you guys are grown-ups. You should be ashamed."

Jenny smirked. "Thanks a lot."

Annja looked around the cave. "Joey, you recognize any of this? Does it look familiar at all?"

"Not really. The woods are filled with caverns like this. Miles of unexplored tunnels crisscross the area. I don't know if anyone has really ever explored them, to be honest."

"Not you?"

Joey shook his head. "I was just mastering the outside world. I wasn't even that curious about the tunnels."

"Maybe this is where the Sasquatch lives," Jenny said.

Annja sighed. "I doubt that. Last I remember reading about the Sasquatch, it doesn't wear a gillie suit, shoot tranquilizer darts or tie people up in secret underground caves."

"This is all the sheriff's doing," Joey said. "And, boy, am I going to enjoy having some words with him."

"But what's the purpose of all this?" Annja asked. "Why bother getting us out here? He could have simply ignored us and done whatever he was planning on doing by himself. What does he need us for?"

"That would be the magic question," Jenny said. "But clearly it's not for anything romantic."

"Safe bet," Annja said. She glanced at Joey. "Any ideas there, Einstein?"

Joey shook his head. "All I know is Dave has been a decent guy since I've known him. That's not all that long and all, but he's always been cool with me. This is completely out of left field. I don't get it."

"None of us do," Annja said. "So let's hear some theories."

"You think this is connected with Simpson and Baker?" Jenny asked.

Annja shrugged. "Could be, I guess." She knew she'd have trouble summoning the sword with her hands bound behind her. Instead, she started looking around for a sharp rock to cut the ropes on. They couldn't just sit there, waiting for someone to come and hurt them. They had to get out and quick.

"Either Simpson or Baker could easily have a gillie suit and tranquilizer darts. That's not out of their ballpark."

"So if they're working together, then to what end? To capture the Sasquatch? David didn't strike me as all that supportive of their mission," Annja said.

"Well, that was before he lured us out to his house and had his friend shoot us with those darts," Jenny replied.

"Good point."

Annja spotted an outcropping of jagged granite ten feet away. "We need to get these ropes off."

Joey squirmed his way over to Jenny and sat up, using her

back for support. "So if Dave is with those two Feds, then that would mean one of them shot us even though we weren't doing anything illegal. That doesn't strike me as being kosher."

Annja smiled. "None of this is kosher, pal. This is the big wide world of evil people." She got herself situated and starting moving up and down, rubbing the small space between her hands against the rocks. She felt the sharp edges bite in her flesh.

"Damn, cut myself."

Jenny looked at her. "You okay?"

"Fine." Annja kept the friction on. She couldn't afford to give in to the pain. David and his buddies might be on their way to finish them off. "How long has David been the sheriff around here?"

Joey shrugged. "I don't know, maybe three years or so."

"Where did he come from before that? Does anyone know?"

"I'm the wrong guy to ask, to be honest. I've had my nose in the woods too much to know what his background is. All I know is he came, wooed everyone and got the job."

"What are you thinking, Annja?" Jenny asked.

"I don't know. Maybe he was sent here for some purpose that we don't know about. Maybe this isn't the first time he's done this." She kept the pressure on and felt some of the rope start to give a little bit.

"Well, whoever he is, he can't get away with it," Joey said. "Someone has to find out and make him pay."

"Like who?" Jenny asked. "State Police are more than an hour away. Who would come out here in time to rescue us?"

"She's right," Annja said. "If we're going to stop David and whatever it is he's up to, we're on our own. Unless there's anyone else we can find to help us."

Jenny frowned. "Who are you thinking of?"

"Sheila."

"From the hotel? I thought she was a nutcase."

Annja felt another bit of rope start to give way. "I thought so, too. But she was the one who warned me about David. That's got to count for something, don't you think?"

"I guess, but how are we going to get to her? I don't have a cell phone on me and I doubt it would work underground, anyway," Jenny said.

One of the ropes fell free and Annja gritted her teeth, working on shredding the remaining ropes. "Just let me finish this and we'll work that out. If we can find some way out of here and get back to town, then we'll be all set."

Joey watched her. "Once we're out of here, I'll need a minute or two to look around and get my bearings. Once I do, I can get you back to town as fast as you can run."

"What happens if I run faster than you?"

Joey shook his head. "No one runs faster than me."

Jenny started. "Did you hear that?"

Annja stopped moving. Her ears strained to make out whatever it was that Jenny thought she'd heard. "I don't hear anything."

"I could have sworn I heard something."

Annja went back to grinding the ropes. "Keep your ears open. If you think someone's coming, tell me. We'll need the element of surprise if they do come in here to check on us."

Joey looked around them. "You know, there's something vaguely familiar about this place."

"You've been here before?"

He frowned. "No, not really. Just something seems really familiar. I just can't place it."

"Well, hurry up," Jenny said. "I thought I just heard something again."

"What did it sound like?" Annja asked.

"Almost like a snore. But really constant." Jenny frowned. "I can't explain it properly."

"A snore?" Annja grinned. "Great. That helps a lot."

"Well, you try listening, then."

"I'd gladly switch places," Annja said. "But I'm a bit busy right now."

Joey tried to get to his feet. "That's not a snore she heard."

"What do you mean?" Annja asked.

Joey struggled to rise, but bumped his head on the low ceiling and sank back down. "Damn."

"You okay?"

Annja kept rubbing the ropes against the rocks. "Joey, what the hell are you talking about?"

"Jenny's right. In a way. Except it's not a snore she's hearing."

"Well, there's a relief," Jenny said. "It'd be just our luck to get trapped in a cave with a sleeping Sasquatch."

"Jenny! Be quiet," Annja said. She looked at Joey. "Will you just hurry up and explain yourself?"

"The snore she heard? It's water."

"Water?"

"There's a huge river that runs through the back part of the forest. It's really swollen this time of year."

"Rapids?"

"Yeah, but it's worse than that. The dam fifty miles away releases some of the water every few months and it adds to the volume. A lot."

"But shouldn't that just concern the river? How is it going to affect us?" Annja broke through another set of ropes. One more set and she'd be able to get them out of the cave.

"The river runs underground, as well. That roar Jenny heard is the oncoming water. If we stay in this cave, it will smash us against the rocks and we'll drown or be cut to pieces."

Annja glanced at the cavern opening—now she heard the roar.

It was getting louder.

28

"We've got to get out of here," Annja said. The roar was growing louder every second.

Jenny looked at her. "Annja?"

"Give me a second."

"We don't have a second," Joey said. "That water's going to be here any moment, and if we're not free we'll die."

Annja broke through the final binding holding her hands together. She took a breath and said a silent prayer. She closed her eyes. The sword hung in her mind's eye, and she reached out her hands and grabbed it.

"Wow," Jenny said, as the sword appeared from nowhere.

Annja opened her eyes and saw she was holding the sword. She stepped behind Jenny and cut her ropes loose.

Jenny rubbed her wrists. "Thanks."

Joey turned around. Annja cut his ropes and then released the sword to the otherwhere. Joey jumped up and hit his head again, then fell over.

"Help me, Jenny!" Annja grabbed Joey and pulled him upright.

The roar in the cavern grew louder. Joey's body started to shake.

He gulped in air and steadied himself. "We've got to hurry."

Annja looked around. "If there's light in here, we ought to be able to get out—that way, right?"

"Depends on the light source. It could just be a narrow slice in the rock that we can't get through. We've got to find a way out that we can all fit through," Joey said.

"I'm not much of a swimmer," Jenny said. "All these years I've been meaning to take lessons, but I guess I just never got around to it."

Annja held on to her. "You're about to change all that. Try to hold your breath for as long as you can. Joey and I will help you navigate through. Just keep your eyes open so you can see what we're doing, okay?"

"Okay." Jenny looked at her. "Annja, I'm really sorry for the things I said to you. I didn't mean any of it. I was just really upset at myself."

"Forget it," Annja said. "Let's just concentrate on getting out of here alive. Then we can take care of our dear pal David."

"It's coming," Joey said, shouting now above the deafening roar.

Annja could see bits of water splashing the interior of the cavern and then a huge wall of white foamy water rushed right at them.

"Get into the pocket over there!" She pointed at a small depression in the rocks. It would shield them from the initial onslaught and save them from being pummeled against the rocks.

Joey got in first and then Jenny and Annja rounded themselves into the depression. A large outcropping of rock momentarily shielded them from the water. Annja hoped it wouldn't break off and slice their heads off.

The water tore into the cavern. "Hold on!"

And then it was upon them. Annja felt the blast of cold

water hit her and struggled to take a deep breath as the cavern filled from ground to ceiling with water in seconds. Anyone not lucky enough to survive the initial blast would have drowned almost instantly.

The pressure of the water washing over them subsided and the entire cavern was underwater. She glanced at Jenny who looked absolutely terrified.

Joey disengaged from them and swam off under the water, looking for a way out. He waved Annja over to where he saw light filtering in through the frigid water. Annja motioned for Jenny to stay put and then swam to Joey.

He pointed and, in the distance, Annja could see an opening. Bright sunlight cut through the water like some kind of brilliant column. But it was several hundred yards away. Could they make it? Could Jenny?

She looked back and saw Jenny staring at her. Annja knew if the lack of air didn't kill them first, then the freezing water would.

She worked her way back to Jenny and pointed the direction they would be swimming. Jenny nodded and Annja locked her hands in Jenny's. Here we go, she thought.

Joey was already halfway toward the opening, using his strong legs to power himself through the water. Annja had to pump twice as hard and Jenny's output was only minimal, no doubt from the fear and cold temperature.

Joey took a quick glance back, nodded and then swam through the opening up into the light.

Annja followed in his wake, pulling Jenny until they both were into the opening, as well.

A strong current immediately grabbed them and pulled them through. Annja could barely hold on to Jenny's hands, but Jenny's grip stayed tight. Far ahead, she could see Joey spinning through the maelstrom and then up toward the surface and even brighter light.

Were they out of the cave?

There was a roar in her ears and Jenny started jerking around. She's losing it, Annja thought. We have to surface now!

And then they broke through to the open air. Annja gasped, sucking in air and water at the same time. Next to her, Jenny did the same and then started hacking uncontrollably as she swallowed too much water.

"Hold on!" Annja heard Joey shout. They were in the rapids, and rocks rose out of the water like static dorsal fins of sedimentary sharks waiting to cut them to ribbons.

The river slung them around the rocks and then beyond. The water was deep and cold. But at least they could breathe.

"Annja! Hold on to me!" Jenny's voice sounded terrified, and Annja clung to her friend harder than ever before.

The river swelled, cresting and then tossing them into an even faster-moving current. Then Annja heard a sound she knew well. They were being swept toward a waterfall.

"We're going over," she shouted. Jenny clung on to her tightly. There was nothing to do but wait until they were suddenly falling through the air under the water and then splashing down into a deep pool. They were sucked underneath and torn apart from one another.

Annja searched the depths and then felt herself floating upward, finally breaking free of the water again. She gasped.

"Annja!"

She turned in the water. The roar was subsiding and she saw Jenny sputtering in the smaller waves. Annja swam over and grabbed her, then dragged her over to the beach. Joey lay on the wet sand, coughing and hacking up the water he'd swallowed.

Jenny collapsed on the sand and vomited a clear stream of water. Annja coughed some out of her lungs and then turned over, letting the sun warm her.

"I'm freezing," Jenny said, her teeth chattering.

Annja looked at Joey. "We need a fire and quick. We'll die from hypothermia if we don't get out of these wet clothes."

Joey nodded and shook some of the water off himself. "I'll get the wood. Give me a second."

Annja helped Jenny up. "You need to get out of your clothes."

Jenny looked at her. "What about Joey?"

"What about him? He needs to get warm, too."

"But he'll see us naked."

Annja took a deep breath. "We can't care about that now. If we don't get warm, we'll die. All of us."

"Fine. But I'm only stripping down to my underwear," Jenny said.

Annja nodded. "That's fine."

Joey came back with a bundle of wood. Annja could tell from the way he was walking that the cold had affected him badly. "I just…need a minute to get it going," he said through chattering teeth.

"You sure you can do it?" Annja asked.

He nodded. "Like one of the tests…my grandfather set up for me in the winter…trying to stay warm…" He used one of his shoelaces and set up a bow drill. He stroked it furiously, and within thirty seconds he had a small coal that he tipped into the bundle. It started to smoke and he grinned. "Fire."

Annja helped him build the fire into a raging blast of heat. "Get your clothes off, pal, you've got to get warm."

He nodded and yanked off his wet jeans followed by his shirt. He didn't seem the least bit fazed by the sight of Annja and Jenny standing there in their underwear.

After a few minutes, Annja could feel the heat returning to her bones. She and Jenny started draping their clothes nearby. "They have to get dry before we can put them back on or we've just wasted our time," Annja said. Fortunately,

Joey had found enough wood that the fire soon had their clothes steaming and drying in the sunlight.

Jenny looked a bit worse for wear. It was the second time in as many days that she'd been exposed to the threat of hypothermia. And nearly drowning in the freezing water hadn't helped boost her morale, either.

As they stood warming themselves by the fire, she turned to Annja. "Is this what your life is usually like?"

Annja nodded. "More or less."

"How in the world do you put up with it?"

Annja turned her face to the sun poking through the trees and shrugged. "It's not really a question of putting up with it. I don't have any control, so there's not a lot I can do except hold on tight and see where life takes me."

Jenny shook her head. "I don't mind telling you this now, but there was a time not so long ago that I really wished I had your life."

"And now?"

Jenny smiled. "Forget it. I'll take my stuffy old existence at the university any day of the week."

"I don't blame you," Annja said. "It's a lot nicer knowing that the crazy stuff is happening to someone else. I envy you in that regard."

"But not entirely."

Annja sighed. "You know, it's a weird thing. I crave the peace and security you enjoy but, at the same time, I guess that's just not my role in life. And sometimes I kind of like it that way."

"Sometimes?"

"Well," Annja said. "I could do without the hypothermia, nearly drowning, gun battles, knife fights, crazed fanatics and various other things that seem to conspire to kill me on a regular basis."

"You forgot the sword," Joey said. "What about that?"

"I don't know about that," Annja replied. "It's all part of the learning process. I'm never sure where it will take me or why. I'm not even sure of all it can and can't do."

Joey tested their clothes. "They're almost done drying."

"Good," Annja said. "Once they're dry, we can get dressed and head back to town. We need to find Sheila and see if we can figure out exactly what is happening around here."

29

It took just under an hour for them to completely dry out and feel stong enough to move on. Joey was a perfect gentleman and left to let Annja and Jenny get dressed, returning only after he was sure they were fully clothed.

Jenny glanced at the river. "It might take me a long time before I think about swimming again."

"Everyone should learn how to swim," Annja said. "You never know when you might find yourself in a raging river."

"Or trapped in an underground cavern," Joey said. "These things happen."

"Don't you have some orienteering to do?" Jenny asked. "Aren't you supposed to be finding us a way back to town?"

Joey shrugged. "Already did while you guys were getting dressed."

"How close are we?" Annja asked.

"Three miles as the crow flies," Joey said. "Not that far. We can cover it in an hour or so."

"Then lead the way. The sooner we get to Sheila, the sooner she can tell us what's going on."

"You really think she knows?' Jenny asked. "And if she does, why haven't they silenced her yet?"

"Maybe the crackpot thing is just a cover." Annja shrugged. "If she knows the heat is on, it might just be a convenient ruse she uses to deflect their attention."

"Yeah, but she's still implicating David. I wouldn't think he'd put up with that," Jenny said.

"If he killed her, then maybe he thinks that would make people assume Sheila was right," Joey said. "He can't afford to have the townspeople suspect that he's a bad guy. But if he brushes Sheila off as a nut, then no one will ever believe her."

"Except us," Annja said.

"Exactly," Jenny said.

Joey led them down a slope that looked mostly overgrown. He picked his way down the trail as if he'd walked it a thousand times. He probably has, Annja thought.

"This isn't one of the trails used by hikers, is it?" she said.

Joey shook his head. "Nope. This is used by some of the larger animals in the area. It's not really a trail, just a large run of sorts."

"It leads toward town?"

"In the general direction." He glanced back over his shoulder. "I haven't led you guys wrong yet, have I?"

"Not yet," Annja said. "Just don't start, okay?"

"Sure."

Jenny walked along next to Annja. "Is this going to be good for you?"

"What?"

"The walking? You should be resting. That explosion really took a toll on you."

Annja smiled and called out to Joey. "Hey, Joey?"

"Yeah?"

"You feel like carrying me all the way back to town on your shoulders?"

He laughed. "Hell, no."

Annja looked at Jenny. "That's me walking, then."

"Everything we've been through could be doing physical damage to you," Jenny said.

Annja nodded. "You're not telling me anything I haven't thought of, Jenny. I appreciate it, but I don't have a choice right now. We need to get back to town and find Sheila. We can't sit around and wait for my batteries to recharge."

"So tell me what happens. Have you ever not been able to summon the sword?"

"Well, yeah, a few times. It seems not to operate in certain environments like small rooms and stuff. But I've also found it gives me a lot of strength, agility, reflexes, that kind of thing."

"So, like anything else, this…power, if you want to call it that, isn't limitless. There have got to be some parameters for usage. Even if you haven't discovered them all yet."

Annja sighed. "That's about right. I learn as I go."

"Guess it wouldn't be as much of a challenge if you found out about it while eating ice cream in front of the television."

Annja frowned. "I can't remember the last time I did that."

Jenny sighed. "I do that a couple of times a week."

Annja smiled. "Okay, well, we've determined David is a scumbag. But I promise you that a good guy will come along sooner or later and then you'll be much happier."

Jenny giggled. "I'll wait until Joey gets to be eighteen."

Annja smirked. "Right."

"I heard that," Joey called out.

Annja laughed. "Of course you did. How are we doing?"

He looked back. "You tell me. You're the one with the dead batteries."

"They're not dead. They're just…run-down."

"Right. You want to take a rest or are you still good to go?"

Annja took a deep breath. The walk was actually making her feel pretty good. "I'm fine. Just keep us on track, okay?"

"You got it."

The hour passed more quickly than Annja would have thought. Joey led them down the animal run toward a smaller pond and then circled around that to a larger trail. He stopped them at that point and held a finger to his lips.

"We're on a main trail now. I can't guarantee we won't run into Dave and company. If they're out looking for us, this is where they'll be," he whispered.

"Why would they be looking for us?" Annja asked. "If they left us in that cavern to die, they probably think we're already dead."

Joey nodded. "Makes sense. Dave would have known the dam was scheduled to let some of its water reserves out and probably put us down there knowing we'd never be found until it was much too late."

"So they're probably not looking for us?" Jenny asked.

"Maybe not. But they're still going to be doing whatever it is they're planning in the first place. And if that involves being out in the woods, then there's a chance we might run into them," Joey said.

"What we need," Annja said, "is a quick route back to town that avoids any interaction. We're not ready for a confrontation just yet."

Joey looked at her. "I can move us quick, but it might be tiring for you."

"We don't have a choice," Annja said. "Just do what you've got to do and get us back to town."

"All right."

He pushed them hard. Annja found the trail fairly easygoing at first, but it soon gave way to rougher terrain and larger boulders that had to be sidestepped or else she would risk spraining an ankle.

Jenny had trouble, too, but managed to keep going pretty well. Only Joey sailed over the trail with ease.

"He probably knows where every rock in this whole forest is," Jenny grumbled. "Lucky for him."

Annja glanced at her. "I thought you were going to wait for him to grow up?"

"Not anymore. I hate guys who make everything look easy."

Joey turned back. "Will you two stop talking? I'm trying to listen up ahead so we don't have any unpleasant encounters."

Annja nodded. "Sorry."

Joey led them down the side of one of the mountains and then stopped by a cluster of pines. Something about the area felt familiar to Annja. "Have we been here before?" she whispered.

Joey nodded. "Yep. Last night. It was dark, though, so I didn't think you'd remember. But good for you for doing so." He glanced around. "Here's the plan. We're close to the main road, probably not far from where you guys ran into Dave. There's a trail that runs alongside part of the main road."

Jenny nodded. "We took that into town after the truck exploded."

"Good," Joey said. "So you know it runs right into town. We're going to stay on that until we reach the bridge and then peel off on a side trail that very few people know about. It's one I use to skirt the street and avoid being seen."

"You do that often?" Annja asked.

Joey shrugged. "Sometimes it's better not being seen. The less people know, the better."

"And you can get us to the hotel that way?" Annja asked.

"Right up to the back of the building. At that point, we can choose our next move."

"Sounds good," Annja said.

Joey held up his hand. "Wait here while I see if it's all clear. We'll need to move across the road fast and get down to the trail on the other side. The quicker we do so, the less risk of being seen. Agreed?"

Jenny and Annja nodded.

Joey crawled out through the trees and was back in thirty seconds. "We're good. Let's go."

Annja and Jenny followed him back through the woods. As soon as Annja felt asphalt under her hands, she got to her feet and sprinted across the road. Her lungs heaved as she did so and she wondered if she really needed more than just a few hours of sleep to overcome the energy deficiency she was suffering.

Jenny and Joey scampered down the hill in front of her to reach the trail. Annja followed them down and then bent over, sucking some air into her lungs.

"You okay?"

Annja looked up at Joey. "Keep going."

Joey's face looked tight but he nodded. "People know about this trail. If at any time I think we're going to run into someone, I'll take us off the trail until it's safe. Okay?"

"Let's go," Jenny said. "I think Annja needs a long rest."

"It won't be long now, Annja," Joey said. "Maybe a mile. Not much more."

"I'm fine. Just do it."

Joey led them down the trail. Annja found herself remembering the lay of it now that she'd traveled it twice. But earlier yesterday, she'd been burnt and dirty and exhausted from nearly having been crushed by David's truck.

That must be it, she thought. The sheer immediacy of me almost dying taxed my system to the brink. I need some time to recover.

How long is it going to take to get back to where I feel one hundred percent? And can I afford to wait that long? If David and his goons show up now, I'm toast. And so are Jenny and Joey. I can't let anything happen to them.

She pressed on, trying to stay close to Jenny, who had apparently gotten her second wind. She seemed to be moving faster than Annja was. Annja struggled to keep up with her.

Jenny looked back. "Can you keep going?"

Annja nodded, but she felt queasy and foggy at the same time. I am not in good shape, she thought to herself.

Her face felt hot and sweaty. Her heart thundered in her chest. If they hadn't swallowed a lot of river water, she might have thought she was dehydrated. But she knew she wasn't. She'd had lots to drink.

But she hadn't had plenty of rest. And that's what she needed more than anything else.

If she could sleep for even a few hours, it might go a long way toward recharging her. Even being knocked unconscious by the tranquilizer dart hadn't given her enough rest.

Could she take a nap at the hotel before they confronted David? It seemed unlikely.

Joey led them up to the footbridge and then veered to the right. A large rhododendron bush blocked their path but he pushed through it. Annja followed Jenny and then saw a smaller animal run in front of them. Thorny bushes poked out into the run, making travel difficult, but twenty yards farther on it suddenly got easier.

Joey stopped and motioned them to squat nearby. "I planted those to help discourage anyone else from using the trail. Now that we're close to town, make sure you keep your voice down. You'd be surprised how many conversations I've heard lurking back here, hiding from people in town."

"You were spying on them?" Annja asked.

Joey shook his head. "Nope. They were being noisy and I was just listening." He winked once and then kept walking.

Annja felt like her legs were starting to melt. Each step seemed to sink into the ground and get harder to pull back out. Her breathing felt labored and awkward, as if she couldn't get enough oxygen into her system.

The run sloped up and then Annja saw the roof of the hotel over the top of the trees. The hotel.

She almost smiled. If they could just get to Sheila.

"Annja?"

Jenny peered into her face. Why does she look so odd? Annja wondered. But had she voiced the question at all? She couldn't remember.

Annja took another deep breath.

"Annja?"

Another step.

She collapsed into nothingness.

30

Annja swam slowly through the blackness of her mind. It was as if she simply couldn't move her arms and legs fast enough to generate any kind of momentum and she was stuck.

Her body drifted aimlessly, slowly spinning over and over but not fast enough to make her feel ill. She had no real sensation of which way was up, anyhow. Her limbs felt numb. She couldn't hear anything. She couldn't see anything.

It was almost like being in some sort of sensory deprivation tank.

My eyes are open, she thought. And yet I can't see anything around me. There's no way to penetrate the inky black darkness that surrounds me.

She tried stopping herself and spinning in the opposite direction, but it didn't work. In some ways, she thought she was like an orbiting planet, powered by the gravitational force of some unseen sun far off in the outer reaches of her galactic mind.

Is this what I did to myself? she wondered. Had she taxed her system so far and to such a great extent that she had just switched off? The truck explosion, the day of trekking, being ambushed, nearly being drowned and having to swim both herself and Jenny to safety prior to another long hike. Had it all simply been too much?

One thing felt certain, wherever she was, she didn't feel tired any longer. This place, this quiet refuge, may have been some sort of resting point for her to come to when things got truly bad.

Annja smiled, or at least she thought she smiled. It's good to know I at least have this.

She wondered how long it would take to fully recuperate her strength. How long had she been floating here? Had she been gone for hours or, when she woke up, would she find that only minutes had passed since she fell to the ground back on the side trail by the hotel?

A thought occurred to her and she didn't like it. What if she didn't wake up? What if she was like the sword, trapped beyond the reach of normal life in some weird other dimension? What if no one could get her back?

Was it possible that she was dead?

She took a breath and felt her lungs expand and then contract. So far so good. She tried flexing her limbs, but they were so numb she couldn't tell if they were moving or not.

This is weird, she thought. And then she quickly mocked herself for being a master of the understatement.

If I'm supposed to stay here until I'm rested, then what in the world are Jenny and Joey thinking right now? She imagined Jenny freaking, trying to figure out what was wrong. Annja felt a small measure of relief that both of them had seen the sword. If they hadn't, they might just think Annja was dead and have her carted off to the morgue for an autopsy.

This is probably the only time it was good they saw the sword, she thought. Any other time, pulling it out for the world to see isn't.

"Annja!"

From somewhere off in the distance, Annja heard the voice. And then something jolted her awake and it sounded like a huge roar in her ears. She winced and clamped her eyes shut. When she opened them again—

Jenny's face hovered over hers. "Annja!"

"All right, all right, take it easy, will you?" Annja tried to sit up but found her body was still somewhat like jelly.

"Easy, Annja." Joey's voice sounded in her ear, but much softer than Jenny's. She felt his arms under her back and then she was propped up into a sitting position. Joey looked at her. "You okay?"

"I think so."

"Jesus," Jenny said, "you scared the hell out of us."

"Out of you," Joey corrected. "I knew she'd be okay."

"Oh, sure you did, you big liar." Jenny stooped closer to Annja. "What happened to you?"

Annja shook her head. "I don't know. I was looking at the hotel and then I tried to take another step and I just couldn't do it. I went down and kept going straight into...I don't know where."

Joey nodded. "You were beyond exhausted. Your physical body had been taxed to its limits and your spirit took over to protect you. Very interesting."

Jenny frowned. "I thought we'd lost you, Annja."

"I didn't do it deliberately, Jenny." She looked around. "Where are we?"

"Still on the trail behind the hotel," Joey said. "You want some water?"

Annja nodded. "That would be great." Joey offered her a small cup of water and she drank it down, tasting the cold against the back of her throat. She gulped a few sips and then paused. "Thanks."

Joey glanced at his watch. "We should get going."

"How long was I out?"

"A few minutes."

Annja stretched. She felt as if she'd spent a long day napping in her apartment in Brooklyn, surrounded by a plush comforter and the throw pillows she liked to keep on her couch. A yawn welled up from within her and she let it out, stretching as she did so. Small pops sounded in her back.

Joey eyed her. "You look…rested."

Annja nodded. "I actually feel pretty amazing."

Jenny frowned. "Nice you could take a nap and all. I'm certainly tired, too, but you don't see me lying down on the job."

"Well, after I had to save your butt from certain death, I figured I deserved it," Annja said. "Help me up, will you?"

Jenny pulled her to her feet and Annja brushed her pants off. "Thanks."

Jenny smiled. "Glad you're okay."

"You and me both. For a while there, I didn't know what was happening to me."

"Where were you?"

Annja shook her head. "It was completely and utterly black. I couldn't see anything. Couldn't feel anything, either. It wasn't until I heard you shouting that I suddenly felt something snap me back to life."

"Yeah," Joey said, "Jenny slapped you across the face pretty hard."

Annja put a hand to her face and felt the tender area by her cheek. "Hey."

Jenny held up her hands. "I was worried. And besides, you know you would have done the exact same thing to me if you were in my position."

"I don't know," Annja said. "Let's test that theory out, shall we?"

"Ladies," Joey said. "Can we just get to the hotel? The sooner we hook up with Sheila, the better."

Annja eyed Jenny. "I'm not forgetting about that, slap happy."

Jenny tried to grin. "Yeah, I know you won't."

Joey led them closer to the hotel. Annja felt much stronger. Her muscles responded well. She could feel the energy coursing through her veins now like liquid heat.

Joey paused. "This is it. We follow this path up and there's a back door we can access that leads right into the kitchen. If Tom's in there, we can get his attention and he'll bring Sheila to us."

Annja nodded. "Okay. Let's do it."

Jenny followed Joey up the slope and Annja came next. As she scampered up the slope, she glanced left and then right but their approach was well concealed. She smiled. Joey would never have used a trail that would potentially expose them to observers. That would betray everything his grandfather had taught him over the years.

They scurried up to the back door and then paused. Jenny was out of breath but Annja felt fine. Joey looked at them. "Give me a second to get in there and check things out."

"How are you going to do that without Tom seeing you?" Jenny asked.

Joey smirked. "Jenny, no one sees me if I don't want them to. Tom won't notice me until I'm ready."

"Are you sure?"

"Of course." Joey nodded at Annja and then eased himself through the screened back door. It opened without a sound and Joey vanished inside.

Jenny glanced at Annja. "What do you think?"

Annja shrugged. "He'll do fine."

"Not that, about you? Are you really okay now? You don't have to be brave in front of me. Just tell me the truth."

Annja smiled. Despite their differences and the confusion of this entire trip, Jenny was still a friend. "I'm actually feeling great. Wherever I was, it really gave me some of my strength back."

Jenny slumped against her. "Thank God for that. The way things are going, we're going to need it."

"I'm going to need it," Annja said. "If things go bad, you take care of Joey and let me handle the bad guys, okay?"

"You won't get an argument from me on that one," Jenny said with a grin. "I don't know the first thing about fighting, anyway."

"Unfortunately, I do," Annja said. "Sometimes I wish I didn't, but there you go."

Jenny watched the back door. "What's taking him so long?"

Annja looked up. "He's probably just checking things out, is all. Give him another minute and then we'll take a closer look."

"I don't like it. What if David was in there and grabbed him? They could be waiting for us right now. Or they could be coming around the back here."

"Calm down. There's no way Joey would give us up."

"Unless he happened to be one of them." Jenny frowned. "I mean, we have to consider it, right?"

"No," Annja said. "We don't. Joey's not with anyone but himself. And maybe the forest."

The screen door slid open and Joey's face appeared. He came down the steps and squatted next to them. "Tom's in the kitchen, but just as I was going to say something to him, someone came in. I waited but didn't get a chance."

Annja frowned. "So what now?"

Joey shrugged. "I guess we take a chance and head on inside."

"Just like that?" Jenny asked. "We're not even going to see if it's all clear?"

"I did the best I could," Joey said. "We'll just have to risk it."

Annja nodded. "Okay. I'll lead the way this time." She rose on her haunches and stalked up the back steps. The screen door opened easily and she was glad it didn't squeak.

Inside the back pantry, shelves lined with all sorts of food-stuffs loomed over them as they kept close to the ground. Annja could hear voices ahead of them in the main kitchen area.

She recognized Tom's deep voice. But whose voice was the other one? It seemed somewhat familiar but then she couldn't be sure.

She peered around the stainless steel cabinet and spotted Sheila. A wave of relief washed over her. All she had to do was stand and call to her.

Annja held her hand out behind her to signal Joey and Jenny to hold their positions. Something strange was going on.

She heard Sheila speaking clearly. But the tone of her voice was very different. And she wasn't addressing Tom as if he was her husband at all, more like he was her slave.

"I don't care if you don't want to make it, I said just do it!" And then she spun and marched out of the kitchen through the swinging door that led to the dining room.

That exchange didn't sound like the Sheila she'd met, Annja thought. What was that all about?

She peeked around the corner, but Tom's back was to her. Good.

She darted out from her hiding spot and raced to the swinging doors. Small porthole windows were cut into each door. Annja rose and looked through one of them.

Out in the dining room, she saw a surprising scene.

Sheila sat at a table nursing a cup of coffee.

Across from her, holding her hand, was David.

31

Annja pulled back from the window. What in the world was going on? David was with Sheila? But how? And why?

"Hey."

She wheeled around and found herself staring at Tom. He looked her up and down and frowned. "Aren't you one of the girls who came in here yesterday?"

"Annja, yes."

He nodded. "What are you doing here in the kitchen? You look like you're sneaking around."

Annja smiled. "You wouldn't believe it if I told you."

"Try me."

Annja gestured outside to the dining room. "I thought you were married to Sheila."

"Unfortunately, yes. That's true. What about it?"

Annja shrugged. "Aren't you a bit upset that the sheriff is holding her hand right now?"

Tom grimaced. "Is that all he's doing? Then it's a pleasant change from the way things normally are."

"What do you mean?"

He turned and went back to working the grill. "Those two can't keep their hands off each other. Ever since they hooked up, it's as if I haven't existed except to fulfill whatever demands they make on me."

"What kinds of demands?"

"Usually has to do with what Dave wants to eat. Apparently the items on the menu aren't good enough for him anymore. Now Sheila wants me to make things I haven't cooked in years. All that foo-foo stuff that has no place being served in a joint like this."

"David's got expensive tastes?" Annja asked.

Tom nodded. "Ever since he started traveling. He became a bit of a globe hopper a few years back. Never seemed right to most of us in town, how he came into all that money to take those trips, but the town's bookkeeper can't find any money gone missing, so we don't think he's robbing us blind."

"So where's he getting it all, then?"

"Don't know. I do know that ever since he gave Sheila a little gift one time, she hasn't been able to stop falling all over him. Literally. They spend so many nights together, it's a wonder she even remembers that this place is her real home."

"You haven't divorced her yet?"

Tom didn't say anything for a minute and then he cleared his throat. "Guess I'm a damn fool romantic. Maybe I keep thinking she's going to wake up and come to her senses, see that he's not the guy for her and that she ought to be with me, instead. Like it used to be."

Annja frowned. Seeing the way David held Sheila's hands out there, that didn't seem likely. "You might just be better off without her. Did you ever think of that?"

"Yeah. Sure. I guess. But who's going to want a guy like me? I'm a grill jockey at a backwater hotel in the middle of nowhere. No wonder Sheila fell for Dave. Even though he lives here, he travels and can take her places and give her stuff I never could."

"There's more than stuff to making a marriage work."

Tom glared at her. "You think I don't know that?"

"When did they start hooking up?"

"About a year back. Right after he came back from some-place abroad. He said Europe, but I thought he went north to Canada for some reason."

"Why?"

"Kinda slipped one time and mentioned he'd once seen parts of British Columbia. Seemed odd to me since I'd never heard him talk about Canada before. But I think he's been there. A lot."

Annja frowned. If David was getting money from some-where other than the town, then he had to either have something of value or be doing something that made him money. But what?

"Annja!"

The harsh whisper broke her concentration. She turned and saw Jenny waving her over. Tom noticed.

"You got more friends back there?"

"Yeah, this is Jenny."

Tom smiled. "Hi."

Jenny smiled back. "Hi." She turned to Annja. "What's going on?"

Annja thumbed toward the door. "Sheila and David are in the dining room, huddling like lovers." She blanched and looked at Tom. "Sorry."

He shrugged. "No matter. I know it as much as anyone in town. It just took longer to admit it to myself."

Jenny looked sad. "Poor thing, to have a wife do that to you."

"They're here for lunch," Tom said. "Want some of that nouveau cuisine I was telling you about. She says if it's not good, Dave will shoot me."

"He can't threaten to do that," Jenny said.

Tom shrugged. "Why not? Everyone in town knows that something's going on. They don't like messing with him at all. Nice guy on the exterior, but if you cross him he's a dangerous snake."

"You don't say." Annja shook her head. "Looks like your sheriff might just need to be replaced."

Tom sighed. "No one around here has the guts to run against him. Last guy who did went missing and that was about the last brave hurrah we ever had. Now most folks have either moved away or stay up in their homes unless there's no choice but to come down for supplies or something."

"This is crazy," Annja said. "We've got to do something."

Joey snuck over to the door. "Wow, that's quite a kiss."

Annja groaned. "Joey."

Tom caught his breath. "Oh, hell, I have to face facts. And I know that kissing's about the least of it, anyway, so no harm done. At least not by young Joey there." He bowed his head. "Nice to see you again, Joe."

"You, too, Tom. Sorry we had to sneak in like this."

Tom shrugged. "No matter. I'm glad for the company. But what brings you in this way, anyhow?"

"Dave tried to kill us last night," Joey said.

Tom leaned against the grill. "All of you? How so?"

"Shot us with tranquilizer darts and then stowed us in the underground cavern up by the river."

Tom's face grew stern. "They flushed the dam earlier today."

Joey nodded. "We found out."

"Rather abruptly," said Annja.

Tom shook his head. "Killing an adult is one thing. But a kid's another. Don't that guy have any kind of morals?"

"Pretty sure he doesn't," Joey said. "But he's got to be working with somebody. Someone else pulled the trigger last night, not him."

Annja moved closer to Tom. "Does Sheila know how to shoot?"

"Most women in these parts do. It's always good to know how to use a shotgun in case a bear gets too nosy."

"And Sheila?"

"Better than most, I'd say," Tom said. "She grew up in the Southwest before coming north with her mom a long time back. She told me her daddy used to teach her how to handle a gun when she was a kid."

Annja glanced at Jenny. "I think we just found our trigger-man."

"Agreed. But what's she helping him with? What's the goal in David's whole enterprise?"

Annja looked back at Tom. "You said she's been gone a lot lately?"

"Been gone a lot ever since the two of them started carrying on together. I don't know whether she's at his house or just out somewhere else with him. She doesn't exactly come home and regale me with tales of their relationship, if you get my meaning."

"Probably better that way," Annja said.

"I'd say so," Tom said. "Bad enough that my wife is shacking up with some other man. I don't need updates about it."

"I wonder what they're up to," Jenny said. "It's got to be something that has the potential for a lot of money."

"We could just stroll out there and ask them," Annja said. "After all, they're sitting right there."

"And risk Dave shooting us on sight?" Joey said. "No, thanks. I'm not really looking to see my life ended before I even get to date a girl."

"You could stay here," Annja said. "That way, in case we get into trouble, you come in with the cavalry."

Joey frowned. "Great choice of words."

Annja blanched. "Sorry."

"Forget it. But if that's how you two want to play this, be my guest. Tom and I will stay here and watch from a distance."

Annja glanced at Jenny. "What do you think?"

Jenny took a deep breath. "At this point, I'm honestly so confused about everything, I don't really care what we do provided we have a fair chance of going home safe and sound when this is all done."

Annja looked at Joey and Tom. "I don't think that will be a problem now."

"Then let's do it."

Annja pushed through the swinging doors and headed straight for the table. Sheila and David turned at almost the same time, the shock of seeing her clearly registering on both their faces.

Sheila started to sputter something.

David reached for his gun.

Annja covered the distance fast and slammed the side of her hand down on David's wrist, hearing a snap as she did so.

David shrieked and grabbed his wounded wrist. "What the hell!"

Jenny slapped Sheila across the face. "That's for lying to us."

David cradled his gun hand and frowned. "You're supposed to be dead."

"They would be if you did it properly," Sheila said.

"I tied those ropes tighter than anyone could have gotten loose. They must have had help," David said.

Did we ever, Annja thought. "You're a real piece of work, David. Not only are you a loathsome scumbag, but you'd kill a child as easily as draw a breath. Real nice, aren't you?"

"Joey would have told someone. I couldn't take the chance. He had to go just like you two."

Annja leaned forward and put her face inches from

David's. "And all that sweet talk last night on your porch? About how you lured me out here through Jenny? What was that all about?"

"Whatever it takes to achieve the goal," he said.

But Annja could see her comment had hit the mark. Sheila didn't look happy. Annja saw her face darken momentarily. "Your man here has a bit of a libido problem, doesn't he?" she said pressing the point.

"I don't know what you're talking about," Sheila snapped.

"Don't you? You think you're the only woman he's led astray? He's probably got a dozen more dumb chicks like you in Canada."

Sheila looked at Dave. "Tell her that's not true."

"It's not. There's only you, babe."

Annja laughed. "I'll bet."

David frowned. "Don't listen to her. She's just trying to get you upset so you'll turn on me."

Annja pulled up a chair and sat down. "Do you mind telling me what this is all about in the first place? We're all a bit tired of guessing and you clearing up some of this would be greatly appreciated."

David smirked. "You haven't figured it out?"

"There hasn't been much to figure out. We've got you contacting Jenny, but for what reason I can't fathom. Simpson and Baker are intent on capturing big foot. And then there's you two running some kind of illegal operation here and trying to get us all killed. I can't connect the dots, so why don't you do it for me?"

"Why would I make your life any easier?" David said.

Annja smiled and then leaned forward to grab his hand. He yelped as she did so. Annja held his wrist. "I think the bone's broken here."

"Which one," David said. "You nailed it good."

Annja twisted the wrist a little and David screamed.

"Wow, you're right. Maybe I did get a couple of them. I guess I just don't know my own strength sometimes, huh?"

David's face paled. "Stop it. You're killing me!"

Annja shook her head. "Not yet, sweetheart. But I will if you don't start talking about what you two are cooking up around here."

David looked at Sheila. "Ask her."

"Why would I do that?" Annja asked.

"Because she's in charge of the entire thing, that's why!"

Annja frowned. Sheila shook her head. "He's delusional from the pain of his broken wrist. I don't know what he's talking about."

"She does! You have to believe me. I'm not the one who knows everything. She is. *They* are!"

"They?"

David nodded furiously. "Of course. I couldn't pull this off without their help. You've got to believe me."

"Who are *they?*"

David eyed Annja. "God, are you really so stupid? Tom! Him and Sheila are running this show, not me."

Jenny started to speak. "But Tom just told us—"

The sound of a ratcheted shotgun behind them made both Annja and Jenny turn around. Tom stood there, leveling the mean-looking Mossberg pump action on them. "I guess you might as well stop torturing that poor man," Tom said.

"You sure don't look brokenhearted anymore," Annja said.

Tom smiled. "Time heals all wounds. Isn't that what they say?"

"Some people say that, yeah."

"Wise folks, those people," Tom said. "Now, slowly get on up and stand over by that wall on the far side of the room. I think it's about time we all had ourselves a nice little chat."

32

Annja edged over to the wall and Jenny followed. I hope Joey's okay, she thought.

"Your friend Joey has been taken care of," Tom said.

"You killed him?" Annja shouted.

Tom shook his head. "I gave him a rap on the head and he's likely got a concussion. He won't be a problem for a while." He sighed. "Eventually, though, we're going to have to make a decision about what to do with him."

"He's a child," Jenny said.

"He's a pain in the ass," David replied. "Just like that damn wolf of his before I shot him. Things'll be better when they're both gone." He got up from the table and walked over to Tom. "You got any bandages or something? I'm going to have to get this thing set down in Maynard at the clinic," he said, holding his wrist.

Tom eyed him. "You're going to leave now to get that set?"

David held up his useless hand. "What would you suggest I do? I can't handle my piece if my hand's useless."

"You won't be able to handle it, anyway, once you get a cast on it," Tom said.

David shrugged. "So just kill them all now and be done with it."

"If you'd done your job properly," Tom said, "they'd already be dead and we'd be finished with this thing."

David sighed. "Look, like I told Sheila, I did my best. They must have somehow gotten help to get free. I made sure that the tranquilizer drug you shot them with was strong enough to knock them out cold."

Annja looked at Tom. "You shot us last night?"

Tom smiled. "I suppose I ought to come clean about that. Name's Tom Slackmore. Former sniper with the Marines. It's kind of a skill of mine."

"That explains the gillie suit," Annja said.

Tom raised an eyebrow. "You know about gillie suits?"

"I met a Marines sniper once—a far better man that you'll ever be apparently—who taught me about what it meant to do his job. He had honor about him. Courage, too. Both of those traits seem absent in you."

Tom laughed. "Yeah, maybe you're right. I served my country and my country forgot about me. I got wounded in a little war no one ever wanted to know about, so they kicked me out and I wound up in this dump with nothing to show for all my hard work. You think honor's something special? It's not. At the end of the day, it doesn't get you a damn thing, except a flag on your casket when you die."

"Touching," Annja said. "I'm sure that will go over real well with the judge and jury when you're brought up on charges."

Tom laughed louder. "And who exactly is going to do that?"

Annja smiled. "Day's not over yet."

David grunted. "This damn thing's killing me."

Tom glanced at Sheila. "Get his gun."

David looked at him. Tom smiled again. "Relax. No sense in you having it if you can't even use it, right?"

"Yeah. Guess so."

Sheila unholstered the automatic pistol and slid it into her waistband. She looked at Tom. "What now?"

Tom motioned at David. "Didn't I tell you this guy was going to be trouble?"

"We needed him. How else could we bring the stuff in?"

"Yeah, well, he's a liability now."

David looked up. "What did you say?"

"Uh-oh," Annja said.

But her voice was drowned out by the sudden explosion in the dining room that took David clean off his feet as the shotgun barked once and cut him open at the midsection. He fell over backward and lay there in a spreading pool of blood.

Sheila gasped. "You know, I used to like him. A lot. Now you killed him!"

"You never did have good taste in men," Tom said. "And he's served his purpose."

"You just killed a cop," Annja said. "That's not going to go over well with the authorities."

Sheila stared at David's body. "She's right."

Tom shook his head. "What difference does it make? By the time anyone clues in we'll be long gone. They can chase us all they want but they'll never find us. Not with what we've got."

Annja looked at Sheila. "You could stop this right now. Just shoot him and be done with the whole thing. Jenny and I will back you up. We'll tell them that it was all his plan. That you were just a hapless wife who got herself mixed up in something she couldn't control."

"Hapless wife." Tom chuckled. "That's a good one."

Annja looked at him and then back at Sheila. "You can do it, Sheila. Just shoot him now and set us free. Come on. We can call in the State Police."

Sheila looked at her and frowned. "I can't do that. I love him."

Annja shook her head. "But I thought you just said you liked Dave."

"I did."

Annja sighed. "Man, things sure get weird in these small towns."

Sheila frowned. "Tom's my brother."

"Weirder still," Jenny said, rolling her eyes. "And people thought rednecks were inbred."

"Don't be gross," Tom said. "We only pretended to be husband and wife in public. It helped create the illusion we needed."

"Illusion for what?" Annja asked.

Tom shook his head. "Aren't you supposed to be some type of scholar? And aren't you a teacher or something?"

Jenny nodded. "I am a teacher."

"Well, both of you are a little dense."

"You should see it from our perspective," Annja said. "We've almost died several times in the past few days. People are stalking big foot and we don't know what the hell is going on."

"Drugs," Tom said. "The ultimate entertainment product."

"This is all about drugs?"

Tom shrugged. "Does it need to be about anything else? We bring them in from Canada through the woods and hold them in the underground cavern you saw earlier today. The one that should have been your grave site until idiot boy over there wrecked the whole thing."

"And what happens after that? You sell them?" Annja asked.

Tom smiled. "Every few weeks we have a visitor come in to stock the hotel kitchen. They bring us supplies, they take back the drugs. And they leave us a little extra cabbage, as well."

"A little?" Sheila smiled. "It's more than that."

"Well, they get the picture," Tom said.

"And what about Simpson and Baker? What are they—your hired muscle?"

Tom shrugged. "No idea what those two idiots are doing." He looked at Sheila. "Didn't you say that Ellen said they were here to trap big foot?"

"Yep."

Tom shook his head. "Damn fools. There's no big foot in these hills."

Jenny cleared her throat. "There isn't?"

"Of course not. But it helps keep folks from buying up land and settling here. Plus, the state's real big on conservation land. That enables us to have a ready space to store our product until it gets picked up."

"How do you get it from the cavern to the hotel?"

"Nothing that a little hike can't help."

"And no big foot?" Jenny asked.

Tom smiled. "Sorry, sweetheart. I've been all up in these woods for years. I know every inch of the ground and I've never seen a big foot in all my travels."

Jenny fell silent. Annja wanted to scream at her to forget the damn big foot and concentrate on getting out of there alive, but she could see that Jenny's hopes were dashed.

"What are you going to do with David's body?" Annja asked.

Tom gestured with the gun. "You two are going to drag him into the back so he's out of view in case someone happens to wander by."

"There's a lot of blood on the wall and the floor. Anyone who sees that will know what happened," Annja said, stalling for time.

"In that case," Tom said. "You and your friend had better be real good at using sponges to clean up. Because if it's not perfect, there will be two more blood splatters on that wall."

"And two more bodies to clean up after," Annja said. "You're not that stupid, are you?"

"Don't try to find out," Tom said. "Now get to work."

Annja glanced at Jenny. She's not going to cope well with this, she thought. But they walked over. Annja reached down and got her hands under David's armpits and pulled. Jenny vomited and Annja blanched, choking back the rising tide of bile in her throat.

"Hurry up," Tom said. "Drag him in the back."

Annja tugged David's body into the kitchen. The corpse left a trail of blood behind, staining the floor a brownish red. It was all Annja could do not to heave her guts all over the place.

Jenny followed her into the kitchen with Sheila bringing up the rear, David's gun trained on them both.

Tom gestured with the shotgun. "In the back there. Just leave him be."

"The smell's going to let everyone in town know you killed him," Annja said.

Tom shook his head. "Don't matter. We'll be gone after tonight. And then as far as anyone knows, we just left."

"Cop killers will provoke an international manhunt," Annja said. "They'll find you."

"I don't think so," Tom said. "It will be too much trouble and they'll eventually give up."

Sheila pointed with her gun. "Get the sponges under the sink and the bucket that's in there, too. Fill it with hot water and follow me back outside."

Annja leaned under the sink, looking for anything that might help them. Tom kept the shotgun trained on her. If she tried to pull the sword out, she'd risk taking all that buckshot in the face. She had to wait until Tom had his focus diverted.

But when?

She got the sponges and tipped the bucket under the sink, running hot water into it. She'd never cleaned up after a corpse before, and it wasn't something she was looking forward to doing.

In the dining room, Sheila went to the front door and put the closed sign in place on the window, pulled the blinds and then turned and smiled. "So we won't be disturbed by anyone."

Annja and Jenny got down on their hands and knees, scrubbing the floor. Jenny gagged several more times.

"Keep it together," Annja said. "I don't want to have to clean up any more than necessary here."

"Can't help it," Jenny said. "The smell is awful."

"It's not as bad as it will be if we don't hurry up."

Jenny leaned into the scrubbing, her hands already red with David's blood. "What are we going to do?" she asked in a whisper.

"I just need a second when Tom isn't looking at us and then we'll make our move."

The barrel of the shotgun edged up under Annja's nose. "Keep your mind on cleaning that floor and less on any thoughts of escape."

Annja nodded. She'd have to time her move perfectly or she and Jenny would be the next to die.

Sheila checked the slide on David's gun. "You know he didn't even have a round chambered? What a moron."

"He was your boyfriend," Tom said. "You never said he was a genius."

"I still don't understand why David wanted Jenny to come

out here," Annja said. "Why was there a need to involve her in all of this?"

"What better way to sell the case for preserving the conservation land around here than by having an expert on big foot declare that there was a high probability that the creature lives in the area? With her endorsement, we would have virtual control of the surrounding countryside."

"Or a huge influx of gawkers desperate to see the creature themselves," Annja said. "It's not the brightest plan I've ever heard."

"Shut up and keep cleaning," Tom said. "Yours isn't to question the plan. It's to do as we say until you've outlived your usefulness, too."

"At which point you'll kill us," Annja said.

"At which point you're absolutely right," Tom said.

Annja frowned. There wasn't much time left. She just hoped that the fact she hadn't seen Joey when they dragged David's body into the kitchen meant that he was out getting reinforcements.

Otherwise, Annja would have to handle two gun-wielding drug runners by herself.

And that didn't sound like a good plan at all.

33

With the mess at the hotel cleaned up, Tom and Sheila ushered Annja and Jenny to the back of the hotel. The sun was starting to set, and as it dipped toward the horizon it painted the area in reds and oranges.

Annja looked at Tom. "So is this where you're going to do it? Right out here in the open?"

Tom smirked. "You must really think we're stupid."

"It's crossed my mind a few times. Hooking up with someone like David. All of this for the sake of peddling narcotics. Yeah, I guess it's reasonable to suggest I think you're both dumb as rocks."

Sheila put her pistol up to Jenny's head. "Shut your mouth, or I'll put a slug through your pal's head."

"That's original."

Tom pointed to the Chevy Tahoe. "Get in the truck."

"You're taking David's ride?" Annja said.

"He doesn't need it anymore."

Annja nodded. "Good point."

Tom glanced at Sheila. "You drive while I keep a gun on these two."

Sheila frowned. "With that thing? Make sure you put them both in the backseat. If that cannon goes off, better to blast the back than me."

"Don't worry about it. I got it under control."

"Sure you do."

Tom frowned but didn't retort as he gestured for Annja and Jenny to get in. Then he shut their door and hopped into the front seat, training the shotgun on them from there. Without taking his eyes off them, he said to Sheila, "Go slow getting us out of town and watch the bumps. I don't want my trigger finger accidentally squeezing too much." He grinned at Annja. "That'd be a shame, huh?"

"I'm sure you'd lose sleep over it," she said.

Sheila started the engine and slipped the truck into Drive before pulling out onto the main road. Annja glanced around but, as usual, the place seemed pretty deserted. "How long have you two been here intimidating people and stuff?"

"Few years. But Dave was the guy who intimidated folks. Give people an authority figure they think they can't fight and folks either accept it or else they just up and move away. If we tried to do it, they'd just go to the cops in another town. In that case, our plans would have been screwed."

"Smart," Annja said. "Smarter than I would have given you all credit for."

Jenny looked out of the window. Her face looked gloomy. Tom nodded at her. "What's her problem?"

"Man trouble," Annja said.

Jenny glared at her. "Annja, how could you?"

Annja shrugged. "No sense lying to the guy."

"Let me guess, was it Dave?"

Annja nodded. "Yeah. Guy was a charmer. And he got his hooks in good with Jenny."

"It was all an act," Sheila said from the front seat. "Dave was with me the entire time. Jenny was just a pawn in the plan."

"Which one of you cooked that up, anyway?" Annja asked.

"Dave did," Sheila said.

"I kind of thought he did," Annja replied.

"What's that mean?" Sheila asked.

Annja shrugged. "Just that for someone so devoted to you, it sure seems like he made a big effort to get any other women out here that he could. You should have seen the way he was talking to me last night at his place. You would have thought the guy had never been with a woman before he was so eager."

"You're lying again," Sheila said.

"Think that if you want, but the guy had a roving eye. It's probably better your brother shot him dead without consulting you first. Saved you both a whole lot of trouble."

Sheila glared at Tom. "You didn't have to kill him."

"Yes, I did. He was becoming a problem. Besides, this drug thing was never meant to be a long-term partnership. Just enough to make us a few million so we could go south and disappear forever. We've got that."

"But Dave was supposed to come with me," Sheila said.

Tom sighed. "Look, sis, you're going down to Latin America. You'll find another guy there."

"But Dave was the first guy to love me for who I am, weight and all."

"And those Latin dudes think chunky women are hot. Trust me, okay? By the time you get down there, you'll forget all about Dave and his broken wrist."

"I'd better." Sheila snapped her eyes to the front and stared hard out of the windshield.

Tom kept his eyes focused on Annja. "You're not going to turn her against me. Might as well stop trying."

Annja ignored him. "Where are we going, anyway?"

"Back to the site of your untimely escape earlier this morning."

"The cavern? Why not shoot us someplace else? What's so special about that place?"

"It's not you guys," Tom said. "We've got another reason for needing to go back there. Our final shipment of drugs is waiting for us to pick up. Once we have it, we'll make the rendezvous and the exchange. In the morning, Sheila and me will drive down to the bank in Edison and make our final withdrawal."

"Taking the money and running, huh?"

"You got it. We've got an appointment to pick up our new passports tomorrow afternoon and then an evening flight down the coast to San Francisco. From there, we pick our choice of destinations, preferably someplace with no extradition treaty. Then we vanish into the pages of history."

"You've got it all worked out," Annja said. "Congratulations."

Tom shrugged. "Sorry you and your friend here will have to be a rather bloody part of our legacy."

"That's how it goes," Sheila said. "You guys were just a casualty of this whole thing."

"Like your Dave," Annja said. "Such a shame he won't be with you. But at least this way you get to split the money only two ways instead of three." She looked at Tom. "That's the real reason you shot him back there, wasn't it?"

"No, it was not," Tom said. "Now keep your mouth shut."

Annja smiled. "Just checking. Sure seemed like an opportune time to get rid of that extra baggage and ensure a few extra million for you and Sheila. At least until she becomes a liability, as well. Who knows, maybe that will be tonight."

Tom aimed the shotgun at Annja. "Say anything else and I'll blow your head off. Sheila and I are in this together."

Annja nodded. "Is that what you told Dave?"

Sheila looked at Tom. "Is it?"

Tom frowned. "Would you stop focusing on Dave? He's gone, okay? I did what we had to do to make sure you and I are safe. That's the point, isn't it? That we get out of this thing alive. Who cares about Dave, anyway?"

"I did," Sheila said. "A lot. He was the first guy to be kind to me."

Tom shook his head. "You're a damn fool sometimes, sis. He was playing you like he played every other chick he came into contact with. Ask this one what that was like."

Sheila glanced in the rearview mirror at Jenny. "Did he really convince you that you were special?"

Jenny looked at Tom and then frowned. "Yes. He did. And he never mentioned you at all. I don't know if that counts for anything, but to me he was a big liar. Who knows how many other women he hurt?"

"You see?" Tom glanced at Sheila. "I told you. He was no good for you. You can do much better and you will once we get to where we're going."

The truck jumped over a big pothole in the road and Annja winced as the barrel of the shotgun jerked in Tom's hands. "Better be careful or that thing's going to go off in your hands," she said.

"That'd be shame, wouldn't it?" Tom asked with a grin.

"It would make a big mess," Annja said.

"Then you should do what I told you and stop trying to infuriate my sister. She doesn't know what's best for her, anyway. I do."

Sheila frowned. "You pulling that one out now? You know what's best for me? Just like always, huh? You've always got to take care of me. Like I'm some invalid who can't look after herself."

"That's not what I meant and you know it."

"I don't know what you meant," Sheila said. "But that sure as hell didn't come out sounding right."

"Sorry." Tom sighed. "Look, can we just get to the cave and find our drugs and kill these two and leave before anyone else knows what's going on?"

Sheila nodded. "We're almost there. A few miles more."

The truck bounced along the rough track of the road. Annja and Jenny were jostled in the backseat but Tom fortunately didn't blow them away as the truck careened around the curves.

He frowned at Sheila. "Slow down, would you?"

"You told me to hurry."

"Yeah, but keep my spine in one piece, too, okay?"

Sheila frowned again. "You're too picky."

"I want to get to Belize in one piece," Tom said. "Being bounced around while sitting backward isn't the best way to do that."

Annja smiled. "Belize is nice. Good diving. Are you guys much into diving? Snorkeling? That kind of thing?"

"He is," Sheila said. "That's why we're going there."

"Was that another decision he made for you guys? In the best interests of the two of you? Or just in the best interests of Tom?"

"He made the decision," Sheila admitted.

Tom glared at Annja. "I'm not going to say it again. You speak up once more and I won't wait until we're underground. I will shoot you and your friend dead right here, right now."

Jenny put a hand on Annja's arm. "Maybe you should be quiet."

"Prolonging the inevitable," Annja said. But she nodded at Tom. "I'll keep to myself."

"What a refreshing change," Tom said. He glanced at Sheila. "We agreed that Belize was the best place to go."

"I wanted Panama. The shopping's better."

"We settle in Belize, you can drive down to Panama, or even charter a plane, for all I care. Then you can shop to your heart's content, okay? Will you just trust me on this? God."

Sheila pointed through the windshield. "We're almost there."

Annja looked ahead of the truck. The road had turned into hard track, packed gravel that crunched underneath the truck tires. She could see that it ended some distance ahead. But it wasn't that far away, maybe only a few hundred yards.

Thick stands of pine trees barred the road, but a small pathway cut through them. That was probably the route they'd take into the caves.

"Is that the entrance?" she asked.

Tom nodded. "Through there, just a short walk away. I wouldn't dream of tiring you guys out before I shoot you. I'm considerate like that."

"Wonderful."

The sun bled a deep red across the sky. Night would descend soon all over the surrounding landscape. Annja would have to time things just right if she had any hope of subduing the brother-and-sister team before they got a chance to fulfill their dreams.

She glanced at Jenny. "You okay?"

Jenny nodded. "Be better if we weren't in this truck right now."

"Yeah, I know what you mean."

The truck came to a sudden stop and Sheila wrenched the gear stick into Park. "Well, now we've stopped so you two can stop your complaining and hop on out. Make sure you take some nice deep breaths of the pines here. They smell sweet and lovely."

Tom smirked. "Don't get all sentimental on me now. We've got work to do before we send these two off to meet their ancestors."

"Work?" Annja frowned. "I thought we did all that back at the hotel."

"Well, there's more here," Tom said. "I'm not much into carrying large amounts of narcotics by myself. And with you two here, there's no reason for either Sheila or me to do it. You guys will make fine pack mules for a few trips."

"Nice," Annja said.

"Don't be down. If you're good, I'll even let you two snort a few lines before I shoot you."

"What the hell will that do?" Jenny asked.

Tom shrugged. "I don't know, maybe numb your brains long enough for me to kill you. Least that way you won't feel anything when you die."

34

The wind whistled as it blew through the thick evergreen boughs. Annja took a deep breath and found that Sheila's suggestion had been a good one. The air smelled sweet with the scent of pine. Overhead, dark storm clouds drifted in, and every now and again Annja could feel a few drops of rain sting down from the heavens.

Tom never strayed far with his shotgun, however, and even as Jenny clambered out of the back of the vehicle, he nudged them along. "Trail's over this way. Let's not waste any time."

Annja glared at him. "Got a schedule to keep, have we?"

"You know we do," Tom said. "The path is through those trees."

"And you won't shoot us in the back?" Annja asked.

Tom grinned. "Trust me when I say that I will at least give you the respect of telling you when I'm going to do it. But that time isn't now. We need you to carry out the parcels first and put them in the truck."

Annja could see through the trees that there was a small trail ahead of her. She and Jenny poked through the branches and started walking. Another stiff breeze blew in, carrying with it the scent of pine, but Annja could also smell the nearby river and heard the rushing roar of the water flowing over the dangerous rapids.

"It's a little different being here at night," she said quietly to Jenny.

"I'm sure we were here last night but we don't remember it, thanks to David drugging us."

Annja nodded. "Good point."

Sheila led the way and Annja spotted a large outcropping of boulders that sat right near the bank of the river. Sheila turned. "It's over here." She shined a flashlight over the rocks and high up off the trail, Annja could see a cleft in the rock.

"Through there," Sheila said as she scampered up as if she'd done it numerous times before.

Annja climbed first and then reached back to help Jenny scramble up the rock face. Once there, Sheila pointed the way inside. "I'll get some lights on."

Tom stayed down below, his shotgun still trained on the opening. "Sheila will tell you which packages to get and then you'll bring them out here. Don't try anything stupid. At least, not yet."

Annja ducked into the opening and found Sheila holding the pistol. "The packages are over there beyond the bend in the tunnel."

Annja walked over and saw that the cavern opened up much more once you got around the bend. In fact, looking back, she could see why this was such a great hiding spot. At first glance, the cave looked as if it ended where Sheila stood.

Jenny came down and stood next to her. "What is this stuff?"

Annja knelt down and opened one of the boxes. Small bags of white powder filled the container. "Looks like cocaine."

"I thought that all came up from South America. How's it coming in through Canada?" Jenny asked.

Annja shrugged. "I don't really know. Maybe with the 9/11 crackdowns, it's easier transporting it into Canada and then smuggling it across the border. Whatever the case, they've got a lot of it here. Probably worth a couple of million on the street, easy."

Jenny frowned. "I can't stand drugs."

"Not my game of choice, either," Annja said.

Sheila appeared around the corner. "Just get the cases and carry them back. You two don't have time for a sample of the product."

Annja frowned. "You really think he's not going to turn on you just like he did David?"

"He won't," Sheila said. "He's my brother, after all."

Annja smirked. "Sheila, family doesn't mean anything. People have been killing one another for far less and for much longer than you and your brother have been around. You thinking he won't doesn't mean it can't happen. That's just being naive."

"That's me being loyal," Sheila said. "Maybe you don't understand that, but it's got to count for something. Now, let's go. Get those packages and start hauling them out to the truck."

Annja grabbed a bag and slung it over her shoulder. It must have weighed about twenty pounds, loaded down with the cocaine. Jenny slung one over her back and promptly fell down.

Annja helped her to her feet. "Take it easy, okay? I don't need you getting hurt right now."

She walked outside and saw Tom standing there with a frown on his face. "What's taking so long up there?"

"Just helping Jenny make sure she doesn't break an ankle before you have a chance to kill us."

"That's kind of you. Now stop horsing around." Tom stood

back, allowing Annja to get down the rock slope with the bag over her shoulder.

Annja frowned. Tom knew the importance of distance. By not being too close to Annja, he could make sure that he saw any move she tried and cut her down before she succeeded in getting to him. Of course, he didn't know all of her tricks, and Annja suspected that the sudden appearance of the sword might give her just the edge she needed to turn the tables.

But that would only take care of Tom. Sheila remained a viable threat, as well. And her reluctance to go against her brother meant that Annja would need to take her out, too.

Tom guided her to the truck and Annja laid the first bag down in the back. "How are you going to deliver this to your friends? You'd better not get a speeding ticket."

Tom shook his head. "I don't think we'll be stopped with that blue-light bar on top of the truck. Remember, we've got Dave's ride."

"And they won't stop a police car, is that it?"

"Exactly."

Annja looked at him. "You've thought of everything, haven't you?"

Tom smiled. "I've had a lot of time to think things through." He gestured with the shotgun. "Now, let's go. There are plenty more bags to haul out here."

Jenny and Sheila appeared on the trail. Jenny was struggling with her bag and Annja grabbed it from her.

Tom frowned. "She's supposed to carry her own load."

Annja shrugged. "I'm more physically fit than she is. She's a desk jockey. Pushes paper all day long."

"If that's so, then why is she out in the field?"

"Change of pace," Annja said. "You want these things hauled properly or what?"

"Of course I do."

"Then let me get her load. She can hand them down to me from the cave entrance and I'll carry them the rest of the way."

Tom eyed Jenny. "You okay with that?"

"Sure."

"All right." He looked at Annja. "Just don't forget that the gun is trained on you all the time. There's something about you that I don't trust. And if you give me the slightest reason to do it, I'll gun you down. And then your physically inept friend there won't have any choice but to carry the bags. Understand?"

"We've been through this already," Annja said. "I'm not trying anything. I just want to get this over with. Maybe you'll find some compassion in your heart and let us live. Tie us up for all I care and get your head start. There's no real reason to shoot us, though."

Tom smiled but Annja knew he wasn't really going to consider it. "I'll think about it. If you keep your end of the deal, who knows? You might just get out of this alive."

Yeah, right. But if Annja could keep him thinking she wasn't going to try anything funny, it might give her the chance she needed.

As she and Jenny walked back down the trail, Annja kept bumping into her friend. As she did so, she whispered. "You'll have to take out Sheila."

"What?"

"I can't handle them both at the same time. And Tom's the more dangerous one. That shotgun can kill us both with one shot."

"I can't do it. Sheila's bigger than I am," Jenny said.

"Just get close enough and kick her hard in the knee. When she goes down, stomp her hand and get the gun away. I'll come to you as soon as I can but I'll have my hands full dealing with Tom."

"You two keep quiet," Tom said from behind. "Don't make me start feeling all nervous inside."

"I was asking her how her ankle was," Annja said. "Stop being paranoid."

They marched back to the cave and Jenny climbed back up. Sheila followed. After a minute, Jenny reappeared, grunting under the strain of another heavy bag. She tossed it down, which made Tom hop around, waving the gun.

"Don't throw the damn bags! If the contents spill, it'll make a huge mess and we won't get our money. Hand them down carefully!"

Jenny looked meek. "Sorry. It slipped."

"I'll bet it did." Tom shook his head and then looked at Annja. "You'd better tell your friend not to screw this thing up or else she'll be the first one who gets shot. You understand me?"

"Perfectly."

Annja picked up the bag and started walking back to the car. She would have to make her move soon. Tom was already growing impatient with the handling of the drugs. He could snap at any moment.

Annja took a deep breath and walked up the trail. She wondered where Joey was. Had Tom killed him? Had he stowed the body so Annja and Jenny wouldn't see that he'd killed a child? Or was Joey still alive and rounding up some sort of rescue party?

It was probably too much to hope for given everything that they'd been through. And yet Annja felt something deep inside that told her Joey was okay.

But where was he?

For that matter, what were the odds that Simpson and Baker were somewhere close by, hunting their elusive Sasquatch? If she could run into them right now, armed as they were, it would help things tremendously. Even their sudden appearance would be enough to give Annja the opening she needed to take down Tom.

She could always explain things to Simpson and Baker later after it was all over.

But for now, she needed an opening.

I'll have to take him on the trail, before we get back to the cave entrance. When we're away, Jenny can take Sheila out.

Annja approached the Tahoe and laid the next bag in the back. She looked over her shoulder at Tom. "How many more of these things are there?"

"About two dozen."

"That's a big shipment of stuff. How did you get it into Canada?"

Tom shook his head. "I don't smuggle it into Canada. I just take it over the border and then get it into the hands of the distributors in this part of the country. I have no idea how the drugs get into Canada. My job is a small one, but it's a critical part of the supply chain."

"So who's going to replace you when you and Sheila take off for parts unknown?"

Tom shrugged. "I don't know. It's not really my problem."

"Isn't it, though?" Annja frowned. "If I was a drug supplier and I had a good thing going, I wouldn't want my supply lines being disrupted because one of my mules decided that things were getting too hot and they wanted to bail. I'd make them stay."

"I've already discussed it with the bosses. They don't have a problem letting us go. They're even loaning us their jet."

"Really? Is there a bomb on the plane?" Annja asked.

"Why would you say that?"

"You think drug kingpins are just going to let you walk away? They can't afford to have anyone who knows their program out there in the world. You could get busted for a speeding ticket and flip like that. Their best option is to kill you. I can't believe you seem so shocked by that idea. Maybe you really are stupid."

"Maybe you underestimate the relationship we have with our network of people."

"Or maybe I underestimate how naive you and your sister are. Although, to be honest, she strikes me as a shade more intelligent than you. At least where matters of the heart aren't concerned."

"All right, that's enough out of you. Get back to the cave."

Annja nodded. The next time through she'd do something. She'd signal Jenny at the handoff that the time had come for them to make their move.

35

Annja walked back to the cave, aware of how much more the sky had been blotted out by the arrival of the dense black clouds overhead. Drizzle was falling and she shook her head to ward off some of the spray. I'm spending more time on this venture being wet than any of the other ones I've been on thus far, she thought.

Behind her, she heard Tom sniff. "Sorry, we didn't bring any umbrellas with us tonight."

"Like you'd hold one over me while I did my work, anyway," Annja said. "I don't think you would."

"You're right, but only because I think you're far too dangerous to let out of my sight."

"What's that supposed to mean?" Annja asked. She had to keep him talking. It might just take his mind off her a little bit and give her the opening she'd need when the time came.

"I saw how you were with Dave back at the hotel. He wasn't a timid guy and yet you handled him like he was easy prey. Broke his wrist even."

"He had that coming, believe me. The way he acted last night at his place, I was lucky he didn't try to rape me while we were waiting for you to show up and shoot us with your dart gun."

"Yeah, I always wondered about that. I never could figure out what he saw in my sister, aside from a convenient lay, I suppose."

"Is that why you killed him? Because he disrespected her?"

"You were closer to the mark before. More money for us. I don't want my sister wanting for anything in life. But she does make some stupid decisions. That's why I've got to call the shots."

"Even if she doesn't happen to agree with them?"

"Even if," Tom said. "You know that old saying that some people don't know what's best for them? My sister fits that bill perfectly."

Annja shook her head. The rain was increasing. She could hear the drops smacking into the ground as they passed through the pine trees again, heading back toward the cave opening.

Jenny was already waiting for Annja. "Where have you been?"

"These bags are heavy," Annja said. "It's not exactly the easiest thing in the world to pull your share of the work."

"My share? You volunteered!"

"You didn't put up a fight," Annja said. She winked at Jenny and nodded once. Jenny nodded back. Message received.

"Get the bag and stop your yapping, you two," Tom said. He looked at Sheila. "You okay?"

Sheila frowned. "Why on earth wouldn't I be?"

"I was just checking," Tom said. "Relax, okay?"

Sheila shook her head. "I'm fine and you don't need to keep checking on me. I can handle my end of this without your constant supervision."

"Fine, fine." Tom glared at Annja. "You got that bag yet?"

Annja heaved the sack over her shoulder. "Yeah, let's go."

They turned toward the truck and walked down the trail. Annja cleared her throat. She could feel the adrenaline starting to course through her. She'd have to time this just right, hopefully catching Tom before he could fire off a round from the gun and alert Sheila to the possibility of the attack. Annja just hoped that Jenny could do her part; otherwise, Annja would be walking back into a potential ambush.

"Your sister sounds pretty mad at you," she said.

"She always gets that way when I have to decide on something."

"Really?"

"Like we were talking about before. She resents the fact that I make all the decisions in the family."

"No other siblings?"

"Nah. Our parents died when we were young and from then on it's always been just the two of us. I took care of her. Sheltered her and looked after her. Even when I was in the service, I made sure she was always fine. Friends of mine would watch over her."

"So, in other words, she's never had the chance to make her own decisions about anything," Annja said.

"You see it one way. I see it another."

"I see her feeling incredibly suffocated," Annja said. "No wonder she's so pissed off at you."

"She'll get over it," Tom said. "She always does."

"What if you're wrong?"

"Wrong about her getting over it? Not likely. You don't know my sister very well."

Annja shifted the bag on her shoulder. "Well, maybe I don't know Sheila all that well, but I know how women think. And here's the thing, Tom. You just killed the only man she might have ever loved."

"Like I told her, there are other fish in the sea."

"Yeah, yeah, I know that line. But what you're missing here is the fact that David was probably the first guy she's ever made up her own mind about. All through her life she's had you watching over her."

Tom was quiet and Annja kept going. "How many boyfriends has she had?"

"I don't know."

"Probably not many," Annja said. "And probably because you scared them all away, didn't you?"

"Not necessarily. A lot of the ones who came nosing around were losers who didn't mean to do anything, except get in her pants."

"So what business is it of yours what she chooses to do and with whom? We all need to make our own mistakes," Annja said.

"Not my sister. She doesn't need to make mistakes. I've made enough of them for both of us."

Annja smirked. "I'm sure you have. But that doesn't mean there hasn't been an incredible reservoir of resentment building up within Sheila's heart. She probably hasn't voiced it to you yet, but then there's what happened tonight. And your actions back at the hotel might just cause the dam to break, releasing all of that pent-up emotion. Anger. Hatred, even."

"My sister doesn't hate me."

They'd reached the truck and Annja set the package down on top of the others. She looked at Tom. "Look, you don't have to listen to me. That's cool. But if I were you, I'd watch my back really carefully these next few days. Sheila's a volcano about to explode, and if you're in the path of her destruction you're toast, pal."

Tom frowned. "Are you finished analyzing my life?"

Annja shrugged. "Like I said, take it or leave it. Makes no difference to me. I'll be dead."

Tom smiled. "That you will."

Annja eyed him. "Not even going to attempt to lie to me about the possibility of getting out of this with my life, are you?"

"Nope. Call it a sign of respect. You don't buy my bullshit, anyway. No sense in pretending about tonight's outcome."

Annja nodded. "I suppose I should thank you for that."

"Yeah, why's that?"

Annja smiled. "It just makes everything that much clearer. That's all."

Tom nodded toward the pine trees. "You've still got a lot of carrying to do. Let's get back."

"How will you know where to meet these people that you do business with?"

Tom patted his shirt pocket. "Got the map and directions right here. It's just a short skip down the old interstate. It's always nice driving into the city, anyway. We do the drop and then Sheila and I continue on to our new home."

"So you say." Annja started walking away from the truck. She stumbled once on some loose rock.

She heard Tom snicker behind her. "Careful there. Wouldn't want you to get hurt and have to struggle through the pain."

Annja closed her eyes and saw the sword hanging there, ready to draw out at a moment's notice. She wanted to wrap her hands around it right now, but the time wasn't right.

Not yet.

She continued walking down the trail. The rain had increased and now the steady shower coated everything. The ground grew muddy underfoot. Annja would have to remember to watch her footing or she'd risk a fall in the mud.

"I'm going to miss this place," Tom said suddenly from behind her.

"So why don't you stay and turn yourself in?"

He laughed. "Prison's not an option for me."

Annja nodded. "Yeah, I think that way about death, too."

"Death's inevitable," Tom said. "The only question is when we're all going to go."

"Don't tell me you're philosophical about the murders you commit."

"Whatever helps keep the demons at bay," Tom said.

"I suppose you're right," Annja said. "It is all just a big question of when, isn't it?"

"Yep."

She glanced back at him. "And if we knew the when of it all, I wonder if we'd live our lives any differently than we have to this point?"

Tom shook his head. "I wouldn't. I'm pretty happy with how things have turned out so far."

"You should see it from my perspective," Annja said.

"No, thanks. I prefer my viewpoint. You know, it's the one with the big nasty shotgun and all. The view's much nicer back here."

Annja shrugged. "Oh, I don't know about that."

"Why?"

Annja dropped suddenly to one knee and pivoted, sweeping one of her legs out and back at Tom's legs.

She caught him at just the right moment as his full body weight was coming down onto his right leg. She swept the leg and he toppled backward, falling into the mud.

Annja was up instantly. She summoned the sword and charged.

Tom saw the sword coming for him and swept the shotgun up, trying to get a shot at Annja.

He was too slow and Annja cut across the barrel and heard the sharp clang as the sword blade bit through the barrel and the stock. The force of the impact knocked the shotgun out of Tom's hands and sent it skittering across the rocks and gravel until it came to rest under a tree.

But Tom didn't stop moving and Annja marveled at his speed as he rolled off the ground and came up, kicking out at her face.

Annja ducked under the kick and tried to cut at Tom's leg but he retracted it quickly and retreated some distance away.

Annja charged again, leaping into the air. She brought the sword high overhead, trying to cleave Tom in two as she came down.

But Tom threw a handful of gravel into her face and she swore as the tiny stones and dirt clouded her vision and stung her eyes.

She swung the sword wildly but missed. Then she felt a thundering side kick explode into her rib cage. She heard a snap and then her lung heaved as she fought to grab a breath. Tom's kick must have broken several ribs.

Annja swung the sword back, trying to catch Tom's leg. She felt the blade bite into something but then the sensation was gone.

Annja wiped her free hand across her face, desperate to get the gravel out of her eyes. Tears streamed down her face, clouding her vision. If she didn't clear her eyesight, Tom would go for his gun and shoot her before she could finish the job.

Another kick thundered into her opposite side and this time it was all Annja could do to keep from dropping the sword and collapsing in pain.

I hope Jenny's having better luck with Sheila, she thought.

Annja cut back again, trying to find a target. She heard Tom laugh. "Can't hit what you can't see."

Annja held the blade in front of her. The blindness worked against her and she couldn't find Tom in the rain and darkness.

A sound reached her ears.

He's going to the gun.

She had one chance.

She flipped the sword over and heaved it like a javelin. She heard the blade hiss through the air.

At the same time, a single gunshot tore through the night.

36

Annja wiped the grit from her face. Her hand came away moist with the tears that had been trying to flush her eyes. And then her vision finally cleared and she could see at last.

Tom's body lay in a crumpled heap about fifteen feet away, a pool of blood staining the ground beneath him. Annja's sword jutted out of the tree trunk nearby.

"I missed," she said, confused.

"I didn't," a voice said from behind her.

She turned and saw Jenny standing there with David's gun in her hands.

Annja smiled weakly. "Great timing."

Jenny nodded. "Well, life has always been about timing, hasn't it? You just have to know when to do the things you need to do."

Annja got to her feet. "The bastard threw sand into my face. It got into my eyes and I couldn't see a thing."

"You okay now?"

Annja wiped her face on her sleeve some more. "I think so."

"He might have killed you," Jenny said.

Annja looked at Tom. There was a neat hole in the center of his forehead. "You made an incredible shot for someone who's never used a gun before."

"What makes you think I've never used a gun?" Jenny asked.

Annja shrugged. "I just thought you hadn't. You never seemed comfortable around them."

"Well, not when Tom was aiming that huge cannon at us from the front seat of his truck. I don't think anyone would be cool in that situation. Except maybe for the great Annja Creed."

Annja shook her head. "I'm not great." She checked Tom's pulse but he was already dead. "What did you do with Sheila?"

Jenny pointed over her shoulder. "Back at the cave. I broke her neck."

"How'd you manage that?"

Jenny grinned. "Just a little trick I picked up along the road of life. A single woman needs to know how to take care of herself. Nothing to it, really. You just step up, elbow them in the face and then loop your arm and—"

Annja held up her hand. "I get it."

Jenny smiled. "So they're both out of the way now. At last."

"That means we can get the hell out of here," Annja said. "I'm buying the first drink at the airport."

But Jenny wasn't smiling anymore. "What about the bodies?"

Annja glanced back. The thought of cleaning up two more corpses was appalling. But she couldn't just leave them where they were. They'd get ravaged by the forest animals. And if they didn't explain themselves to the police—the real police—there was a chance they'd be implicated in some type of murder charge.

Jenny was right. They had to clean things up.

"Where did David say the nearest state cops were? An hour away or something like that?"

Jenny nodded. "Yeah."

"I guess we should call them, huh? At least when we get back to town and talk to Ellen."

"And what about the other stuff?"

"The drugs?" Annja shrugged. "Beats me. The cops'll take it, I guess. That's their thing. I sure don't want anything to do with it."

"It's worth a lot of money, though, isn't it?"

Annja nodded. "Probably worth millions on the street."

"They were planning on heading down to South America, weren't they? Someplace where they could set up shop without the fear of being extradited back to the U.S. That's quite a plan for them."

Annja brushed her knees. "Yeah, well, their plans are ruined now. Just goes to prove that you can't stop the forces of good." She glanced up. "That'd be you and me."

Jenny smiled. "Yeah, I got it."

Annja looked at her sword sticking out of the tree and then smiled back at Jenny. "I guess I'd better yank that thing out of there, huh? Can't leave it like that for some innocent person to stumble over. That'd be messy."

Annja started to walk over to the tree and then heard the sound of a hammer being pulled back on a gun. "Don't do that."

She turned. "What are you doing?"

Jenny held the gun aimed at Annja. "I'm finally taking control of my life. That's what."

"By shooting me?"

"I don't want to have to do that," Jenny said. "But that sword is far too dangerous. I can't let you get it back in your hands or you'll use it on me."

"Why would I do that?"

Jenny sneered. "Because you're Miss Goody-Goody. There's no way you're going to let me walk out of here with those drugs. You'll try to stop me. And I'm done with people imposing themselves on my personal destiny."

Annja frowned. "You think those drugs are your destiny? Don't be ridiculous. You've already got a great life."

"I don't have a life," Jenny said. "I have an existence. And it's a meager one at that. I've got no real career path other than making tenure at some university no one even cares about. My romantic world is a sham. I'm struggling to make ends meet on my crappy salary and I'm a miserable wreck."

Annja frowned. "If you need money, I'll loan you some to get you back on your feet."

"It's not just about the money. Can't you see that? I'm tired. So tired. Of everything. The daily struggle to survive. And it's all based on the hope that one day things will finally get better. Well, when do they get better? I'm not a young girl anymore. The world isn't my oyster. Hell, it never was my oyster. All it ever turned out to be was a big pile of crap. And I'm sick of it, Annja. "

"And you think this is the answer to your problems? Stealing drugs and then selling them and taking the money to go run off somewhere and live like the spoiled princess you've always wanted to be?"

"Being spoiled has nothing to do with it."

Annja sat down on the ground. "You think your life is tough, Jenny? You should try seeing things from my side of the coin. I don't have any family. I don't have many close friends aside from folks like you."

"Yeah, but you've got a career in television. That's got to count for something. Lots of fans and all that."

"I don't have many fans. The coanchor on that show gets more fan mail in a day than I do all year. And it's all because she lost her top once during filming. You think I want to sacrifice my journalistic integrity for some pieces of mail? And yet that's the world we live in these days."

"You're paid well, at least."

"Sure. The money's nice. But it doesn't make all the lone-liness go away when it's just me alone in my bed at night." Annja shook her head. "You think I have the life, don't you? That all of this travel is a great adventure for me."

"Isn't it?"

"No, it's not. Did you ever wonder why I spend so much of my time traipsing around the world?"

Jenny shrugged. "It's pretty obvious, isn't it? You love what you do. The quest for relics and all that stuff. It's your obsession."

"Yeah, it's my obsession." Annja sighed. "That's only part of the story, Jenny. The other part is that I am so scared of ever settling down and committing myself to one thing, one person, one ideal, that I run away from anything that even remotely looks as if it could be a solid foundation in my life. And I run right toward danger and anything else that looks as volatile as nitroglycerin."

"If that's the case, then why did that sword choose you to be its holder and caretaker?"

"Isn't it obvious? It knows I'll never stop running toward the bad guys. That there will always be a chance for me to fight and use it for the powers of good. Of course it chose me. The last thing that sword would ever want was someone with a regular job, a spouse and two kids at home. Can you imagine that? It would never get used."

"And presumably evil would triumph," Jenny said.

"That's my guess."

Jenny shrugged. "All right, so you've got a crappy life, too. Why don't you change it?"

"Who says I can?"

"I do."

Annja smiled. "Yeah, I wish it was that easy. It's not. The same powers that brought this sword to me will make sure that I never have a moment's rest as long as I try to avoid my destiny and that of this sword."

Jenny sighed. "I wish I could take it from you."

"Don't say that. You don't want this thing. I don't even know if I want this thing."

Jenny lowered the gun. "I don't want to hurt you, Annja."

"You don't have to hurt me. But you don't have to take those drugs, either. There's always a better way."

"Is there? I've heard people tell me that all the time. And I never seem to find it. People say to have faith and yet my faith is never rewarded. I've prayed to every deity I can think of. I've prayed to every ancestor in my family. I don't ask for much. Just a little bit. And yet, time after time, there's no help from beyond. No help from those who are supposed to have the power to help us."

"I know what you mean."

Jenny frowned. "And then every day I hear stories of people who are bad, unjust or evil who are living a great life. Criminals with more money than God. Women falling all over themselves to be with them. Even law-abiding people who are frugal, cheap bastards and would never give a dime to charity. Even they have the life."

Annja nodded. She'd seen it enough times to know that Jenny spoke the truth. Her friend took a stuttering breath and then continued.

"So when does it all end, Annja? When do I get the rewards of living an honest, hard-working life? When do I wake up and see that all the struggle has been worth the pain and agony that I've endured? When?"

"Maybe tomorrow. Maybe never," Annja said.

"I'm tired of the maybes. I'm tired of saying to myself, 'tomorrow's going to be the day this all gets taken care of.' I'm tired of wishing so hard that I make my head hurt. And I'm tired of the endless disappointment."

"I don't know what to tell you, Jenny." Annja shook her head. "I wish I had the power to make all your pain go away. But I don't. None of us do."

"I do now," Jenny said. "And I'm not walking away from the chance just because it's not the right thing to do in someone else's book. For me, this is the right thing to do and it's the right time to do it."

Annja looked at the ground. "I can't let you take the drugs, Jenny."

"Why not? After everything I've just told you. I poured my heart out to you. I'm dying here and you still cling to some supposedly noble ideology? How is that your decision to make?"

Annja shook her head. "I don't know. But it's a decision that has to be made and I'm the person here, right now, standing in your way."

Jenny raised the gun. "Like I said, I don't want to hurt you, Annja. But so help me, God, if you try to stop me from achieving my happiness, I will put a bullet in you. I'm not going to go back to my crummy life and try to spend the next forty years telling myself that it would have been wrong to take the drugs and give myself the life I've always wanted. No way."

Annja got up from the ground. "I can't let you do that, Jenny. You'd never forgive yourself if you did. That junk only hurts more people than it saves. The money those criminal kingpins have is taken from the suffering of others. You don't want to be any part of that."

"I do now." Jenny shrugged. "I just do not care about anyone else anymore except myself."

"In that case," Annja said. "You'll have to shoot me."

37

Jenny shook her head. "I don't want to do that."

"You're not taking the drugs, Jenny. So if you're determined to do that, then I'll have to stop you," Annja said.

"After everything we've been through together. You'd really try to stop me?"

"I wouldn't *try*. I would do it," Annja replied honestly.

Jenny shook her head. "I thought you'd understand my reasons for doing this."

"I do understand your reasons. But that doesn't mean I have to condone them. And I can't. I hope you'll understand that."

Jenny shook her head. "Actually, I can't understand why you'd stand in my way. That's equal to you telling me that I don't have the right to live my life the way I want to."

"No, that's you saying you don't care if living your life comes from the suffering of others."

"What about *my* suffering? Doesn't anyone care about that? Isn't that important, as well? Or am I just going to be forgotten again like every other time?"

Annja looked Jenny in the eye. "You're starting to annoy me with the woe-is-me stuff. You're no different from millions of other people. We all struggle in some way, shape or form to make our way through life. No one ever said it was going to be an easy thing."

"No one ever said it was going to be this difficult, either."

"Granted. But what's the choice? You're going to abandon all your morals now just because you've got the chance to take advantage of a situation that you'd normally steer clear of?"

"I've got the chance to make my life what I've always wanted it to be. My visions have the chance to become reality now."

"And how are you going to manage that? You're just going to waltz down to their contacts and sell them the drugs?"

"Why not?"

"You think they'd even deal with you?"

"I've got the merchandise."

"But they don't know you from anyone. You could be a cop. You could be wearing a wire or something. Trust me when I tell you that drug dealers aren't the kind of people you want to be messing around with."

Jenny ratcheted the slide on the pistol. "Well, maybe this is the new Jenny. And frankly, the new Jenny just might have some tricks up her sleeve that the old one didn't."

"You're going to need them if you hope to come out of that meeting alive and intact."

Jenny smiled. "Why don't you come with me?"

"Me? No way."

"Why not? You could be the security blanket I need. Keep an eye on things and make sure it all goes to plan. I'll split the money with you. There's more than enough for both of us to go anywhere we want and live like queens."

Annja shook her head. "You haven't been listening to me,

have you? Didn't you hear what I said earlier? I can't live my life the way I want to. The sword controls me now. It's not overt, but I can feel the pressure from it to journey where there's evil and help rout it."

"Throw the sword away, then."

Annja shook her head. "As if it was that easy."

"You threw it easily enough at Tom there."

Annja nodded. "And look where it ended up."

Jenny glanced to her right and so did Annja. But the sword wasn't embedded in the trunk of the tree anymore.

Jenny frowned. "Where is it?"

Annja tapped her chest. "Back with me now. Inside. Always with me. No matter what."

Jenny pointed the gun at her. "Don't even think about pulling it out. I won't hesitate to shoot you."

"Yes, you will."

The explosion made Annja wince as the air broke near her left ear. A single shell casing spun out of the ejector port on the side of the pistol and spiraled to the ground.

Jenny regarded her now with a certain detachment. "I don't think you want to make a wrong assumption again, Annja."

"Guess not."

Jenny nodded at the truck. "How much have you placed inside?"

"A few bags. Not that much."

"And what do you think the street value would be?"

"I have no idea. But it's not enough. Remember, these guys you'd be dealing with are expecting a full shipment of drugs. You show up with just a few bags and they'll think you're holding out on them. That's not the kind of thing that endears you to criminals."

"So you'll help me load the rest of it, then. Just like we were doing before."

Annja shook her head. "I won't."

Jenny waggled the gun. "Don't make me shoot you. I'm getting tired of saying it."

"I'm getting tired of hearing it." Annja sat down. "You're going to have to accept the fact that I am not going to be a party to your new criminal enterprise."

"So that's it?"

"That's it."

Jenny looked down over the pistol. "This isn't how I wanted things to end with you, Annja."

"Could have fooled me. You seem perfectly at ease with what you're about to do."

"I suppose stress and anxiety have a way of making you reconcile the certain necessary evils of life." She shrugged. "And I'm sure it's nothing that a couple million dollars won't help me forget all about."

Annja shook her head. "If you think for one split second that you'll ever forget about this, then you're sadly mistaken."

"Am I really? And how would you know?"

"Because I carry the memory of every person I've ever killed. They never leave you. They never go away or dull over time. They're always there in your mind. Whenever you think they're not, they just come back even stronger than before."

"I guess I'll have to learn to live with it. Just like you did, huh?"

Annja nodded. "Yeah, but the people I've killed have all been bad. The world was better off without them." She looked at Jenny. "I've never had to kill a friend before. I've never done what you're about to do."

Jenny was quiet for a moment. She frowned when she looked back at Annja. "All of this talk is just designed to get me to think twice about my actions."

"I'm trying to talk some sense into you before you make the biggest mistake of your life."

Jenny shook her head. "The biggest mistake I ever made was not doing a better audition for *Chasing History's Monsters*. I could be where you are right now."

"They came to me," Annja said. "I never searched them out at all."

Jenny smiled. "Oh, sure. I read all about it in the newspaper. How you were chosen out of a hundred or so hopefuls. I was one of those hopefuls. I thought I had a legitimate shot at the role. I didn't know at the time that the fix was already in."

Annja shook her head. "I didn't know about that. I figured it was just propaganda put out by the studios to help sell the show. No one really expects anyone to believe it. I didn't know you tried out for the show. I never knew what it was that made them pick me. I'm sure you would be a huge hit on the show."

"Stop trying to butter me up. It won't work."

Annja sighed. "This is getting us nowhere. You're going to shoot me so you can run off with bags of drugs, sell them to people you've never even met, think that they won't smoke you as soon as they get a shot and then ride off into the sunset on some *Fantasy Island* regurgitation."

"Yep."

"You realize the entire thing sounds ridiculous."

Jenny laughed. "My life's been ridiculous so far. Why stop now?"

"Because I'm asking you to. Does that count for anything? Anything at all?"

Jenny chewed her lip. "Not anymore, Annja. I'm sorry. But it doesn't. The time has come. The needs of the one now outweigh the needs of the many."

Annja nodded. "I can't entirely find fault with you wanting to do this. I just wish you'd see how unlikely it is that you'll be successful."

Jenny looked up. The drizzle had tapered off and the clouds had started to part. "Weather's getting better. That should make loading the truck easier."

"For you," Annja said.

"Still not going to help?"

"No."

"And I can't buy your loyalty?"

Annja sniffed. "My loyalty was never for sale. It was given unconditionally as a result of being your friend. Your good friend."

"We were good friends," Jenny said. "It's a shame that after all we've been though it has to end this way."

"Just get on with it, then."

Jenny nodded. "All right. If that's what you want."

"It's better than sitting here trying to talk some sense into you. That's obviously not going to work."

"I'm beyond reason at this point. All I can see is what I need to do in order to make my life what I want it to be."

"If you say so."

"I do."

Annja leaned back on her hands. "Make sure you aim properly. I don't want an abdominal wound. Those suck."

Jenny positioned the pistol in both of her hands and adopted a solid shooter's stance. "I'll put two in your heart. It will be over soon enough."

Annja looked at her. "I want you to do me a favor."

"A last request? That seems a little trite. Especially coming from someone like you."

"What's that supposed to mean?"

Jenny shrugged. "You don't seem like the type who would beg for something at the last moment."

"I'm not begging for anything," Annja said. "I'm only making a small request for you to remember something.

That's all. No steak dinner or anything like that. Just a tiny favor."

"And what would you like me to remember?"

"That I saved your life."

Jenny looked at her. "Joey saved my life. Not you."

Annja shook her head. "No. If I hadn't taken the spirit walk with Joey's grandfather, we never would have found you."

"Why didn't you tell me that before?"

Annja sighed. "Because when I do these things I'm not looking for bragging rights. I do them because I don't have any other choice. It's who I am, how I'm wired. I can't not help people."

Jenny nodded. "I understand."

"Do you?"

"Yes. But I still have to do what I have to do. You must be able to understand that."

"I can understand the thought process but not the eventual outcome. I think you're committing suicide here."

Jenny shook her head. "I disagree. But even if I am, at least I'm finally living my life on my terms. It's felt as if I've been living in a fantasy future world for so long, I don't even remember the last time one of my decisions was made by me for me."

"And this decision you're making now, the one to kill me? That's all for you, huh?"

"Yes. It is."

Annja nodded. "Then I wish you the very best of luck with your life."

"Thanks."

Annja closed her eyes. "See you on the other side, my friend."

She heard Jenny's voice. "Goodbye, Annja."

Annja steeled herself.

She would summon the sword and be ready to move as soon as Jenny did.

Before she reacted, Annja heard the explosions of the two gunshots in rapid succession.

And then she felt the impact in her chest.

38

Annja looked down at her chest.

There was no blood. And the blade of the sword hovered in front of her, flat side toward Jenny. She frowned.

What had happened?

Annja looked at Jenny.

Jenny's shirt had two dark, blossoming stains on it. She looked down and gasped. "What happened?"

Annja groaned. The sword had deflected the bullets and sent them back into Jenny's chest instead of Annja's.

"No," she said. Annja got to her feet and ran to Jenny. The gun had fallen when the bullets impacted. Annja kicked it away.

She helped ease Jenny down to the ground. Jenny tried to smile but a pinkish stream of blood oozed out of her mouth. "I guess things didn't work out quite like I wanted them to, huh?"

"I guess not," Annja said.

Jenny gripped Annja's hand. "I'm sorry I tried to kill you."

Annja nodded. "Forget it. It's done and over with now."

Jenny laughed. "You were always the master of the understatement, weren't you?"

"Old habits die hard," Annja said. "I'm sorry things turned out this way. I couldn't let you do it. You would have died with regrets."

Jenny shrugged and winced as she did so. "I'm not exactly dying with good times etched into my memory."

"No. I guess you're not."

"I only wanted what I thought I deserved. What anyone thinks they ought to deserve. Is that so wrong?"

Annja shook her head. "You did what you thought was best for you. I don't think anyone can find fault with that."

"Do you?"

"No." Annja smiled. "Some of us just don't have the guts to do what you tried to do."

Jenny smiled. "I'll tell you one thing."

"What's that?"

She coughed and Annja could see the pain on her friend's face. "When I get to the other side, I'm going to have a serious sit-down with the man in charge. I've got a lot of questions I want answers to."

"Any chance you'll come back and clue me in?"

Jenny started to cry. "No. I don't think they'd let me even if I wanted to. I've never gotten anything I wanted so far, why start now?"

Annja cradled Jenny in her arms and looked down. Life was rapidly fading from her eyes. "I'm sorry."

Jenny shook her head. "Nothing to be sorry about. I did this all to myself. I guess that's the biggest lesson from all of this, huh?"

"What's that?" Annja felt her eyes starting to well up. Tears rolled down her face.

"That we're always in control of our lives. Even when it seems like we're not. We have power over every decision and choice, if we just accept the responsibility that goes along with them."

Annja nodded. "Wisdom is a treasure hard earned."

Jenny clutched her hand. "I'm sorry."

"Me, too." More tears flowed from Annja's eyes. Why did it have to end like this? Why this way?

Jenny's eyes rolled over white and a final breath escaped her chest. Annja closed her eyelids and then let her body down gently. She sat there, crying softly for another minute, looking at the peaceful expression on Jenny's face.

Annja used her sleeve to wipe the bloody trail from Jenny's mouth. There, she thought, at least she doesn't look so gruesome now.

She glanced at Tom's body and then back. So much death, she thought. And for what purpose?

Those damn drugs.

Annja hauled herself up and squatted next to Tom's body, pulling a sheaf of papers from his shirt pocket. Then she walked over to the back of the Tahoe. She fished out one of the sacks she'd carried, opened it. The plastic bags of white powder stared up at her.

No more, Annja thought.

She turned back to the trail and headed toward the cave. She passed Sheila's body on the way inside and found the woman's head bent at an odd angle. Jenny had done a damn good job of dispatching her.

Another life lost to the pull of greed and drugs.

Annja heaved two of the bags on her shoulders and carted them down to the Tahoe. She dumped them inside and then repeated the process ten more times. Each time the bags got too heavy, Annja simply remembered how Jenny's face had looked as she died and her anger gave her strength.

Annja finished packing up the truck. The rain had started

again, clouds blew in quickly and she could hear thunder in the distance.

A storm's brewing, she thought. And it's not just out here in the wild forests of the Pacific Northwest.

Annja looked at Jenny's body. She had to see someone about this. But who? Who would believe her? And what would they say when they saw all the corpses?

Her options weren't good.

What do I do now? she wondered.

"Annja?"

She turned. Joey walked out of the darkness.

Annja ran to him and hugged him close. He wore a bandage on his head. She felt the lump underneath it. "I thought you were dead!"

Joey grinned. "Yeah, well, Tom sure swung for the fences when he hit me. Where is the jerk, anyway?"

"He's dead. Over there."

Joey looked beyond Annja's shoulder and nodded. "Serves him right. I can't believe he was using this place. Disgusting that he soiled the beauty of nature so much." Joey looked around. "Where's his partner in crime?"

"In the cave they stashed us in this morning. She's dead, too."

"You killed her?"

Annja shook her head. "Not me. Jenny."

Joey grinned. "Nice one for her. Where is she?"

Annja pointed. "She's dead, Joey."

Joey looked back at Annja. "What? How?"

"She made a bad decision. And it cost her her life."

"*You* killed her?"

Annja shook her head. "No. In a way, she killed herself."

Joey sighed. "So much death."

"Too much death, my friend. But I am glad to see you."

Joey smiled. "Likewise. I heard those shots and we came running—"

"We?"

From behind Joey, two men stepped into the clearing. One of them smiled and held up his hand. "Hello, Annja."

"Agent Simpson?"

He shrugged. "Name's Davis, actually. But you can call me Simpson if you want."

Baker came out into the open, as well. "Nice to see you again, Annja. Shame it's under these circumstances," he said.

"You have a different name, too?" Annja moved Joey behind her, ready to unleash the sword. The way she was feeling, they'd be lucky if she left anything larger than a thimble with which to identify them.

"My name's Connor. But like Davis said, if you feel better calling me Baker, then so be it."

"Annja."

She shook her head. "Not now, Joey. Let me handle this."

Davis held his hands up. "I think you might want to listen to him. He's got plenty of things to tell you."

Annja frowned, but kept her eyes on the two men. "What do you want to tell me, Joey?"

"They're not here to trap the Sasquatch."

"What?"

"They're not. They're special agents with the Drug Enforcement Agency."

"DEA?"

Davis nodded. "We knew there was a heavy drug flow coming into this area but no one knew exactly where. Several towns border this forest, so we decided to set up shop and see what we could find out."

"That's why we had to run you and your friends out of the woods the other day. We didn't want anyone getting hurt in case we found the dealers."

"And the big foot thing—" she glanced at Joey "—sorry, the Sasquatch thing, was just a cover story?"

Both men nodded. "It's amazing what you can sell as a cover story given the hysteria that swept the country since 9/11. Paranoia's at an all-time high. We're not happy about that, but we're not beyond using it for our own purposes, either."

"Swell."

Davis pointed at Tom's body. "He was the ringleader?"

Annja shrugged. "I guess so. His sister Sheila's up in the cave down the trail there. And there's another body back at the hotel in town. David, the sheriff. Seems the partners had a little dispute and he lost out."

"He was in on it?"

Annja nodded. "Yep."

Connor sighed. "Good lawmen are tough to find these days."

"Whatever." Annja wasn't in the mood to discuss the moral ambiguities of law enforcement. She pointed to Jenny. "I was trying to figure out how to handle the body of my friend."

Connor frowned. "The cute one?"

"She would have liked hearing you say that," Annja said.

"I would have liked taking her out on a date." He sighed. "How did she die?"

"Not as happy as she would have been if she'd known you were interested in her," Annja said. "But I guess that's the way it goes."

Davis pursed his lips. "We need to clean things up here. Call in the state authorities. You have anything else to add to what we've seen so far? Any sign of where they stashed their drugs?"

Annja considered the packages in the back of the truck. She thought about how many people would suffer once those drugs hit the streets. And she thought about how the criminals who peddled them would laugh all the way to the bank.

She shook her head. "No. Nothing else to add. I think you guys have got it all sewn up here."

"We have any questions," Davis said, "we'll call you. Make sure you leave your number with Ellen back in town before you go anywhere. Okay?"

Annja shrugged. "I'm easy enough to find, anyway. You just have to look me up online."

"Well, give us a number so we can call you."

Annja nodded. "Fine."

She glanced at Joey. "You must be ready to sleep for a week."

"My head hurts, but overall I feel pretty good. Nothing a few days' rest won't help me get over." He looked at Jenny's body. "It's a real shame she's not still with us."

Annja nodded. "I know. But hopefully she's finally at rest. And happy."

"You think she is?"

"I don't know," Annja said. "I just don't know."

"By the way," Davis called out to Annja again. "What exactly were they doing up here with you guys, anyway?"

Annja frowned. "They brought us here to kill us. Like they did this morning. Only this time, they actually succeeded in taking one of us down." Annja pointed at the truck. "I'm going to give Joey a ride back to his grandfather's. Any problems with me doing that?"

Connor pointed at Jenny. "Leave her here. We'll have the State Police take good care of her."

"You're sure?"

"Least we can do," Connor said.

The rain had tapered off, but still dotted their faces.

Connor looked at Annja. "This is the part of the drug war people never really see—the invisible casualties."

Annja nodded. "Maybe it's time someone let the criminals know they can't get away with this stuff."

Connor eyed the truck for a moment and then looked back at Annja. "Maybe you're right."

Annja backed away. "Get in the truck, Joey."

Connor nodded at Annja. "Good luck."

"I'm not the one who's going to need it," Annja said quietly. Then she hopped in the truck and gunned the engine. In seconds, she and Joey were speeding down the road in the rain-slicked darkness.

39

Annja dropped Joey off at Dancing Deer's house. Joey jumped out of the truck and looked at her as the rain continued to fall. "You're going off on your own, aren't you?"

Annja nodded. "It's something I have to do, I'm afraid."

Joey smirked. "You're not afraid. You don't seem to be afraid of anything. At least to me."

"I'm afraid of plenty of things," Annja said. "But I can't let that fear stop me from doing what's right."

Joey looked up into the rain. "Even if it means you might die in the process of doing what's right?"

"Even if."

Joey looked back at her. "If I was older, you know I'd insist on coming with you."

"I know you would, Creeping Wolf. And I would be grateful for your help. But tonight, this is going to have to be all about me. Any other time and I'd welcome your assistance."

Joey nodded. "I understand. Sometimes the path of the warrior is surrounded on all sides by many foes. But only the warrior can fight his way out of the bad situation. Help is not help at all."

"That another one of your grandfather's sage sayings?"

Joey shook his head. "Nope. Mine. I'm trying some out to see how they sound."

Annja smiled. "I'll keep that in mind. You'd better get inside now before you catch a cold to go along with that concussion."

"Will you come back?"

Annja shrugged. "I don't know. What I'm about to do might just be the last thing I ever attempt."

"In that case, I hope the spirits of all my ancestors travel with you and help you on your quest. Even if the final battle is yours alone."

"Thank you."

Joey shut the door and stood in the rain while Annja backed out of the driveway. A light came on over the porch and she saw Dancing Deer with his right hand upraised. She held up her hand and felt a sensation of warmth come over her.

Joey stood there for a second and then turned and ran into the house. In another moment, the light was off and the night reclaimed its dominance.

Annja took a deep breath and then slid the Tahoe into Drive.

As she drove down the road, she took the map and directions out of her pocket. She pulled over and studied them briefly. She hadn't driven in this part of the country before, but the directions seemed easy enough to follow.

She made it back to the interstate after twenty minutes of hard driving. Every once in a while, she flipped the blue lights on to pass a car on the stretch of road leading to the highway, but otherwise the dense rain seemed to keep everyone at home.

Annja hoped it stayed that way.

She drove south through small towns and hamlets of scattered homes and ranch houses. People worked hard for very little in these parts, it seemed. To Annja's mind, it just enraged her all the more that someone was polluting their area with the drugs she was transporting.

It ends tonight, she thought.

Annja reached for the glove compartment and found a cell phone in the box. She flipped it open and dialed the number on the paper that had been in Tom's pocket. It rang three times on the other end before picking up.

"Yeah?" a voice said.

"I'm coming to you now. I've got the merchandise." Annja frowned. She felt like she was on an episode of *Miami Vice*.

The voice on the other end sounded gruff. "Good. You know the place?"

"I've got the address."

"How long?"

"Maybe forty minutes until I get there."

"Tom with you?"

"Nope, just me."

The voice chuckled. "He's making you do all the legwork now, huh?"

"I guess so. What else are brothers for, huh?"

"You sound different. You okay?"

Annja frowned. Damn. "Just a cold. Been out in the rain all damn night getting the stuff. Now I'm coming down with something."

"Well, we finish up our business maybe we can get a drink."

"Sure."

"It'll be nice to see you again, Sheila."

"Yeah. Gotta go."

Annja disconnected the call. So much for the idea that maybe she could pull this off without anyone knowing about it. If the guy on the other end of the phone knew Sheila and what she looked like, then Annja's plan would be up the moment they saw her.

She took a deep breath and checked her speed. While she doubted any State Police would haul her over, given that she was driving a police vehicle, she had to make sure she didn't chance it. Getting busted with drugs would not help her situation.

Annja navigated her way to the outskirts of the city and then pulled over long enough to check the map again for the directions. Fortunately, they'd been written well and Annja found the signs easily enough. After another twenty minutes of travel, she rolled into the rendezvous site.

She didn't expect anyone to be there yet. She'd told the guy on the phone that she was still forty minutes away to buy herself some time. Getting there first, Annja could check out the environment and see if there was any way she could pull off a successful ambush.

The pickings were slim. She looked around and saw that the meeting place was in the middle of a parking lot at the end of an alley next to a warehouse. The warehouse was long boarded up and shuttered so Annja wouldn't have access to it during the meet.

Just as bad was the fact that the parking lot was wide open from all sides. It would have been tough positioning a sniper at distance for this meet, let alone finding a way to handle the group who were no doubt already on their way.

Great, she thought. What am I going to do now?

Another burst of rain opened up on the car and the water fell down so hard that it drummed a steady rhythm onto the roof of the Tahoe. Annja was glad she wasn't out in the rain.

But it did give her an idea.

She would have to stay inside the truck until the last possible second. Once her contacts arrived, they wouldn't be able to see inside the car because of the rain-streaked windows. They wouldn't know who she was until she got out.

So she would have to throw herself out of the truck and come up attacking them as they arrived.

It was the only way.

If she could get to them before they all got out of their cars, then she'd have a fighting chance. But if she messed up and they were all out, they could simply mow her down as she came at them.

It was not what she had in mind when she'd decided to follow this trail to the end. She realized she hadn't had anything in mind other than doing *something*.

The timing would be critical.

The cell phone chirped and Annja put it up to her ear. "Yeah?"

"It's me. We're five minutes out. You there?"

"Just got here. It's pouring down."

"I know."

"How do you want to do this? You want to come to me or you want me to come to you?"

She heard the chuckle in her ear. "I'll come to you. I wouldn't want you getting wet. We do the deal and then my guys take the stuff from you while we conclude our paperwork."

"Paperwork. Right."

"See you in five minutes."

The line went dead and Annja stuffed the phone back into the glove compartment. She closed her eyes and saw the sword in her mind's eye, right where it should be.

If he was going to come to her, then that might tip the odds in Annja's favor. She could even hold him hostage.

Maybe.

She frowned. Once they arrived, they'd want to finish

things up fast and get out of there. No sense hanging around, waiting for the local cops to cruise by.

A set of lights cut through the darkness.

Annja frowned. Had it already been five minutes? She didn't think so. That meant someone else was arriving.

But who?

She started the engine just in case she needed to get out quickly. The car coming across the parking lot slowed down. Annja couldn't see a thing aside from its lights with all the rain sluicing down.

Is this them?

It couldn't be. What happened if they showed up while this car was there? Would more innocent people be killed?

Maybe it's just a pair of high-school kids looking for a place to make out, she thought. Talk about bad timing.

But then the car turned and headed right for Annja. So much for that, she thought.

The car slowed to a stop and the headlights remained on. Annja licked her lips and steeled herself. She checked the sword again and felt a measure of relief seeing it right where it belonged.

This is going to get messy, she thought.

She heard a car door open and then close. In the rainy night she saw a figure walking over, but he seemed completely unconcerned about the rain that must have been drenching him.

Annja heard the tap on her window and nearly jumped through the roof. She lowered the window just a crack. "Yeah?"

"You going to let me in?"

"Why would I do that?"

A laugh filtered in through the crack in the window. "Because I'm getting soaked standing out here in the damn rain, that's why."

"Hang on a second."

Annja slid the power window back up and checked herself out in the mirror. She looked a mess. Dirt streaked her face. Her hair was a shambles.

Maybe this guy hadn't seen Sheila in a long time. Maybe he forgot what she looked like. Any one of those things could help Annja out.

But it was a big chance.

From outside the truck she heard the guy call out. "Hurry up."

Annja unlocked the doors.

She heard footsteps going around to the other side of the truck where Joey had been sitting only an hour or so before. But Joey was a great kid. The person about to sit there was a drug dealer.

Annja heard the door start to open and she turned away toward her own window. She wanted to keep this going until the very last second.

In a rush, the guy hopped into the front seat and started brushing himself off. "Damn, it's a mess out there tonight. You weren't kidding. Maybe we should have just arranged to do this tomorrow, huh?"

Annja nodded.

"Hey, you okay?"

"Yeah."

"It's been a while, Sheila. How have you been?"

Annja turned and looked at the man sitting next to her. "I've been good, thanks. Unfortunately, I don't think you'll be saying the same thing in a few moments."

40

Shock froze the scarred and battered face of the man sitting next to Annja. But experienced reflexes made him immediately throw his left elbow directly at Annja's face. She had just enough time to shift to her left to avoid the blow.

The man followed it by letting his left hand swing free, chopping Annja across the bridge of her nose. She grunted and heard the bone snap and then the blood started to flow. Annja tasted the copper and frowned.

"Bad move."

But the man sitting next to her didn't stop. As he punched at her with his left, his right hand clawed at the door handle, trying desperately to get out so he could order his men to open fire.

"You're not going anywhere," Annja said. She hauled him back and the truck started to shake.

Annja flipped him around and he head butted her in the face. Annja wondered if he'd cracked some of her teeth. She heard the dull sound of a blade opening in the close space between them.

I need room to move, she thought.

The man stabbed at her heart, pumping the blade in and out fast.

Annja deflected his arms and the blade, then punched straight into his solar plexus, trying to disrupt his diaphragm so he wouldn't be able to breathe properly. He grunted and tried to slash her across the throat.

Annja leaned back over her seat and then felt her own door swing open, sending the upper part of her body out into the rain upside down.

Instantly, the doors on the other car opened and men started to pour out. All of them were armed with submachine guns.

This is not good, Annja thought.

She slid out of the truck and then rolled behind it as the first bullets ricocheted off the asphalt near her. Annja closed her eyes and summoned her sword. I hope I'm strong enough for this, she thought.

The man Annja had been fighting with came out of the truck screaming. "Shoot her, shoot her! That's not Sheila!"

The men wasted no time. All around the Tahoe, the air exploded as bullets pinged and splanged off every surface. Annja huddled near the back, trying to use the truck's bulk to shield her.

I can't stay here. They'll close on the truck and cut me down, she thought.

There was a brief pause as magazines ran dry and some of the men started shouting that they had to reload.

Annja came out of her squat and ran around the side of the truck, holding the sword high. She swung and cleaved the closest man who was busy fiddling with his magazine release. He glanced up, saw Annja and screamed as she cut through him, spilling his blood in a splash on the ground.

Annja kept moving, her eyes rapidly cataloging the scene. Six men.

All armed.

The next man was faster than his predecessor and he snapped his magazine home, ratcheted the slide and started to bring up the barrel of the gun as Annja ducked down, spun and cut horizontally, nearly slicing him open across the chest. She heard a sickening gurgle in his throat as he started to drown on the explosion of blood and bile erupting from the heinous sword gash.

Annja leaped into the air, bringing the sword high overhead and cutting down at the next man who was armed with an assault rifle with a much longer barrel. But instead of trying to shoot at her, he anticipated the downward cut and used the barrel of his gun to deflect her move to the side.

She cut back horizontally, trying to take him across the midsection. But he jerked his legs back, gaining distance from Annja.

I'm exposed here, she realized. Annja dove forward, narrowing the distance between her and the man as more shots rang out. She felt a nick by her ear and felt a warm flow of blood as a bullet or a piece of asphalt cut her.

She rolled and came up under the arms of the man in front of her. Annja stabbed straight up, but again the man arched back, letting the blade fly past his sternum. He used his momentum to pivot, drop and kick Annja squarely in the chest.

Air flew out of Annja's lungs as she struggled to regain her breath. She aimed a fist at the man's head and this time scored two blistering punches on his nose. She heard the crack and smiled. Now she'd given him something to think about.

Annja dropped low and then plunged the sword in deep, hearing the sharp release of air. She yanked the sword free as the man slid to his death on the asphalt below.

But she had an immediate problem punctuated by the sound

of rapid gunfire. She jerked the sword up in front of her and felt the bullets slam into the blade, making it twist in her hands.

Annja kept moving, certain that if she stopped, she'd be a dead mark. She ran toward the closest gunman and slashed his hand. She heard his weapon fall to the ground with a clang and then swung her blade back up, slicing into the man from his hip up to his neck. He started to retch and gurgle as he slid to the ground dead.

Annja was in her zone now. Her eyes impassively surveyed the scene, assessing every remaining target. By her count, she had just three to go and then this band of drug dealers would be vanquished from the earth.

She felt the stab of a bullet puncture her thigh.

"Dammit!"

There was no way to tell if it was a bad hit or not. She knew if the round struck her femoral artery, she could be bleeding to death even as she closed with the man who had shot her. His eyes widened as Annja screamed and drove the sword at him, cutting down and then back up, using her momentum to slice the air faster than he could even try to keep up with.

He staggered back and Annja pressed her attack until he tripped and fell. Annja impaled him with the sword, running it into his chest and his heart. He stiffened and then dropped his gun and died.

Annja's reflexes took over and she jerked her body to the right, tucking into a tight ball as she rolled and came up, launching her sword at the last of the henchmen. He started to dodge but the blade hit him first, thrusting into his midsection. The momentum of the throw drove it all the way to the hilt. The man looked down and his eyes rolled back. He slipped to the ground on his own blood.

Annja pulled the sword free and finally turned to the last

man standing in the parking lot, the man who had initially been in the truck with her.

"Who are you?" he asked.

"Annja Creed."

He watched her for a moment. "Have we done something to you or to your family? Something that drove you to come after us like this? Because I can't remember leaving anyone alive who could take out my guys like this."

"You don't know me," Annja said. "But I know the disease you help spread. The pain and the heartache."

"A man's got to make a living."

"Not like this."

He smirked. "So, what, you're some do-gooder out on her own little mission to clean up the streets? Is that it?"

"What if it is?"

"It's a horrible cliché."

Annja shrugged. "I don't much care what it seems like. I've lost a close friend tonight because of the drugs you were going to buy from Tom and Sheila."

"Tonight? Your friend died tonight?"

"That's right."

"Because she got involved with Tom and Sheila?"

Annja nodded. "And she got seduced by the thought of all that money you were going to pay them."

The man smiled. "We weren't going to pay them a dime. We were going to kill them. The higher-ups don't like it when folks decide to retire early. Messes things up for the rest of us. What we worked so hard to get in place here. People are making money. They don't like when someone fucks that up."

"I told them you'd kill them if they came down here," Annja said.

The man nodded. "Yeah, you got all the answers, huh? So where are they? They take the smack and run away? It's not going to help them. If they double-crossed us, the bosses will find them. Doesn't matter where they go. Everyone can be bought."

"Is that so?"

"Yeah, even you, babe. I'll bet you've got a price. I name a number and if you like it, why don't you and me work something out? I'll even let you take over Tom and Sheila's route if you want. You can do good with it."

"I can't be bought," Annja said. "Because some things aren't worth any money at all."

"Yeah, yeah, okay. Whatever. So did Tom and Sheila think you could kill us and that would be it?"

"Tom and Sheila are dead."

He eyed her. "Anyone else told me that, I wouldn't believe them. But seeing what you just managed to do to my guys, I'm inclined to think otherwise." He spat a wad of bloody spit onto the ground. "You killed them?"

"Just Tom," Annja said.

"And Sheila? Who killed her?"

"My friend. The one who died tonight."

The man laughed. "Sounds like you guys had quite the party up in the sticks. Anyone left alive?"

"You mean Dave."

"You know about Dave, too, huh?"

"Yes."

"All right, is he still breathing?"

"Not after Tom used a shotgun on him."

The man whistled. "I always knew that guy had more than a few screws loose. Shotgun, huh? Messy."

"I had to clean it up."

He smiled. "Was that before or after you killed Tom?"

"Before."

"No shit."

He looked around. Six bodies were spread out near the car they'd driven up in. The stench of death hung in the air, a tension of violence still eager for one last victim to call its own.

"Just you and me now, huh?" the man said.

Annja nodded. "Not for much longer."

"That's some blade. How come I didn't see it when I got into the truck with you?"

"It was raining."

"So you gonna do me with that the way you did my guys? Stab me through the heart? Some sort of symbolic death?"

Annja shook her head. "Nope."

"You're not?"

Annja nodded at the truck. "I think I've got some stuff that belongs to you."

The man regarded her for a minute and then walked over to the Tahoe. Annja gripped the sword in her right hand and eased the back door open with her left. Inside, piles of bags filled with cocaine lay on the floor.

His eyes lit up. "Yeah, that's the stuff. Looks like you brought all of it, too. Good girl."

Annja frowned. "This is what you wanted, right?"

"Yeah."

Annja used the sword blade to slice open one of the bags and display the contents. Brilliant white powder spilled out.

"Pretty sight," the man said. "Some people call it heaven."

"In that case," Annja said. "Why don't you pay it a visit."

"What?"

Annja grabbed the back of his head with her left hand and shoved him face-first into the powder. He struggled but she felt the rage coursing through her veins at the thought of how something so stupid had so easily seduced Jenny.

She could hear the coughing and retching as the man was forced to inhale the cocaine. His body trembled and his legs jerked in an awful death spasm before Annja finally let him slide away to the ground.

He landed face up, coated in the white powder he'd ingested.

"I hope you like heaven," Annja said.

She spent the next few minutes gathering the bags into a pile and then she found a lighter in the glove compartment. She used the spare gas can to soak the entire parcel and then set it all ablaze. In seconds, the drugs were cooking in the drizzly night air.

Annja took a final look at the scene and walked away, leaving it all behind her.

epilogue

"So the leg's okay?"

Annja sat in the police station looking at Ellen. "Seems to be fine. Luckily, there was no damage to the artery." Annja smiled. "That uniform looks good on you."

Ellen grinned. "I'm still getting used to people calling me Sheriff, and I don't exactly know if it feels right, all things considered."

"What do you mean?"

Ellen shrugged. "Well, here I was working right under Dave and yet I had no clue that he, Sheila and Tom were all involved in the drug business. I mean, I was more than a little shocked."

"No one sees everything all the time," Annja said. "That's just the way it goes." She smiled. "In any event, you'll have plenty of opportunities to make sure things go well here in town now."

"Davis and Connor said you left in an awful hurry when they last saw you."

Annja nodded. "I had some unfinished business I had to attend to. They know where to reach me if they need.to."

Ellen eyed her. "I heard something interesting on the police bulletin wire. Apparently there was a scene at some parking lot down in the city. Seven dead bodies, a few abandoned cars, including one belonging to the late sheriff, and a smoldering pile of luggage with chemical residue consistent with cocaine."

Annja looked around the office. "Yeah, well, you know how dangerous life can be in the big city."

Ellen nodded. "That I do. It's one reason I stay out here in the backwater of civilization."

"Maybe you'll have a chance to get some more folks coming through here now. Pick up the joint a little bit."

"That'd be great. We've got an abandoned hotel down at the end of Main Street. Might be nice if someone bought it and reopened it for business."

Annja smirked. "Not me. I've got too many other things I need to take care of."

Ellen's eyes glanced down to the package on the desk. "That her stuff?"

Annja looked at the envelope containing Jenny's personal effects. "Yes. I have to take them to her family and explain what happened. I figure it's the least I can do for her, considering all the stuff she went through."

"We never really know, do we?"

"What's that?"

"What people are like. We make friends, we live with them, we love them, but deep down inside they're always a mystery. And sometimes the only way to unravel it is when they die on us."

Annja nodded. "Sometimes death is no solution to any mystery. Only the start of it."

Ellen stood. "You come back anytime, you hear? I'd be honored to call you my friend."

Annja shook her hand and then gave her a hug. "Consider it my honor, as well. You take care of yourself, Sheriff."

Annja scooped up the envelope and walked outside to her rental car.

Joey was leaning against the car with his arms crossed. "I heard you'd come back to town."

"I was going to come see you."

"Were you?"

Annja smiled. "Come on, I'll give you a lift."

Annja climbed into the car and started the engine. As she slid the car into gear, she looked at Joey. "How are you?"

He shrugged. "Fine. Everyone's trying to get over the shock of what happened. Even though Dave never necessarily came out and kept everyone under his thumb, people still felt it. And since Tom and Sheila were in on it, that just reinforced the effect. With them gone, things will blossom."

"Blossom?"

"Yeah."

Annja smiled. "Nice choice of words." She paused. "I found out that it was David who killed Cheehawk. He must have been tracking us that night."

"I eventually figured out it was him, as well. I'm glad I tried to blow up his truck."

Annja whirled. "That was you? Jenny and I were in that truck!"

"Yeah, I didn't know you two would stumble across him or that he'd switched vehicles with the Feds. Obviously, I never meant for that to happen to you."

"Yeah, thanks, pal." Annja had to laugh. "That was a close one."

"Sorry, okay? I was so upset when Cheehawk died, it was all I could do not to freak out."

"I'd have to say that trying to blow up someone's truck comes pretty damn close to freaking out."

"Yeah, I guess so."

"Why didn't you confront him on it?"

"What, and risk him shooting me?"

"He almost did, anyway."

"Good point."

Annja nodded. "When you're an adult you'll learn all about foresight."

"But apparently not the dangers of hitchhiking."

"Wiseass. So where are we going?"

"I know a place, and I want to show you something before you leave town for good." Joey gave her directions and Annja drove for about two miles outside of town. Joey motioned to a spot near a sharp rock face. "Park there."

Annja slid the car into park and they both got out.

"I think you need this. From up here, we can see for quite a distance. It's one of my favorite places to come. Whenever I need to be with my friends."

Annja smiled. "I think we all need a place like that."

She walked to the edge of the precipice. Far below, she could see the swirling waters of the river that had nearly claimed their lives. She could see the mountains and the forests that had both ravaged and sheltered them. And overhead, clouds and sun mingled in the pale blue sky.

"It's time to say goodbye, Annja."

Annja nodded. "I wish things could have been different at the end with Jenny." Annja wiped her eyes. "See you on the other side," she said quietly.

Joey stood out on the edge and whispered a chant of some sort before turning back to Annja. "If it's all the same to you, I think I'll stay here for a while."

"Really?"

Joey nodded. "I'll find my own way back home."

"I know you will."

"It's been an adventure, Annja Creed." He wrapped his arms around her and squeezed her tight.

Annja smiled, fresh tears flowing out of her eyes. "It sure has, Creeping Wolf. You take care of yourself," she said.

He looked at her. "Don't forget the journey you took when you were here. We're connected now, you and me. We'll keep each other's secrets. Don't ever forget."

"I won't," she said.

He nodded. "In that case, it's time to say farewell. For now."

Annja kissed his cheek and turned back toward her car. "Be well, Joey."

"You, too."

She walked to the car and slid into the seat behind the steering wheel. A thought occurred to her and she got back out of the car. "What's your secret, Joey?" she called out.

She looked around.

Joey was gone.

But something nearby drew Annja's eye. She walked to the edge of the path where the grass met it and crouched down. In the dirt, she could see the marked impressions of a track.

A big track.

Five splayed toes topped a footprint that must have been at least fifteen inches long. And some distance farther on, Annja found another one, leading off toward the same rock face that she and Joey had just climbed.

Whenever I need to be with my friends.

Joey's words came back to Annja. She smiled. He knew all along, she thought. Creeping Wolf wasn't just some crazy kid who liked to run around in the woods. As he'd said himself, he was the caretaker of this place, this little piece of Eden on earth.

No wonder he'd been so quick to dismiss the reports and

the sightings and everything else that went with the legends. To say otherwise would have meant a rush of thrill seekers. And that would have meant the forest and the creatures—all the creatures—that inhabited it would be at risk.

Annja walked back to the car and got in. She put her hands on the steering wheel and stared off into the world around her for a moment. Then she started the engine, slid the car into Reverse and backed up, swinging it around until it was aimed back toward the main road.

And the world beyond it.

She took one final glance over her shoulder. "Your secret's safe with me," she said.

The Executioner
Don Pendleton's
FIRE ZONE

A U.S. gold heist turns an African nation into a war zone.

After the leader of an African rebel group hijacks a shipment of enough gold to fund a revolution, Mack Bolan must retrieve it before the killing starts. Unable to trust even the CIA, the Executioner must put his combat and survival skills to the test to infiltrate the rebel base and destroy the key players.

Available October wherever books are sold.

GOLD EAGLE®

GEX371

www.readgoldeagle.blogspot.com